# SHANE

*for Elma*

With thanks to Lisa, Arno, Charlie, Martin, Boguś and everybody who helped me to get this book out into the world.

# SHANE

## Tim Orchard

fiction direct

FICTION DIRECT

Shane

First published in Great Britain by Fiction Direct 2007

ISBN: 978-0-9555503-0-3

British Library Cataloguing-in-Publication Data
A catalogue record for this book is available from the
British Library

Set in Garamond

Printed in Great Britain by
TJ International Ltd., Padstow, Cornwall

Fiction Direct
20 Brockwell Court
Effra Road
Brixton, London SW2 1NA

www.fictiondirect.com

## ∞ 1 ∞

Shane left the station, a sports bag hanging from one shoulder and strolled to the mini–cab office, opposite. A couple of guys rested against a car, checking the racing page. They eyed him as he entered the office. The controller raised his chin and said. "Where to mate?" Shane told him. "The Temple Estate." Pointing outside, the controller said. "Front car." They went by East Hill, the driver casual, asking the usual questions, which Shane ignored or gave out noncommittal answers. As he paid the driver, the man said. "Don't live around here, do you?" Shane shook his head and hefted the bag onto his shoulder, he said. "Just come to see a friend." The taxi guy said. "Was alright up here one-time, shit hole now, but." He handed Shane a card. "Got my mobile number on there. Give me a call when you need to get back to the station." Shane looked at the card and put it in his pocket, lifted his hand in farewell and turned into Circle Road.

The Temple Estate isn't big or modern. Built soon after the Second World War, to house bombed out Londoners, there were no tower blocks and every house had a front and back garden. The only flats were above the shops, on the precinct and those distinctly low rise. In Shane's memory the estate had been populated by people his mother would have derided as respectable working class. Something his own family definitely were not. But everything changes, even the Temple Estate. Circle Road rings the estate in a necklace of semi's, the bulk of the houses set inside its internal circumference, in a series of cul–de–sacs and crescents. At the centre of the estate, a pub and a shopping precinct. And to Shane, in the quiet of the sunny afternoon, walking along Circle Road, with old smells and old sights, the estate seemed pretty much as it always had. More rundown maybe, the occasional house boarded up, a few big youth hanging out. Usual stuff.

Shane was going to see Gerry and Louise and their two kids and as he'd thought on the way here, ten years is a long time, maybe now there were three children. He wasn't worried about not having been in touch, because Gerry had been the last person he'd seen before leaving the country, so Gerry knew. Now though, only the people Shane had done the favour for, knew he was in the country but even they did not know where he was. He would leave the same way as he'd come. No–one was looking for him. He'd been back dozens of times over the years and he'd come to realise the cops had more than enough, they didn't even see him. Shane did what he was paid to do and faded away. This was the last time. He knew he wouldn't be coming back. Something in his thinking had changed, before, now, again. He wanted to see if there was still something in their friendship and if there was – well, good. Gerry and Shane had been friends for as long as Shane could remember. From the first few days at school, when he'd been impressed by the other five year old and his barrel-chested impersonation of John Wayne.

Through their childhood the boys had built dens together, made fires, collected newts and fished the gravel and chalk pits on the acres and acres of waste ground between the town and the Thames. They had done all the kid and teenage stuff together. Got drunk together, took their first drugs together. Gerry had even worked in Shane's Dad's scrap yard when he first left school but the sly mixture of the legal and the illegal, that was inherent in the business, did not suit his basically honest nature and he soon left for a factory job. They stayed tight, even as Shane, who enjoyed the buzz of crime, had used his father's connections to push himself forwards. Shane moved to London and Gerry met Louise. It was love. When they got married, they camped out at Gerry's parents until the council gave them a place on the estate. Gerry had always lived on Temple Estate and he didn't want to live anywhere else. Although they had taken different paths in life, it did not affect the trust and affection of years. The brutality of Shane's life was in stark contrast to the normality of Gerry and his family's life. It was a bolt hole for Shane. Somewhere he came to lay low, to disappear, hide-out and he had stayed with them many times.

The house looked like a lot of other houses, except for the burnt out car sat in the front garden. As he skirted the blackened blob and rang the doorbell, it suddenly dawned on him, what a long time ten years was. He cast a glance at the rest of the garden. It was all overgrown and wild, tall weeds and nettles dying against each other. No-one came. He tried again, strained to catch a sound. Nothing. Wondering if the pub on the precinct was open, he pushed again, not expecting an answer. Shane turned and looked past the garden and the car, to the street and the four young guys, sitting on the wall near the entrance to the cul–de–sac opposite. He was thinking of the alley, the short cut to the pub at the end of the cul–de–sac. The young guys stared at Shane. Shane stared back.

The door opened and a boy's voice, said. "Who

are you?" A crop haired kid of about eight or ten or some age like that which he couldn't gage, stared up at Shane. He smiled down at the boy and said. "I'm Shane. Who are you?" The boy did not give his name but said. "I'm not supposed to talk to strangers." Shane said. "I'm not strange. Is Gerry or Louise, your dad or mum there?" The boy looked at Shane as though they were speaking different languages. He wasn't giving anything away and they looked at each other in silence. Shane shifted the bag from one shoulder to the other. From inside the house, a woman's voice shouted. "Billy! What have I told you about answering the door!" Billy pulled a cheeky face, eyes rolling up in his head, he said. "Oops." Then she was looking, hard faced, through the same crack in the door as Billy. A handsome woman in her early thirties, black hair cut in a neat bob, dark eyes wary, she hustled Billy behind her. She said. "My husband told the other one – we don't want trouble – just leave us alone." Holding up his hands in a sign of peace, Shane said, quickly. "I think we're at crossed purposes, here. I'm looking for a mate and his family. Lived here for years." Billy said. "His name's Shane, mum." Her face softened, she opened the door, she smiled. Behind him a deep male voice, said. "We've only been here a couple of months and to be honest it ain't been that easy."

Billy shouted. "Dad!" Dad was a biggish man

knocking forty, with full plastic bags hanging from his hands. He looked Shane up and down. "Don't look like you got that tan around here." Shane shrugged. The man said. "You must have come from somewhere warm." As he spoke, he glanced over his shoulder at the four youths on the corner and Shane followed his gaze. The guys whispered to each other and laughed. Billy's dad said. "Come inside, for a cup of tea." He motioned Shane forwards and said. "I'm Craig." As they passed the woman in the doorway, he said. "My wife and my love, Lisa." Craig kissed her and she cracked a smile and a nod. Billy said, again. "His name's Shane, dad." Craig grinned and said. "And you've met Billy."

Sat at the kitchen table, the adults drank tea and Billy drank juice. There were biscuits. Craig, as if in explanation, said. "Dole day." When Shane explained again, who he was looking for and his surprise at them not being there, Craig breathed an audible sigh of relief. When he told them that Gerry had lived on the estate his whole life and that he couldn't imagine him and Louise, living anywhere else, Lisa folded her arms and said. "You could if you lived here." Craig took her hand and caressed it, he said. "Like I said, we haven't been here very long." Billy said. "Mum don't like it here, 'cause they burned dad's car." Lisa scolded Billy. Craig said. "Seriously. If you don't want to sit quiet, you can go into the garden or the other room." Looking from one adult to another and not seeing a smile, Billy dropped his eyes and sucked noisily at the rim of his glass. With a sour smile, Craig said. "But I guess that's why I invited you in. Those fuckers across the street are part of it." Billy slid his hand palm up over the table top, towards his father, he said. "Dad." Lisa laughed. Fishing 10p from his pocket, Craig slapped it into Billy's palm and said, to Shane. "Money grabbing little wotsit's the living, breathing, swear box. 10p a pop. Anyway, we've had excrement through the letter-box, windows smashed, the car was last week and I don't want them over there knowing what's going on here, even if it's nothing."

Shane said nothing. Lisa said. "The man next door told me, your friends moved up north. Didn't leave a forwarding address. He didn't say outright but I think they were suffering harassment, as well." Rising from the table, Lisa refilled the men's cups and took her own to the sink and rinsed it. To no–one in particular, she said. "I'm starting the supper." Craig said. "Yeh." Billy chirupped. "Chips." Shane looked at his watch, he told them, he had imposed too long, he had to get off, find a room, you know. But it was like they looked at each other and made a decision and Lisa said. "Would you like to stay for some food, Shane? There's plenty." Craig said. "It's early." Lisa said. "There's plenty of time to find a hotel, later." Travelled out, sick of moving, needing somewhere, Shane was happy to accept this unasked for hospitality.

While Lisa rattled the pots and pans, Billy, Craig and Shane moved to the living room, to watch the TV. The house seemed sparsely furnished. More bare floors than carpet, fifty quid TV, couch and easy chairs battered into submission by other families bodies. Craig said. "Ain't exactly home, yet." He curled his lip. "Only the best, eh?" From the window, both men could see the burnt out car, like the abandoned husk of some gigantic beetle, squatting in the front garden. Craig said. "Mind you, who knows how long we'll be here, really. She plays it tough but it's getting to her." Out of the window the late August evening was closing in slowly towards night, but it was still bright and, somewhere, muted, distant, the voices of children playing on the street. A man and a woman walked by, stared at the car and shook their heads. Shane said. "What did you do about the car?" Craig said. "Police and Fire-brigade. Fire-brigade were great, cops were useless."

When the food was ready, the three adults ate at the kitchen table and Billy took his in by the telly. The food was plain English grub and reminded Shane of times past and things too distant to be regretted and why he enjoyed living abroad. Being a stranger and being invited into Craig and Lisa's home, had surprised Shane. It had happened in rural Spain and in Morocco, people he had only spoken to for moments, insisting he come into their homes and share their food. Shane said. "Do you do this for every 'odd bod' who knocks on your door?" Lisa looked at Craig and they both pulled a face and laughed. Craig said. "Not 'round here."

As they ate they exchanged brief histories. Shane's by necessity, was somewhat vague. Why he had left in the first place or when that was, were dealt with by shrugs and the need for a change of scene, you know how it is sometimes, life just gets too –. They looked back at him like people who didn't ever get that choice. He told them about the different places he had lived, about the food and how he saw the people in Spain, Italy, Morocco. Craig said. "No wonder you've got such a tan. I want your job!" Shane saw the three dead bodies in the Manchester flat and said. "No you don't." He switched, had them laughing about Moroccan traders chasing him down the street, desperate to sell him a carpet or a leather jacket or in some cases a dress for his wife or lover or whoever – sure they didn't give a damn, money was money. Lisa and Craig told him, turn and turn about, of the events, which had washed them up on the Temple Estate.

They were people who had done all the normal things. But as Craig said "These days, normal ain't normal. Normal is a sub-culture. Normal makes you the weirdo." They had been together for twelve years. Saved the deposit for a house on the outskirts of town. Starter home. Got married. Everything is groovy. Eighteen months later, Lisa is pregnant. Not a problem. Both were overjoyed. Both wanted a child. In due course, Lisa had to give up work. Money was a bit tight, okay, but with a new baby on board, they didn't go out so much and their life together became something else. Things evened out. Craig said. "Most people don't want much, to be left alone, for things to be alright, you know." Life rolled on, they were happy, Lisa said. "We had our problems, everyone does. But it's love and trust in the end, that's what I think, anyway – and we're still very much –." She didn't get to finish her sentence, Craig said. "Alright, love. I think he gets the idea." Then he put down his fork and kissed her on the cheek. And things happen and sometimes you do not have any control over the things that happen. Firms get bought and sold, some workers become natural wastage, others faces don't fit. Craig said. "Who knows? I was out on my ear. Seems thirty nine 'ain't that young anymore." Things change and he couldn't get another job that paid decent money and things go wrong when things start to go wrong. It's a slow grind down to losing the house back to the building society and then everything is gone. On the social – where is there to go, what do you do? Eight months in bed and breakfast is a long hard road. Shane said. "Shit!" Craig laughed, he said. "Lucky Billy 'ain't here." And Lisa said. "Believe me it was." Looking around the kitchen with a tight smile, Lisa added. "This was supposed to be a new beginning."

Shane laughed and said. "Sorry Lisa but I just saw Gerry's workshop. I'd forgotten how big it was." He pointed out the back window, to the workshop, which took up half the back garden. Almost in unison, Craig and Lisa said. "That bloody thing!" Shane agreed, he said. "Ugly, but sturdy. Bit of a perfectionist old Gerry, took us two weeks to build." Pulling the plates and knives and forks towards him, Craig gathered them up and ferried them to the sink, he said. "Well, its our problem, now." Shane said. "What do you mean?" Craig turned on the tap, water came out and started to steam, he put the plug in and stood watching the sink fill. "Drugs." Lisa said. "I'll do that, love." Craig shook his head and began to do the washing-up. He said. "I don't care what people do. But it 'ain't me and I don't want nothing to do with it." He stood at the sink, hands hanging in the soapy water and looked straight at Shane. "Especially when they try to intimidate me and my family." Lisa closed the curtains on the kitchen window and went through to the living room, to do the same. Craig said. "Seems like some guy called, Rowlands, runs the estate, 'ain't ever seen him, though. This big bloke came here, smooth as you like, saying, how he knew moving was one of life's most traumatic experiences but they wanted the house and it was best to get it over with before we'd really settled in. Wanted us to do a council swop, for a two-bedroom place in one of the cul–de–sacs. Offered us a cash sweetener. Didn't like it when I told him we were happy here. He said, he was speaking for Mr. Rowlands and maybe, as we were new to the estate, we should ask somebody before we made a decision."

Shane went to his bag in the hall, unzipped it, took out a litre of Jamesons whiskey and carefully zipped up the bag again. He could hear Lisa in the living room, encouraging Billy towards bedtime. Wiping his hands, Craig grinned, he said. "Mmm." The two men sipped their drinks in silence, after a minute, Craig said. "Came back a few days later. I told him, politely like, to piss off. They burned the car the next night. Anyway, forget it. Tell me, Shane, what do you do to earn a crust, cause it looks like, if you don't mind me saying, you do alright." The question always came, eventually and usually Shane didn't care, saying the first thing that came into his head. Property development, finance, anything that explained having money and no business. But there was something quite disarmingly honest about Craig and while he didn't want to lie

– he caressed his bottom lip and was saved. Lisa came into the kitchen, trailing Billy by the hand. The boy was in pyjamas. He went to his father and they wrestled. Craig got Billy in a headlock and tickled him until he screamed. Lisa said. "Craig!" Billy wriggled out of the headlock, took a step back and with a bloodcurdling yell, flung himself at Craig, who tickled him into submission. Craig hugged Billy, Billy kissed his dad, Lisa said. "About time." He stood in front of Shane and held out his hand. They shook formally and smiling shyly, Billy said. "Goodnight Shane." Although he wanted to laugh, Shane said, seriously. "Goodnight and very nice to have met you, Billy."

When she came back to the kitchen, Lisa blew an airy whistle of relief, shook her head and picking up her glass, said. "Cheers." She sipped, they all sipped, she said. "You know what they say about summer holidays lasting forever when you're a kid, well they last forever when you're a parent, as well!" Nodding her head at Shane, she said. "Seems to have taken a shine to you – and believe me, after all those months in the B and B he doesn't like everybody." They drank more whiskey. Talked about this and that, told a couple of jokes and had a laugh. Drank more whiskey. Raising their glasses to the visitor, Craig and Lisa, said. "Cheers!" They told him he was the first real person, not a social security officer, council official, cop, or oh yeh, a fireman, to cross the threshold. Shane poured more drink and saluted the pair of them for their hospitality to a stranger. The whiskey warmth had them in its golden triangle, relaxed, happy. After a while Shane looked at his watch, it was nearly eleven and he rose unsteadily to his feet. "I know I'm like one of the last few people in the entire world, but I don't have a mobile. Never had. Never wanted to be that available." Shane stopped abruptly almost as though he was giving too much away and got the cab drivers card out. He said. "Yeh, well anyway. Can I borrow your phone to get a cab?" Lisa looked at Craig, who raised his eyebrows and gave an unsure cock of his head. Catching their look, Shane said. "Alright? Yeh, I know, I've overstayed my welcome, right? No worries, I'll itty off. Get a cab on the way down the hill." Lisa said. "Well, it's getting late, we were just wondering –." Taking his mobile from his pocket, Craig put it on the table, and said. "You can borrow it if you like but, there's a spare room and a bed upstairs, if you wanted to stay here."

Shane sat down at the table, taken aback, once more, by their simple generosity in the teeth of the fears they obviously had. He couldn't figure whether they recognised what he was or if they didn't or whether they didn't care. That he wasn't one of Rowlands crew, seemed to be enough, for the moment. They had a bit more whiskey. Shane asked what they knew about Rowlands, again. Nothing. Except he definitely controlled the drugs on the estate. And he wanted their house. Lisa told Shane, that Rowlands was probably the reason his friends had fled north. But Shane couldn't believe it. Could not accept that Gerry, head like a brick, could be forced into anything. But did he know Gerry, anymore? There were times but those times were all in the past, when this house had been a second home and he wondered, then, momentarily, about himself, and if his wanderings and what he did, had changed him into someone Gerry would not recognise. Suddenly he didn't know what he was contemplating. A little shift, a rift, a ripple, a rip. Nothing. He said. "No, I don't see it, Gerry was stubborn man." Lifting her chin, to indicate the house they sat in, Lisa said. "You don't know the state this place was in when we first came to see it. If we hadn't been so desperate – the council have completely redecorated, new kitchen units, everything – we wouldn't have considered it. Graffiti everywhere, windows smashed, someone had put burning rags though the door at some point and the hall was soot black, the banister and stairs singed. And that's only the half of it." She wrinkled her nose, Craig said. "And a burned out car, just like ours, in the garden."

They put Shane in the small, twelve by six, bedroom at the front of the house, overlooking the

street. There was a single bed, a cheap bedside cab-
inet and a rug over the bare boards near the bed.
The bed was already made up and the curtains were
drawn. Lisa's handy work. He closed the door,
turned off the light and stood by the side of the
window, looking through the edge of the curtain,
down to the street outside. It was like watching a
cheap reality T.V. show, with the sound down. The
four youth on the corner were going about their
business. And a class A business it was. Shane
could tell by the wraps and rocks. Two lads serving
up and one on a bike, riding around, dropping off
for deliveries, one keeping an eye out. Tick tock
and it don't stop, with dead eyed cunts on foot,
legs all skin and bone, looking for a little credit or
a blow job compromise. Geezers in cars they can't
afford, looking dubious, quick cash over and gone.
Ordinary types, looking sly and giving it the double over the shoulder shot before copping. Couple
of women on bikes, few guys sliding by. Shane
watched for a while and then went to bed.

## 2

The sleep was all whiskey and bone weary tiredness, the long dragged out day clouting him into
easy submission and he was a sucker for it, for the
best of sleeps. Here in a strange bed, in a strange
house, his body felt safe. Safe at last, somewhere
and no–one knew where. Safe to take straight eight
in oblivion. Half waking in a splat of sunlight with
Billy knocking on the door, then in the room, grinning shy and proud, with an un-spilled cup of tea.
Shane propped himself up on his elbows. The tea
was hot and sweet. Billy asked Shane if he could
play draughts. Sipping tea, Shane said. "'Course.
Can you?" Looking at Shane as though he was a
complete fool, Billy went. "Chaa? Play you later!"
Then noticing the shoulder bag on the floor, said.
"Can I get your stuff out for you, Shane, can I?"
Expectantly he reached for the bag. In a double

quick movement, Shane put the tea cup on the floor and pulled the bag up on to the bed. He said. "No!" Too sharp, too final. It was only childish curiosity, Shane knew that and he caught Billy's hurt look, he said. "Sorry Billy, no – point, I'm not staying." Billy dropped his eyes, like he was really hurt but in a cheeky voice, said. "Scared I'll win." Picking up the tea again, Shane gave him a big smile. "Don't worry Billy boy, I reckon we'll fit a couple of games in before I slope off." Billy said. "Best of three." Sucking air through his teeth, Shane feigned pain. "Ooo, aah, you're hard! Three games?" Billy laughed. "Believe it sucker!" Shane laughed too. "Well then, there's something I've got to ask you. Being a little kid like, that don't mean you cry when you get beat, does it? 'cause you are definitely going to get beat." Big snort of laughter from Billy and he spun around in some M.T.V. dance move, pointing his fingers, like guns, at Shane. "No – way!"

From below, Lisa called up the stairs. "Billy!" The boy did a big slow double-take, face full of fake fear. Lisa again. "Billy, get down here and leave Shane in peace." On his way out the door, Billy stopped and with the confidence of his age, said. "Loser." Then he was gone. Putting the tea down, Shane flopped back onto the bed and closed his eyes. He thought about his other life, the tranquillity of his house in Morocco and the different way he was there. He knew what was going on here, like the variation on a theme. So why wasn't he gone? Letting this family and their shit get to him, like they were real friends, like Gerry and Louise. Yet here he was and still not sure what he was going to do. The way Shane saw it, we lived to our natures and the circumstances presented to us, learn to control our natures as best we can and change when circumstances change. Guilt didn't have much of a place in Shane's world because it was usually too late for guilt. Circumstance out paced it every time. He threw back the covers and got dressed.

Bacon, eggs and toast and Lisa said. "Lucky it was dole day, yesterday, else it would just be toast." Billy was telling her how bad he was going to beat Shane and Lisa was smiling at Shane and joking Billy into finishing his cereal. Billy told Lisa, Shane was leaving after their games and flat like it mattered, she said. "Well I expect he has things to do." Scraping his chair back, Billy said. "I'm out of here dudes!" Lisa waved him away and he launched himself from the room, stopping momentarily at the door, to warn Shane he was going to set up the board. Lisa said. "If you want to see Craig before you go, he's down in that shed, says he's going to have it down." Picking up Shane's plate and Billy's dish, Lisa wiped the table, she said. "Craig thought, well we both thought, when we moved here, things would get back to normal. He's a good man – he's put up with a lot. We don't want anything special, we just want to be left alone. That Rowlands and his thugs, they aren't going to leave us in peace, are they?" Tension showed in her face, just as it had when she'd first opened the door to Shane. What could he say that she could not already guess? Things could only get worse. She cocked her head in question. Shane wanted to tell her it would be easier to move or to swap houses with whoever it was Rowlands wanted them to swap with, but somehow he couldn't. He shrugged and looked away, he said. "I don't know, I'm not them." Lisa did not let go, she looked him up and down, like she knew what he was, until he looked at her, she said. "No but –." The telly went on in the living room and some dippy kids treacle mumbled through the house. Lisa said. "You know he won't let you go until he's beaten you, don't you?" Shane said. "That's what I'm afraid of. Look, I'll go and see Craig."

The shed, when he got close up, was looking old. Still sturdy and still dominating the garden but the years were on it. It was ridiculous now to think of the trouble Gerry had gone to, like anything mattered ten years on. The whole dream Gerry had of making furniture. Who was going to buy it? It was a working man's dream of another life and dreams sustain everybody, so Shane had never asked that question. The large windows, designed to let in the optimum light, were blacked out. The interior of the workshop was painted bright white. Craig was sitting on the workbench, studying a yellowed leaf in the palm of his hand, he looked over at Shane, he said. "Looks like your mate changed his hobby." As Shane joined him, Craig spread the large leaf out on the bench and said. "I may be straight but I ain't no fucking muppet." Shane said. "Yeh, right." Craig stared at him and Shane looked casually around the room. A running gantry, for electric lights, hung from the ceiling. It could be raised or lowered and was tied off to a hook on the wall. There were no lights or transformers, though, nor baths or pumps. Gerry had obviously taken any thing of value with him. There was a standpipe in one corner, with an old white, stone sink under it. Shane said. "Yeh, looks like a grow-room to me, too." Craig said. "Lisa reckons I'm gullible, you know, trust people too easily." Shane walked across to the tap, he said. "Lisa seems like a sensible woman to me." He turned on the tap. A splurge of rust-coloured water bounced into the sink. He turned it off and said. "I'd trust her judgement."

He went back to where Craig was sitting. The two men studied each other. Shane said. "Got any tools?" Beside Craig on the bench, were a couple of half-arsed screwdrivers and a three quid hammer, he said. "Not really." He paused, he said. "What you doing here, Shane?" Shane smiled at Craig but even if Craig had been Gerry, it wouldn't make any difference, some things you didn't explain, he said. "I ain't anything to do with Rowlands, if that's what you mean." He picked up the hammer and weighed it in his hand. He'd once killed a man with such a hammer. He placed the hammer back on the bench, he said. "We've all got obligations. I have to earn money. Sometimes I have to come to England, sort a few things out." Shane spoke lightly, but Craig studied him. Shoving his hands in his pockets, Shane began to mooch around the room again, he said. "That's why I'm here. Had things to do I couldn't get out of." Craig said. "Sorted?" With a nod, Shane said. "Yeh, yeh. But I suppose I was feeling lonely. Should have kept in touch with Gerry and Louise." Billy swept into the workshop, making mad war type noises, explosions, screaming laser directed shells, rat tat tat and all that and the two men watched him.

It was game time. Craig sent Billy back to the house and when the two men were alone again, Shane said. "What you going to do about Rowlands? If he's after the house, he'll want the shed as well." With a big sigh, Craig pushed himself off the bench. "Don't know. Don't want to run away, chances are we'd just end up in bed and breakfast, again. We've got nothing to fall back on, you know. Benefits hardly last the week. I want to rip the fucking shed down and tell Rowlands and his crew to piss off." They stepped out of the workshop, into the garden, Shane said. "It would be easier to take Rowlands' offer. Swap houses, screw a few bob out of him for your trouble, get on with living." They stood for a moment, looking at the house, at the pale blue sky and the Simpson clouds painted on it, at the bright sun and the washing hanging on a line, a few gardens down. Birds were singing, the world didn't look like a bad place. Craig said "Is that what you'd do?" There was no edge to it, just a flat statement, neither demanding, hardly questioning. Shane said. "We're different people."

On this part of the estate, the houses, semi-detached, had been built with good sized front and back gardens, as though the post war working classes had as much right to space in their lives, as anyone of their betters. Further into the estate, the gardens were smaller, the houses meaner. An alley, the width of a small truck, ran between each pair of houses, ending like the gardens, at a brick wall. Twenty foot high, behind which the derelict, dead remains of the huge engineering firm that once dominated the town, rotted. A couple of hundred feet on, the brick work turned to chain link, ten feet high, separating the estate from the bevy of DIY superstores, carpet warehouses and giant supermarkets, that now filled the waste ground, around the canal which ran down towards the

Thames.

Shane said. "What about the neighbours?" Looking to the side, where a low, green painted, wooden fence separated their garden from their immediate neighbour, Craig said. "Don't know. There's an old guy lives next door. See him doing his garden, sometimes. Say hello, that's about it." That garden was all immaculate borders, neat clipped lawn, narrow concrete path and dapper little shed and was exactly as Shane remembered it, from ten years ago. On the alley side of Craig and Lisa's, the council had fitted a new fence, about four feet high. On the other side of the alley, the rotted fence of the next house, lay in the rubbish tip of a garden, like the bones of a dead fish. Shane said. "What about over there?" Craig pulled a face. "Bloke and a woman, don't even look at you if you pass them in the street. Their lad is one of the corner boys, lives there with some girl and a kid." Indicating the workshop, Shane said. "Do you want a hand getting that fucking monstrosity down?" He laughed. "'Cause it won't be easy, 'specially with the tools you've got."

In the living room the TV was off and Billy was a picture of concentration. Halfway through the second game now, and he was desperate, determined, as only a child can be, to win. Much to Billy's chagrin, Shane had shaded the first game. A tight win, and one won only when Shane started to play hard and fast and forget that he was playing a child. Somewhere, during that first game, Shane had come to the conclusion that living in a B and B must be a bit like being inside and that the kid was good and was going to beat him, if he didn't kick it. But into the second game and he was on the back foot again. Billy had come out of the traps, quick, double shuffle, look around, restraint enough to draw Shane forward, then bish, bosh. Two pieces of his by Billy's side. Battening down the hatches, blocking, parrying, Shane managed to take a piece but Billy was still one up on events. To Shane, the board looked uncomfortably equal. He tried to move like he wasn't disturbing the balance of the board, like treading water. As he took away his hand, Billy moved on something unseen, this way, that way, taking two more. But Shane was lucky, the game swung towards him. But Billy was lucky and good. He broke open Shane's defence and once kinged, was the master of the back flip and the double dutch sideways leap. Shane was always one step behind. When he was kinged, he could only snap at the heels of Billy's raging monarchs. The boy was too good.

Ra, ra, ra! Billy was ecstatic. He puffed out his chest. Third game. "The last game." Shane said. "The decider." Billy said. He jumped up, did a quick circuit of the room, pointed a finger at Shane and in a tough-guy, American accent, said. "This time it's personal!" He flopped back into the chair, rubbing his hands together and gurning like an old man. "Mugs away." Shane moved. Billy mirrored. Shane moved. Billy mirrored. A long slow front opened up across the board. First blood to Shane. Shane laughed. Billy growled. The desire to win overcame Billy's caution and Shane punished him. Two more. Three make a nice little pile and Shane made a show of getting the plastic disks just how he wanted them, one, two, three. Histrionics akimbo, Billy flopped about in his chair, like a beached fish, pulling faces and having death throws and just as Shane was wondering if he was being cruel by really trying to beat the kid, Billy clicked into action. Now it was really bish bash bosh and Shane was too slow and Billy was on a roll. He bounced around the board, like Shane was standing still. Shane shook his head, tried his best, but it was power plays all the way. Billy gave no quarter. Big grins, emphatic win. Shane had had enough but Billy wanted more. They settled on a friendly.

When it was over, Shane had the distinct impression Billy had let him win. They had talked, on an off, through the games. Billy found out that Shane had a swimming pool and lived by the sea, that he had ridden on a camel and wasn't married. That if he didn't argue about the price of everything, the shopkeeper or stall holder would think he was stupid. Except of course, bread and toilet roll and then they would think he was stupid too. That gave Billy a laugh. Shane was a liar. It was true, Shane told him, he was a liar. That gave Billy another laugh. What Shane learnt was, whenever you left your room in the bed and breakfast, you always made sure the door was locked. That, in a family room there was a telly, a sink, a big bed and a little bed, for Billy. That when he went to the toilet, either his mum or his dad went with him because there are a lot of weirdos out there and it was against the rules to run in the corridors and Billy's best friend had been an Albanian. Shane asked Billy if he had made any friends since they had moved. Billy told Shane no, his mum wouldn't let him play outside the garden anymore because of the bad men that burned dad's car and that would be why it would be really good if Shane stayed a bit longer, then he, Billy, wouldn't get bored so much. Simple. There wasn't any arguing with that kind of logic and anyway, Shane was going to help his dad with the shed and Billy could do him a favour and tell Craig, he had gone to borrow some tools.

When Billy was gone, Shane sat for a few minutes, putting the pieces back in the box. He could hear Lisa moving about upstairs, making the beds or something and there was Craig outside, trying to take down that fucking shed with a three quid hammer. What was happening to this family, was happening on other estates up and down the country. It was a growing tide of shit. And what about himself? No–one could change things, not really but things changed anyway. And why had Gerry started to grow Skunk? Why had the family scarpered up north? A hoover started up above his head, he glanced out the window. Near the top of the cul–de–sac opposite, a few kids had a ramp set up and were skateboarding over it. A car cruised by. A woman with a pushchair and shopping bags was trying to cajole a toddler on a leash, to walk faster. Nothing out there seemed more than normal. Reality was a strange thing.

Quietly closing the front door, Shane nipped across the front of the house, stepped over the low, dividing fence, between the front gardens, and in a moment was ringing the neighbour's doorbell. A skinny, unshaven, wey faced man, in his late sixties, opened the door, he said. "Alright, Shane. Saw you go by, yesterday. Come in." He did, and as he did, Shane said. "You alright, Stan?" They went through to the living room. The house had a quiet feel, the furnishings and decorations, dusty and faded. Seeing Shane glance about, Stan said. "Lacks a woman's touch." Shane said. "Where's the misses?" Flicking a finger towards an armchair, Stan said. "Park your arse." When they were both seated, he said. "Died three years ago. Had a dodgy heart for ages. Since she was a kid." He rolled one hand slowly around the other, his eyes were sad and still surprised at his loss. Shane could see him lost and lonely but he had nothing to say, he said. "I'm sorry, Stan." It wasn't enough. Stan didn't mind, he knew nothing anyone said could ever be enough, he said. "Yeh, well, anyhow, you look like you're doing well. Still living abroad? Well you would be, wouldn't you." Shane nodded, he came forward in his chair, he smiled at Stan, he said. "Looks like you still got your health and by the way you're sussing me out, your brains and all. It's a shame about your wife dying like that. It seems, Stan, things ain't what they used to be, not here or next door."

Standing up, Shane stretched himself and walked around the room looking at its mish mash of styles. The DVD player, all black and modern, the wide screen TV and sitting on top, a framed, black and white photo of some old time wedding, twenties, thirties? Shane didn't know, didn't care, he needed to know a few things and to borrow a nailbar, a saw and a decent hammer. Stan said. "Well they say, what don't kill you makes you stronger. At my age, it seems what don't kill you makes you that bit weaker. You don't come back all the way from some things." Shane came and stood in front of Stan, with his arms folded, he said. "I can believe that." Looking up at Shane, Stan said. "Don't waste your time trying to scare me, I'm too old to give a fuck. What you doing back here? You ain't come to pass the time of day, have you? What you after?

Oh, I know. Your mate next door pissed off up North, five, six months ago, alright." Back in the chair again, Shane said. "Why was that?" Stan said. "Upset the wrong person." He paused and Shane cocked his head. The older man sucked his teeth and glanced involuntarily at the unused ashtray on top of the gas fire, he said. "Gave it up five years ago but you never really get rid of the urge, do you." Never having been a smoker, Shane shrugged. "Guess not." Stan looked again at the ashtray and down at the carpet, and said. "Don't get me wrong, I liked Gerry. Gave me that coffee table." He nodded towards a low hardwood table with stumpy legs. "Things have changed around here, in the last few years and he was a stubborn man." Shane said. "Rowlands, the guys on the corner?" With some effort, Stan pushed himself upright and licked his lips, he said. "What's the time?" There were two clocks in the room, neither worked. Shane showed the old man his watch. Stan went over to a seventies style drinks trolley, with several bottles sitting on it, he said. "I'm having a drink, what about you? Want one?" Shane shook his head. "Too early." The pensioner poured himself a brandy, sipped and sat back down.

He said. "When we, Beth and me, moved in here, it was a step up. First time either of us had a bathroom or an inside toilet. Yeh, it's changed around here alright. Ain't as bad as some of those sink estates you hear about, but it's rough now. Those young blokes, it's drugs, place is rotten with 'em. Been going on for ages. Coppers take them away every once in a while but they're back again the next night." Shane said. "That'd be right." A sip of his drink and Stan said. "The tall skinny one, has cap back to front." Shane said. "I know the one, saw them out there last night." Stan looked Shane in the eye, he said. "They all do that though, don't they?" Shane said. "What?" Stan smiled. Shane chuckled and said. "You old cunt." Stan said. "Anyway, Gerry upset his daddy by beating the shit out of the streak of piss. And his dad ain't the sort of person you really want to upset." Shane said. "Rowlands?" With a nod and a grin, Stan said. "The fat man." Shane laughed, Stan laughed. "That's what he's called by a lot of people around here – The fat man – but not to his face. Funny thing is, when he was a teenager, he was as skinny as that misbegotten son of his. He started porking up in his twenties and never stopped. Reckons he's got a thyroid problem, I reckon he eats too much."

Shane said. "So why did Gerry batter the son?" Looking away at the gas-fire, Stan was reluctant, he swilled the last of the brandy around in the glass and drank it down. He copped a sideways look at Shane and maybe he didn't like what he saw, he said. "I know what you are, Shane. I know how you earn your money, and Gerry wasn't lily white at the end of the day, either." They sat in silence, Shane looked at his fingernails and Stan got another drink. Shane said. "Yeh, I know, been in the workshop, wasn't carpentry." Standing in front of the gas-fire as though it was on, Stan raised his glass, he said. "Drug farmers to the right of me, thugs to the left of me, dealers to the front of me, gangsters behind me – gawd, what a lovely world!" Shane said. "And?" Still in front of the fire, the old man sipped brandy and looked at Shane as though something incomparably fine was passing over his tongue, he said. "He got Gerry's eldest, Mark, on smack. After Gerry did Dean, that's the son, all hell broke loose. Louise couldn't hardly go out of the house, for the abuse and threats of what they were going to do to her. Two or three of them attacked her over by the shops one afternoon, robbed her, roughed her up – next thing I know, they've flitted. But that was just the last straw. Before that it was shit parcels through the letterbox, front of the house graffitied, petrol poured through into the hall, followed by a light. But you know how it goes, don't you?" Evenly, Shane said. "I don't suppose Gerry left a forwarding address or anything?" Without answering, Stan slid back into his chair and gave Shane a queer look.

Shane said. "Alright Stan. I know what I am as well and I've got no beef with you. Just tell me some stuff, Stan. Like, I can understand how things went with Gerry and Rowlands, but why the new people, next door? Why start out on them?" Stan said. "Don't know. Just wants his way, I expect." A long quiet minute ticked by, Stan looked at the gas-fire and Shane stared at Stan. Eventually, without looking up, Stan said. "You can't account for people like the fat man and you know it. There'll always be stupid bastards ready to do what he wants, for drugs or money. There's whole bloody families hooked on one drug or another around here – he's in easy street. I tell you, there ain't no G.H.C's (good honest criminals) anymore." He grinned at Shane, who sneered jokingly and said. "Were there ever?" All serious, Stan said. "No." Shane smiled. Finishing the brandy and standing the glass on top of the fire, Stan said. "Look, I've got to live here. I don't want any trouble from him – him and my son Rod have got an arrangement – but I don't want any trouble from you, either. But like I said, Gerry was very hard headed and before he left, he burnt out Rowlands' new white Merc'. And Gerry was doing very nicely out of the plantation, out back. Maybe the fat cunt just thinks he could make even more money. Maybe he just wants to flex his muscle's, muscles." Shane said. "Yeh, who knows." He wasn't getting anywhere, what was the point? He said. "Got any tools, Stan? Need to borrow, I don't know, a decent hammer, a saw, nail bar, you know."

The tools were all in a cupboard, under the stairs and Shane dragged them out into the hall, for Stan to go through. He gave Shane an old lump hammer, a couple of saws, two cold chisels, a small nail bar and a roofer's axe. As he handed the last item to Shane, he said. "My Rod's a roofer. Handy tool." The axe was about fifteen inches long, rubber grip over a steel shaft, the integral head, axe shaped at the front, had a three inch long spike at the back. Handy tool, Shane agreed, as he passed it back to the old man. Stan looked at him from under his eyebrows. Shane said. "Won't be putting no roofs on, just pulling that old monstrosity down." Putting the axe back in the toolbox, Stan said "And you don't think that will cause more trouble?" "Not my idea. I'm just helping the people who gave me a bed for the night." Unconvinced, Stan said. "Right." Shane looked straight at Stan, who shook his head and said. "You can go out the back way." As they walked through the house to the back garden, he said. "My son, Rod, went to school with Rowlands. They hung about together when they were teenagers. Rod's a big man. He helped Rowlands out, a few years back, when the fat cunt was still thin and didn't have a pot to piss in. That's why I don't get robbed or harassed in the street. When the cops come asking what I've seen, I've never seen nothing. And I'm telling you now, Shane, when they come asking again, it'll be the same." Shane said. "Makes sense. Anyway I ain't never been here or next door, so that suits me." Stan nodded, like he understood, and he probably did. He was an old man and he only wanted to be left alone. Maybe he really just wanted to tell Shane to fuck off and not give him the tools, instead he said. "Most of Rowlands lot are just yobs, not real heavies, but watch out for Wilson and Dalrimple."

# 3

It was nearly mid day by the time the two men began work. Craig had already disconnected the electricity. The water for the tap, in the shed, came from a hose connected to a stand pipe at the back of the house, which neither Craig nor Lisa had even noticed before. Craig had disconnected that also.

Inside the shed, the two men ripped down the running gear for the lights, along with the sheeting material on the ceiling and dragged the lot out onto the overgrown lawn. Then they hacked and smashed the work benches, which lined two of the walls and threw the bits out on top of the other stuff. Next the door was off and the windows out. Craig put the window frames to one side, cold frames, he reckoned. The sun was hot and the work was hot. They pulled off their shirts. They were men of a similar height and build, around six feet, neither gone to fat. But Shane was deeply tanned, his body slick and toned, like a boxers, where Craig was pasty, English white, and his body was softer, less muscled, but still in reasonable shape for a man knocking on forty. Both looked up at the sun, wiped the sweat from their brows and laughed. Shane pulled out some money and stuffed it into Craig's hand, he said. "Maybe, without seeming too macho, you could get Lisa to itty off and get us a few beers, I reckon we may need 'em." They laughed again.

When Lisa and Billy got back from the shops, all the sheds interior cladding was on the heap and Craig and Shane, in the full pleasure of the physical, were battering the ship-lap planks off the outside, in a whirl of flying hammers and wood. Lisa produced sarnies to accompany the beer and everything was hunky-dory, everything was good and the work stopped. Lisa was obviously glad the thing was coming down. She proposed a toast to better times ahead and they clanked cans, even Billy, who was on Tizer. The men slowed down the work to incorporate the boy, who mashed joyfully at the friable planks, dragging his broken successes onto the heap. He raised his fist to the air. "Bonfire, yes!" As they worked, Shane said. "This ain't going to endear you to Rowlands, you know that, don't you?" There was a moment or two, a couple of beats of the hammer, no-more, Craig stopped and said. "That's why it's got to come down. What else can I do? I ain't being pushed any further." Shane said. "You've never seen Rowlands, right?" Craig shook his head. "Know what they call him around here?" Craig shook his head again. With a grin, Shane said. "The fatman." A hoot of laughter erupted from Craig, he said. "The fatman! I like it!" He battered a few more planks and laughed again. Shane said. "They won't let it go. Things could get nasty." Craig said. "I ain't going nowhere. If he is the fatman, then the fat bastard will have to burn the house down!" Voice serious, Shane said. "It could come to that." The two men looked at each other and Craig said. "I know."

Eventually the workshop was nothing more than a four by two frame, topped by a plywood and felt roof, Lisa said. "You could take the roof off and call it a pergola, what do you reckon?" Craig laughed, he said. "You know what they say, pergola today, Indonesian garden furniture tomorrow – it's a slippery slope – a fishpond feature, a rockery and bud-a-bing, suddenly you've got a garden to maintain and you know what? Then you need a shed to keep all the gardening tools in!" Lisa punched Craig on the arm and then hugged and kissed him, Billy said. "Mum, Dad!" Craig grabbed Billy and they had a three way hug, with Billy loving it and going. "You're daft you're silly." Their happiness made Shane happy in himself and he knew he would not be leaving right away. Lisa got more beers from the fridge.

Cutting through most of the uprights, they got behind one corner of the now unstable structure and pushed. All four straining and laughing as the squealing, creaking, structure, teetered and fell like a pole-axed ox, slowly to the ground. It was a good sight to see the great pile of rubbish and they popped cans and said. "Cheers!" A car came slowly down the alley.

Almost without moving, Shane picked up the lump hammer and held it casually, down by his side. Craig tensed and Lisa took his hand as surreptitiously as Shane had picked up the hammer. Billy was running around the wrecked shed, with a length of electric cable as a lasso, going hut, hut, hut. Wilson and Dalrimple were easy to tell apart, the large and the little, the panther and the rat. Moving beside Craig, Shane touched his arm and said. "Don't. Whatever. It don't matter. Leave it." Craig eyes didn't say anything, his nose wrinkled, Shane took that as a good sign and said. "It's only a wind-up mission." It only took moments for Wilson and Shane to recognize each other for what they were. Wilson was bigger than Shane but both knew that in the end, that that didn't count. Dalrimple was skinny, no more than five-five, pinched face with eyes on sticks and a cocaine jaw. If there was going to be trouble, Shane would have him first. Billy stopped running when he saw the two men.

Wilson and Dalrimple stood by the fence. Billy went and stood by his mother. Dalrimple kicked a fence post and rubbed the back of his hand under his nose, bug eyes jumping from face to face, his chawed up, snake smile, dispensed on one and all, like the promise of plague. He giggled under his breath. Wilson just licked his lips and looked at the pile of wood that was the shed. No one spoke, until Wilson said "I told you politely, that we would need that shed when you moved out. I don't like to have to tell people things twice. I don't like it when people I've gone out of my way to be polite to, do things they know will upset me."

Tossing her beer can on to the pile of wood, Lisa said, loudly. "It's our garden and we'll do what we want. Who do you think you are? Coming around to people's houses trying to intimidate them – the council gave us this place, we got it fair and square. You got a problem, go and argue with them – leave us alone!" Although she started off tough Lisa ended sounding what she was, scared. Wilson and Dalrimple exchanged a look. Nodding at Lisa, Wilson sneered and addressed Craig. "Your misses needs to be taught that there's only one time a woman needs to open her mouth – and it ain't to talk." Dalrimple was looking Lisa up and down, giggling, he said. "Sounds like a job for me." Craig made to move, Shane grabbed his forearm and said. "Don't." Wilson laughed, Dalrimple fixed his skittering eyeballs on Craig and through grinding teeth, he said. "You better listen to your pal, pal." Turning his attention to Shane, for the first time, Wilson said. "Whoever your "pal" is." The "pal" was loaded, snide and dismissive. Craig gave Shane a sideways look and so did Lisa and Billy, but Shane wasn't forthcoming. There was nothing to say that wouldn't make things worse and violence, Shane had learned early, should be a chosen not a given, and chosen wherever possible, by him. He smiled blandly at Wilson. Dalrimple said. "The strong silent type." Under his breath, Billy said. "Shane?" Craig said. "Why don't you take Billy inside, love."

On the opposite side of the alley, in the top, back room of the house with the broken down fence, a couple of guys watched the action, for what it was worth, which was shite. Shane had seen them pull back the blanket, which posed as a curtain, when the car had first crunched down the alley. Two at least, he could see the peaks of their baseball caps, featureless in the shadows but young, he guessed. He'd watched them from the corner of his eye, maybe they were tooled up, you never knew – waiting up there, but no. Shane had them pegged as a couple of the corner boys.

Lisa was walking towards the house, with Billy by the hand, as she passed Dalrimple, he wagged a fat, lascivious tongue at her and leered. "Mmm definitely and nice legs too. You can be sure I'll be seeing you." Without warning, Billy jerked free from his mother and wielding the electric cable, like a whip, slashed at Dalrimple's face. The boy was lucky. The end of the flex, where the wire showed copper, caught Dalrimple's ear and drew blood, even as he caught the cable and ripped it viciously from the child's hand. Lisa leapt after Billy. Craig was going the same way when Shane grabbed him in a bear hug. Dalrimple was halfway over the fence before Wilson got to grips with him. The lads in the window laughed and Billy was screaming in anger and Dalrimple, even as he was pulled towards the car, was trying to slash the boy with the cable and only Lisa saved him, dragging him backwards, onto the grass.

Wilson held Dalrimple against the car, Shane heard him growl. "Leave it you cunt. Drop the cable." And Craig heard it too, and Shane loosened his grip. Dalrimple let the cable slide from his hand, to the ground. Wilson said. "Come on." As he pushed his partner towards the driver's seat of the car, Wilson pointed at Shane and said. "You're on the wrong side, pal." Craig said. "Why don't you piss off to your fat friend and tell him we 'ain't movin'." Wilson shook his head, as though he felt sorry for the poor, blind, fuckers who couldn't see common sense when it was set out for them.

Dalrimple had the car door open, he giggled and turning back towards where Lisa still comforted the irate Billy, said. "I'll see you again, sexy legs." Billy scowled and Dalrimple coughed and gobbed a large green ernie over the car roof at the boy. It fell, plop, in the grass a few feet away. Lisa could not hold Billy. He burst from her arms and launched himself at the fence, spitting as he went. A gob of mucus somehow managed to clear the fence and land, in a dribble, on the car's bodywork, but Dalrimple and Wilson were already in the car. Dalrimple revved the engine and spun the wheels, grass and pebbles bashed at the underside and they were gone, out the alley like a cork from a bottle.

## 4

That evening as they ate, gloom hovered over them all, even Billy, who was subdued to the point of silence. Craig fumed angrily and Lisa tried to make the best of it but her smile had died and her eyes were frightened. No one asked Shane if he was going to stay that night, it wasn't necessary. When he'd taken the tools back, Stan had laid a few more bits of information out for him. Like, Dalrimple lived in the house at the entrance of the cul–de–sac opposite, where the corner boys used his garden wall as their office. Further up, Wilson had a house and at the top, in bulb of the cul–de–sac, was Rowlands' place. Stan said. "People owe him money, people are scared of him, well Wilson and Dalrimple really, the rest of the estate turn a black eye." Shane laughed and said. "Don't you mean a blind eye!" Stan curled his lip. "No. Speak out of turn and a black eye's the least of it!" It wasn't what Stan had said as much, as that, an hour after the confrontation with Wilson and Dalrimple, some big youth on small bikes, spun by and paint bombed the front of the house with red, gloss paint.

Rowlands' house at the top of the cul–de–sac, was next to the alley which ran through to Bishops Crescent, which itself runs in a long, slow, curve, through the centre of the estate to the shops and the pub, The Temple Bell, on the precinct. Even after the years he'd been away, Shane could still remember the estate like the back of his hand and could see Rowlands' house was most conveniently placed for the trade he was in and he could almost see the fat fuck sitting there, like a spider at the heart of his web. He knew it wasn't like that and if you spoke to most crim's, they simply saw it as business, especially the drugs trade. Didn't he have a picture of himself at the top of a small mountain of hash blocks, flashing an AK? It was business, like some was legit, some was licensed, some was illegal, and that was down to vested interest, power and who had control, who made the laws. Things could be dressed up any way but empires were built on criminality. See the history books.

Lisa wanted to go out and start cleaning the paint off the front of the house almost as soon as it happened but Craig, slow burn mad now, wouldn't have it, he said. "Why bother? They'll just come back again." And with a practical turn, added. "Anyway, it'll be easier to clean off when it's dry." No one argued, even if he was wrong. The positive sense of achievement engendered by the destruction of the workshop had been wiped out by the run in with Wilson and Dalrimple. They all felt it, but especially Craig. The threats towards Lisa had had the desired effect and left him frustrated. He was a man unable to protect his family. He wanted to strike back, to do something, prove something, however futile. Shane counseled restraint, and said. "Let's think it through." Lisa said. "I would rather go back to the B and B, than have you hurt." Hardening his features, Craig said. "I ain't moving." Billy raised his eyebrows and looked at Shane and Shane ruffled his hair. Billy tried to give Shane a Chinese burn and Lisa said. "Leave it, Billy boy." Billy said. "I'm going upstairs, okay!"

When Billy was out of the room, Shane told them most of what he had learnt from Stan. When he mentioned that Rowlands spent most evenings in the pub, The Temple Bell. That there was a corner in the front bar, that the fat man and his cronies considered their own, like an open plan office, Craig began to chew at the bit. Shane could see the desire for confrontation running through his head, the desire to strike back at the cause of his trouble, whatever the cost. After Shane had said his piece and Lisa had commented, that it was like they were just a bit in someone else's puzzle, Craig got up from the table and hands shoved in his pockets, began to walk around the kitchen. Lisa watched him, and said. "Craig?" Like he was afraid to take his hands out of his pockets and find they had their own violent intentions, Craig stopped, holding his elbows akimbo, a nasty look on his face, he said. "Is that all we ever are! Just some bit in someone else's jigsaw. We've been shoved around from pillar to post and those shits out there today, who do they think they are! They act like there ain't no law – well, and there ain't, is there! Call the cops and they tell you they can't do bugger all without proof. Keep a video diary they say, make a note of every incident, then we'll slap their wrists and set them free to torment you some more."

Hopelessly, Lisa said. "Alright Craig, love." But it wasn't alright, by Craig, who still, hands in pockets, paced the room. He said. "No, it's not alright. Billy's got more guts than me. What am I like, standing there while they insult you?" Lisa said. "I don't care what they say." Standing in front of her, Craig said, vehemently. "I do!" He took his hands out of his pockets and flopped them about, he went. "Aaarg!" Shane and Lisa looked at him. Craig stared back at them as though they were the mad ones and, with a nod, like he had made a decision and knew exactly the right thing to do, said. "Look,

I worked hard today, didn't I?" No one argued. Walking around again, arms making shapes like he could get it for you wholesale, Craig continued. "Made me feel like a man, again and, as a man again, I find I have a dry throat. I feel I deserve a pint, or three. With my co-worker, Shane, if he's interested?"

Lisa studied Shane but Shane didn't give a damn, because he didn't intend to answer Craig. Craig cocked his head at Shane, and said. "Well?" Shane didn't answer. Lisa said. "Why do you want to go to the pub? Do you want to go to the pub, Shane?" Shane shrugged, he knew Lisa was afraid and she had reason and he knew Craig was scared, as well. Once confrontation was decided upon, then there was no going back, and if he must, Shane would go to the pub with Craig. Lisa said. "Anyway, there's still beers in the fridge." Craig wasn't having it, wasn't to be mollified, he said. "And?" Lisa didn't answer, Craig said. "I'm going to the pub." Silence. Upstairs, Billy could be heard, bang, ping, pow, like he'd got some private cowboy game going on for himself. They heard him running on the landing and coming down the stairs, killing as he came, bang, bang, die sucker, pow, zap, and all of a sudden he was in the kitchen doorway, the large, dull, shape of Shane's 9mm, Glock, semi-automatic pistol, held in both hands.

The thing Shane noticed immediately was that

the safety was on and that the clip was in. Billy, legs splayed, had them covered from the hall doorway, ready to zap, bang, pow them, in a blaze of hot lead. Shane didn't wait for Lisa's exclamation of horror or Craig's movement towards his son, in a quiet voice, which brooked no argument, Shane said. "Give that to me now." He reached out and took the gun, barrel first and Billy, the excitement of his game suddenly dead in his eyes, relinquished the weapon without a word. And he looked at Shane knowing he'd done something wrong but only half guessing what, as in a rush of exclamations and questions, Lisa and Craig surrounded him. Shane took the clip from the gun and laid both carefully on the table as he waited, for the comeback to flow his way. Almost in tears, Billy looked from his parents to Shane and in a broken voice, said. "I just, just – it was – in, in –." He didn't have to say much more, Craig and Lisa could guess where this alien object had come from. Lisa clutched Billy to her breast, her eyes, like death stars, turned on Shane. She was almost too angry to speak, but spluttered. "We! You! How!" Then Craig's rage at Rowlands swung pendulum-wise at Shane.

First he bellowed. "I trusted you!" Then pushing Lisa and Billy aside, he screamed. "You! You fucking cunt!" He swooped down and clutched the front of Shane's shirt, their faces now inches apart, and continued yelling. "Spend all day with you, you cunt! Let you stay here, treat you like a friend, you fucking cunt!" Billy shouted. "It's not Shane's fault." Frustration and anger still not spent, he jabbed a finger at Billy. "Shut it! Fucking shut it!" Billy hugged his mother, she didn't know what to do and pleaded. "Craig." Face back in Shane's, Craig wasn't having any. Obviously seething, he controlled himself and said. "Don't tell me nothing! Don't tell me about swearing, when this fucker brings a gun into the house." Shane said nothing and wished now that he had dumped the weapon. He looked at it on the table while Craig ranted and raved and pushed and shoved at him. It didn't matter to Shane, Craig could have really hit him and it wouldn't have mattered. Although Craig was angry, the anger seemed directed at himself and he looked closer to tears than real violence. Billy had started to grizzle and Lisa was sobbing. Once again, she pleaded. "Craig." Looking at them, Craig licked his lips and took a couple of deep, safety first breaths, stepped back and shoved his hands back in his pockets.

Nobody said or did anything, nobody looked at anyone else. Shane stood and picked up the gun and clip, he said. "I'm sorry. I'll get my stuff and leave." Lisa and Craig looked at him then, both hopeless and sad and Billy sobbing a big one and under his breath, said. "It's not fair." As Shane began to climb the stairs he heard Lisa tell Craig she was taking Billy upstairs. Near the top, he heard the spring of Billy's step on the treads and then Lisa admonishing shout. "Billy!" Glancing behind him as he came, the boy rushed up to Shane, going. "Sorry Shane! Sorry!" On the landing, Shane squatted in front of Billy, he said. "It was my fault, Billy boy. You've got nothing to be sorry about." And Lisa was there then, with Craig two steps below and Shane said to them, too. "I'm the one who's sorry." Then he went into the small bedroom, shut the door and sat on the edge of the bed, with his head in his hands.

From the room beside him, Shane could hear the low, mumbling tones of Lisa and Craig, as they talked to Billy. Not words. Sounds and a silence. Could that be Lisa crying? Shane hoped not. He lifted his head and looked through the window. He wondered why the corner boys were not at their post. Eight oclock or there about, he figured. It was like with Lisa crying. A person doesn't always have to see or hear everything. Shane knew what he felt, trusted himself and that, down the years, had made him. That and an ability to kill and maim. It paid the rent and sometimes, in the past, it had given him pleasure. He had tried to change his life but still he could do what he could do and sometimes he still did what he could do. And he thought about the youths looking down on them, from the house across the alley, when Wilson and Dalrimple were there. Why weren't they plying their trade? Time really was money. Maybe it was simply that they did not want to be questioned about the paint bombs, should the police turn up, which they wouldn't. "What was the point." Craig had said. Or it could be that something else was planned. He felt sorry for Craig and Lisa. In the end, despite Craig's attempts at bravado, they would be soon forced out. The world they were rubbing up against was ruthless and Shane was going to walk and leave them to it, and there was a sense of relief in that. To walk away and say, this ain't my problem and why should he feel bad anyway? It really wasn't his problem. He was just sorry to part company with them this way. Shane packed his bag.

He came out of the bedroom, ready to go and as he hesitated on the landing, wondering about a goodbye, Craig came out of the next room. Shane said. "I'm off, then." Closing the door behind him, Craig took a deep breath, raised his eyebrows and sighed, he said. "Don't go. Lisa's scared. We don't know what's going on and we think we need some help. Please." Reaching out, Craig took the bag out of Shane's hand and opening the little bedroom door, pitched it inside. Again, Shane said. "I'm sorry." Craig, a lump in his throat catching his voice said. "Yeh, well, guess I overreacted, too. Sorry." As they went down the stairs, Craig said. "I can't stand seeing Lisa crying."

They sat at the kitchen table again, thrashing out some kind of strategy. Craig still wanted to go to the pub, not for confrontation, but to show we live in a free country. For the first time, in what seemed like hours, Shane laughed. Craig said. "Yeh but, you know what I mean." Shane laughed some more, he said. "Yeh, I know exactly what you mean." Then Shane told Craig about the corner boys, and why maybe, they weren't about. He told Craig that the way he saw it was, it could only get worse. He told him, take the swop, take what money he could get, it was just business. Craig said. "But it's wrong." Shane shrugged, he didn't care, it didn't matter. He said. "There is no wrong to a man like Rowlands. Business is business. What is happening is what it is, it ain't personal, he don't give a shit about you. To him, the fact that you do care, just makes you a plonker." Craig's head bobbed and he drooped a bit, he said. "Right." Shane said. "I ain't saying, I'm just saying." Craig said. "Yeh, yeh, it's okay, but the crap is, you're probably right.I'm this plonker, who just wants to be left alone with his life, not to mention his wife." Shane said. "I don't think we should go to the pub tonight." Craig didn't argue, he said. "That'll cheer Lisa up anyway."

Shane told Craig, people don't understand anything until it's real to them. Craig said. "This is real to me but I don't think I understand it. I want to hurt someone and I haven't felt like that in years." With an ambiguous smile, Shane said. "You wanted to give me one earlier, didn't you?" Craig snorted through his nose, his shoulders shook, he grinned at Shane. "What the fuck do you expect!" Then they talked about what they should do and Lisa came down and they talked some more about giving in and taking the swop and Craig wasn't noisy but he wasn't for moving. What were they going to do, then? Lisa said. "Did you kill anyone with that gun?" Shane held up three fingers. Craig said. "Christ!" Lisa said. "Who were they?" Shane didn't want to go into details, obviously the bodies hadn't been found, yet. With a shrug, he said. "Faeces heads." Craig gave a snuffling little laugh. Lisa gave him the long look. Shane said. "It doesn't matter. Something had to be done, I was the one who done it." Lisa said. "So, you are like Rowlands and the rest, then." Shane said. "If you like." To Craig, he said. "When I said, people don't understand anything until it's real to them. I wasn't talking about you and Lisa. I was talking about Rowlands – and Wilson and Dalrimple. We've got to –" Delving into his pocket, Shane took out a fifty pence piece and slapped it down on the table top. "– Fuck them up."

# 5

Darkness fell and the corner boys were still conspicuous by their absence. Cars crept by and sped on. Others walked, looked about, waited and walked on. As Shane said. "There are others serving up elsewhere on the estate." He didn't bother to explain that it didn't matter if they managed to stop Rowlands, it was a growth business and some other fucker would soon replace him. Lisa was worried about guns, violence, about Billy, about the police, what would happen if they started taking the law into their own hands. Shane didn't have answers. He told them. "Every little thug's got some weapon or the other to do damage with and for sure the likes of Wilson and Dalrimple will have guns. But, for them, it would be easier to force you out, get you to leave, rather than kill you. For a few quid, someone like Rowlands can get your windows broken every day of the week, and worse."

Shane left Craig and Lisa sitting in the living room, with the lights out, waiting. It had been agreed that, providing they managed to get through the night in one piece, Craig and Shane would go to The Temple Bell, to try to come to a compromise with the Fatman. In the meantime, while Craig and Lisa watched for trouble, Shane went out into the night, but not far.

Even before he opened the back door, he could hear the female voice, belligerent, screeching. "Give it to me! You bastard!" Something crashed in an upstairs room. A rumbling, inaudible, male, voice was answered by more screeching. "Fucker! Shithead! Bastard! Give me it! Now! You shit, you fucker, I need it!" Male words. A slap. Female tears. Shane pulled the back door closed. The kitchen was a shit heap. The floor was a slalom of squashed food bits and aged, take-away container lids. Despite a washing machine and a dishwasher, washing-up and filthy clothes covered every surface. The place had a dirty, buttery smell, overlaid by a shit and piss stink from the dirty nappy overload spilling from the open rubbish bag, near the door to the hall. Above, the female voice began its litany, once more and from the open living room doorway a little girl, of about two, peered at Shane.

She came along the hall towards him, bare-foot, sucking her thumb, dressed in a long vest with a cartoon bear on the front. Her head was cocked, curious, her eyes were wide and Shane waited, as she approached, for stranger fear to kick in with vocals and tears but she was silent, and Shane wanted to keep it that way. He didn't like to hurt children but then again, he didn't like all children and there wasn't time to get to know this one. Shane reached out and grabbed her vest in his fist and as he pulled the child towards him, he clapped the other hand over her mouth and smothered her kicks and struggles with his arms and body. He looked into her wide open, frightened, eyes and scanned the kitchen, wondering what the fuck to do with her. He slid across the kitchen floor, to a pile of washing. Keeping his hand firmly over her mouth, he held her writhing body tight against his chest, with the one arm, while delving amongst the dirty clothes for, whatever, with the other. Up came a frilly blouse, too complicated. Up came a tiny, gossamer thin, pair of knickers. Shane put them in his pocket. Up came a pair of bloke type boxers, not long enough. The kid had stopped struggling. The woman upstairs had stopped her pitiful, empty threats and hopeless begging. Up came a t-shirt, perfect. Shane took the knickers from his pocket and as he lowered the kid to the floor, knelt on her legs and forced the knickers in a ball into her mouth and turning her onto her stomach, tied her hands behind her back, with the t-shirt. He dragged her across the kitchen by the back of her vest, opened the washing machine door and stuffed the kid in head first, forcing the rest of her body to follow. He quietly closed the porthole door. Click.

A wide-screen TV, sound down, was making colour in the dim living room. On the couch, nodding out, was a man in his late forties, with long, straggly hair, tied back in a ponytail. In an armchair facing the TV was a woman, younger than the bloke, maybe, greasy, unkempt. She was slumped, legs akimbo, and they were the skinniest legs Shane had ever seen, two pairs of football socks on each foot, pulled up to her knees. Her eyes were open but no one was home. Smacked out she could have been dead. They both could have been dead. They didn't see Shane and they were less real to him than the flickering TV. He quietly shut the door to the room and took the stairs in long silent strides. The door to the main bedroom was ajar, a light was on and he could hear someone moving about. Beside it was the mirror image of the little room Shane was sleeping in, except it was the little girl's room. The door was wide open and a night light was on. There was a mattress on the floor, the duvet was thrown back and a fluffy, pink crocodile lay on the sheet.

The main bedroom was ridiculously, voluptuously, furnished. One wall was a floor to ceiling mirrored wardrobe. Inadequate lighting came from a goldie looking, mini- chandelier, with a bunch of little candle shaped bulbs, half of which weren't working. There was a carpet in what may have been some kind of off white colour, once. It was as deep as an uncut lawn. There was a flouncy canopy hanging from the ceiling like a whore's parachute. The bed was a huge affair. The headboard was of pure leatherette. A great half moon of burnt orange and chocolate, vacuum sucked, into a pair of leaping gazelles and a sunset. There were outrider cabinets on either side of the king-sized mattress, in the same combination of colours as the headboard and painted in a representation of the South African Velt, grass swaying in the wind. Details were picked out in gold paint and the headboard was trimmed in brass metal tubing. By the window was a vanity table and chair, in the same design. There was a home entertainment centre, with a Plasma TV/DVD/CD, and two white leather armchairs. But like the rest of the house, the bedroom was skuzzy, grimy, like someone had got a gallon of cheap cooking oil and smeared the whole house. Even the banister rail had been sticky to the touch, as he'd come upstairs.

They were both young. He was maybe nineteen. She was even younger, seventeen or so. Small and thin, she had rat tail hair that hung down and hid her face, as she bent to her task. He was tall and slim, a baseball cap was perched on his head and his hands were in his pockets. There was a sneer of disgust on his face as he watched her on the bed, fix herself up. It was twenty, maybe thirty seconds before they noticed Shane in the room. He took his hands out of his pockets and tried to look hard. She opened and closed her mouth and swallowed saliva, she pulled the spike from her arm, and said, slowly. "Who the fuck are you!" At the same time, he said. "You're the mate of that cunt next door!" For a moment she thought she was queen of the world and sprang off the bed and dived at Shane, brandishing the syringe. But it was like she was moving in slow motion. As he blocked the first weak punch from the young guy, Shane grabbed her raised arm and jerked her towards him, smashing his forehead into her face and shoving her away and she staggered back, eyes rolling up in her head, on to the bed. Her nose broke and began to bleed but one way or another she felt no pain. Shane walked through the punk's punches and grabbed him by the throat, pushing him back until his head smacked hard against the wall. The youth was flailed about and squealed. "Who the fuck do you think you are." And Shane punched him full in the face and his lip burst, blood ran out of his nose, his arms dropped down by his sides and Shane held him, almost fastidiously, at arms length and back handed him a couple of times. The hat fell off his head. He began to cry. Shane gave him a tolchock in the belly so that his knees buckled a bit, tightened the grip on his throat and said. "Perhaps you're in the wrong job." The youth forgot momentarily what was happening and for the briefest second a ray of hope sparkled in his fearful, tearful eyes and stupidly, he croaked. "You from the job-centre?"

Shane dragged the guy across the room by his hair, kicking him if he squealed or tried to wriggle free. Shane didn't have an overall plan. He needed to garner some information and to start to undermine Rowlands and his cronies. How he would achieve this had not yet come to mind. Already he didn't know how to leave this house without doing more damage. He didn't like to kill children, or even smacked-out grandparents, but in the end, to him, it didn't matter. He knew what he was capable of but in the end he didn't want to hurt anyone. When he left, he wanted Craig and Lisa to be able to live unmolested and they, in the end, were only something that was an image, of something else, something lost. Sometimes Shane didn't like to think, so he thought and didn't think all at the same time and it worked for him. He threw the youth into one of the armchairs and looked down at him. The guy wound his arms around his head and waited for Shane to batter him some more.

When the blows didn't fall and the kicks didn't come, the arms slowly unfolded. Shane squatted in front of him, he took the young man's two wrists gently in a handcuff grip, in one of his own, he took the young man's jaw in his other hand, he said. "Whose is the kid?" For the first time there was a touch of real defiance in the punk and he tried to shove himself upwards and away from Shane. Going on about what would happen if Shane touched her and Shane gripped his wrists like they were some small rodents he was strangling and it hurt and the fear came back into his eyes and Shane hit him and said. "I do what I like." He struggled a bit and Shane hit him a bit. He started to cry again, he said. "That's my daughter! I love her! Don't hurt her. Don't! Where is she!" Shane said. "I'll show you where she is." He tried to get up again. Shane hit him and said. "In a minute."

"You'll need to pack a few clothes." He looked at Shane like he was speaking gobbledegook, he said. "Why?" Taking the young guy's jaw back in his hand, Shane gripped it, until he was writhing in the seat and explained. "Well, you won't want stay here, will you?" Confusion and pain scrunched up the youth's face. Shane said. "What do you think Rowlands and his crew will make of you, when he finds out everything you've told me? I would have thought going away was a top option." Through his twisted gob, he pleaded. "I ain't told you nothing." Dragging him upright by his hair, Shane hit him in the solar plexus and let him fall, choking to the floor, where he vomited. "Get up." Shane kicked him and he groaned. "Get up." Another boot. He didn't get up, he tried to crawl away instead and Shane grabbed the back of his snide designer top and half-lifting and half-dragging him propelled him out of the bedroom and down the stairs. Outside the kitchen, Shane said. "This place is a shithole." Sticking his foot in his arse, Shane sent the guy skidding across the kitchen floor on his hands and knees. The little girl looked panic stricken. The plug to the washing machine was there, on the worktop and Shane pushed it into a socket but did not turn it on. He was crying again and begging Shane and Shane turned the dial to spin and said. "Now tell me things."

Back upstairs some beans had been spilled, but not enough and the little girl was still in the washing machine. But through the time honoured facility of slaps and threats and minor torture, an agreement was arrived at. Shane asked the questions and the young guy answered. "Any of your mates got weapons?" "Fizzy and Dean have got blades." "Which one's Fizzy?" "Guy on the bike." "That all?" "It ain't the Bronx, anyway everybody knows who we're with." "Who's got a strap?" "I don't know." "Don't bother to lie." "Ouch! Alright! Alright! They've got them." "Who?" "Dean's dad." "The fat man?" "Got it all down pat, 'ain't you.

Ouch! Yeh, Rowlands and Wilson, too!" "Dalrimple?" "Don't please, not again! Yes, Dalrimple!" "You lot deal off Dalrimple's wall, right?" "Please! Yes! Yes!" "Give me the low down." "Let me get Suzie out of the fucking washing machine, you bastard! Ahh! She's just a little kid, you –. No! No!" "Tell me everything I want to know and quickly, I don't have long." Shane hit the youth a few times and when he was crying, again, grabbed him by the hair and said. "This world is full of choices, every moment of every day and these are your choices. You can tell me what I want to know and leave here with the girl or you'll tell me anyway, with more pain, and then I'll kill you and her and the two downstairs and the bitch on the bed."

Scared, shamed by his own helplessness, the guy spilled his guts. He went into the bottom of the wardrobe took up a loose board and pulled out his cache of money. About fifteen hundred quid and half-a-dozen ten pound wraps of smack. He told Shane under which house brick, under which bush, in Dalrimple's garden they kept their stash, when they were serving up on the corner. Dalrimple kept more quantity in his house, as did Wilson but he didn't know where. There was another little team serving-up, on the precinct, maybe half-a-dozen guys. Dalrimple collected the money and kept the supply line running. Dean was in charge of their team, going through his father or Dalrimple. The young guy told Shane. "I do what I'm told. Tic toc, know what I mean? Dean's just a skinny version of his dad." By this time, Shane knew Wilson had a girlfriend, that Rowlands was alright, if you didn't cross him and that Dalrimple lived alone and although everybody knew there was often loads of cash in the house, no one would dream of robbing him. When Shane asked. "Why?" A sickly, half-arsed grin glimmered on his face, he said. "He's a fucking nutter, that's why!" Shane hit him and the youth looked at him as though he'd been hit by a friend. So Shane hit him again, and said. "This ain't funny, none of this is funny. Why ain't you work-ing tonight?" Now, pain aside, he looked a bit shaky, nostrils flaired, eyebrows raised. Shane was getting bored, he looked at his watch, almost fif-teen minutes now. Long enough and he wanted out.

Shane looked around the room. It was so fop-pish and cheap, he wanted to set it on fire, burn the room down, the whole house down and all the peo-ple in it. He thought he had finished with all this – crap. He walked over to the wardrobe and opened a door. There was the usual mish mash of stuff inside and Shane pulled a strappy top from a hang-er. Twisted it quickly in his two hands, until it became tight and knotty and stepping back to the youth, dropped it neatly over his head, to his neck and began to gently garrote him. Shane whispered in his ear. "Now, again, why ain't you working tonight?" His arms were flapping and his legs too and, Shane could see the crazy faces, the guy was pulling in a mirror opposite. He eased off and the guy, after coughing, started spitting. Dean's dad had told them to leave it for the night. That was why he'd got the few wraps, in case anyone called. Didn't usually keep nothing in the house. He gestured towards the bed, where the girl had curled foetal, arms wrapped around her head, the syringe still gripped in one hand. "Her and them downstairs are like a bottomless pit." Shane asked him what was going to happen. Lighter fuel through the letterbox, Dean had said, when he'd phoned, earlier. Shane asked him when it was going to happen. He told Shane, probably after the pub shuts. Shane said. "Give me your phone."

Shane put the phone on the floor with the money and drugs, he sighed. The youth looked dubiously from under his eyebrows at him, waiting perhaps for the next clatter. After a moment or two, the guy said, quietly. "Please, can I get Suzie out of the washing machine?" With another sigh, Shane eyed the youth, he said. "We all do what we like, we don't hear other people, not really, most of us are too busy trying to figure out what the fuck's going on, we try to soften our landing by only hearing what we want to hear and only seeing what we want to see. Stop it. Leave it out. Fix up. Tie your laces, know what I'm saying? We all got options these days, all got choices, so they say. So, I gave you yours already. Time to make a decision now. Are you ready to pack?" Like a stranger, the young guy looked around the bedroom, he swallowed and glanced down at Shane's hands. The twisted, strappy top, still dangled from one fist, he said. "I got a bag in the bottom of the wardrobe." Shane couldn't help laughing, he said. "Loyal little fucker ain't you." In a voice that coupled outrage with fear, the guy said. "Why should I die! I don't even come from around here!" He mentioned a village in the Kent countryside and Shane said. "I know, just a poor cracker who got led astray." Indicating the one on the bed, Shane went and stood over the girl. She feigned coma but he knew she was feigning too, he questioned. "What about her?" A look of confusion, tripping into disgust, rippled over the young guy's features, he said. "Is this like one where I get a choice?" Shane said. "You're a stupid cunt, ain't you." The guy cowered in his chair, he said. "No. No, I don't want to take her. I love Suzie, but, like, for fuck sake, her and her family are fucking leeches! I keep the fucking lot of them. Think I would have put up with that bitch, if I'd known what she was like? No-way! Thought I was doing the right thing, moving here when she – we only fucked a couple of times – I thought – anyway I love Suzie, alright!" Shane jabbed the girl in the ribs with his finger, without moving she groaned and looked at him with one gimlet eye. Shane looked into her eye, he said, to the youth. "Better start filling your bag." The young guy swallowed like he didn't believe, but he did, because he got onto his feet and going to the wardrobe, dragged a bag out and began to fill it.

To the girl on the bed, Shane said. "So, that's what's happening." He went over to the drugs and money and picking up the smack and a couple of hundred quid, came back to the bed, he said. "Here." He dropped the money and drugs onto the bed, he said. "Losing your man and your daughter in one go is tragic, this'll ease the pain." Without taking her eye off Shane, she put an arm around the cash and wraps and drew them into her body. Turning to the guy, who was quickly filling his bag, he said. "Enough. Leave some room for the kid's clothes." Shane took the taxi driver's card from his pocket and picked up the phone. The taxi man remembered Shane. "Ten minutes." He said. The girl still eyed him, malevolently, and Shane thought about warning her not to speak to any of Rowlands lot, but knew he would be wasting his time. Instead he grabbed the guy by the hair and dragged him to the little girl's room, to finish filling the bag. Shane said. "Bring a couple her favourite fluffy toys and her coat, poor little fucker'll definitely need some comfort."

On the landing, Shane took the youth by the throat, with one hand and with the other took hold of his testicles and began to exert a gentle pressure with both hands. He was squirming before there was any real pain and in a pain filled world, Shane was comparatively gentle with him, he said. "You're a little tosser, you been thinking you're something you ain't. You got a mother?" The guy nodded. Shane turned the screw just a bit and said. "Why don't you take that little girl you say you love and visit your old mum and make her happy. This is a chance to become something different. Do yourself a favour." Releasing the guy, Shane took out about half of the rest of the money and stuffed it into his hand, he said. "I'll keep what's left and your phone, if that's okay?" The guy nodded his head, giving it like, yeh, whatever, let me out of here. So Shane did.

Down in the kitchen, while the newborn daddy took his daughter from the womb of the washing machine, Shane pulled a distinctive hooded top from the wash pile. It was black, with exposed red stitching all around the seams and a splatter of U.V. paint down the front. At first the kid seemed catatonic, and the young guy started to cry again and saying that she was dead. Shane put his ear to her mouth and could feel her breath. He gave her a gentle slap on the chops and as she came back to life, he pulled on her coat. They went out the back door and up the alley between the houses, on to Circle Road and off the estate. By the time they met the taxi, the little girl was asking questions and the guy was telling her how they were going to see his mother and what a lovely time they would have and Shane thought of pigs flying. The taxi driver said. "Are these your old friends, then?" Shane said. "No, these are my new friends." The driver made a nod towards the young guy, he said. "Is he alright?" Opening a rear door and ushering him and the girl inside, Shane said. "Sweet as. Had a bit of trouble but he's nearly over that now." Shane slammed the door and for some reason waved goodbye as the cab pulled away. When it was out of sight, Shane pulled the hooded top over his head and kept the hood up. On the way down to meet the cab, they had seen no one and on his way back, Circle Road was still deserted. Shane checked his watch. There was still over an hour before the pub chucked out and Shane still had things to do. Apart from a hall light, Dalrimple's house was in darkness.

**6**

Dalrimple may have been "a fucking nutter" but he wasn't nutty enough to leave his back door unlocked. With one of Craig's crap screwdrivers, Shane popped the kitchen window, just the way his dad had first shown him when he was twelve. Simple is best, was his dad's motto. Old school and it had always worked well for the geezer. Fingers in pies and all that, dodgy down to his boots. And when the arse started to fall out of the scrap business, with the E.E.C. rules, and another short stretch for receiving was not to his liking, he had sold the yard to developers and moved to the Canary Islands. His parents had left England before Shane's forced exit and it seemed ironic to Shane, that, with the short hop from Morocco, to the Canaries, he now saw more of them than when just the few miles to London separated them.

The neatness of Dalrimple's house surprised Shane. But then not, too. We all got our little things. It was more than the lack of the usual bloke debris, like washing-up and full ashtrays and beer cans, the sort of things that just accumulate around a bloke, living on his own. It was the food cans in the cupboards all facing label out, the living room, sparse and pristine, where things looked polished in the light from the street and nothing, not even a cushion, was out of place. There were no familiar objects, like photo's, no nick-nacks, and definitely no pets. Unless the large, well fed python, in the glass tank under the window, could be considered a pet. Upstairs had a similar neat tilt to it. The bedroom was all Ikea, like a showroom, like no one had ever had sex in it. The bathroom was all big white tiles and large mirrors. An enclosed power shower, which took up an entire corner of the room. A fancy washbasin of glass, with stainless steel spigots and taps, set in a hardwood stand and an immaculate toilet. The whitest and shiniest of shitholes Shane had seen in a long time.

Shane pulled the top over his head and balling it up, reached down into the toilet bowl and stuffed it up into the bend. He lifted off the cistern lid, adjusted the ball-cock, so it would flow continuously and plugged up the overflow pipe, with a wad of toilet paper. Then he replaced the cistern top and flushed a couple of times, until the toilet bowl was almost full and left it. He went to the glass wash-basin, dropped the glass plug in and opened the taps. He did the same thing with the shower. Before he was out of the room, the toilet and sink were already spilling water over the floor. The bed-room was way too clean. To Shane's eye, it needed ruffling. Shane had contemplated searching for Dalrimple's stash but he reasoned, if he was so obsessively neat in his habits, anything as inani-mately volatile as drugs and money, would be tucked up tight and he didn't have time. Anyway, when it came down to it, Shane really only wanted to annoy Dalrimple. Wanted to see Dalrimple's coke fuelled little body explode in exasperation. It was safe to say he didn't like Dalrimple. He picked up the beautiful, pine bed, with the covers of crisp white linen, all tucked like a mathematical equation around the mattress and tipped it into a heap in the corner. He opened all the doors on the wardrobe. This man pressed his socks! This man pressed his underpants! Shane loved it! He pulled everything from the shelves and coat hangers into a big heap and danced on the lovely creases, kicked those lovely, clean clothes all about the room. He upend-ed the drawers, and the half-arsed contraption that held them. He got hold of a stainless steel lamp standard and smashed all the mirrors, then crashed the thing into the chair, the bed, anything, until it was in bits. The other bedroom in the house had been converted into a computer room, all neat and tidy, with a top of the range P.C. and all the accoutrements, including a web-cam. And again, Shane smiled, as he thought about Dalrimple sitting there coked brainless, with his jeans around his ankles, as he went web-cam to web-cam, with some other misbegotten sod. Shane destroyed the lovely flat screen and opening the window, fucked the little camera out into the night. The computer stack, under the desk, couldn't be easily smashed. So Shane pulled out all the connecting cables and hefted the thing out of the room and across the landing, into the bathroom. There, with the floor already awash with water, he pitched the computer into the overflowing shower tray. Annoyance value, just stuff to set Dalrimple seething. Simple mindless vandalism against his pristine little castle. Anything and enough to make him stupid with rage. Water was beginning to run out of the bathroom into the hall and trickle across the varnished boards and between the cracks. Shane forced the little locks on the computer desk drawers, took them to the hall and up-ended the contents into the growing stream. A lovely flash of pinkie-red among the fluttering papers. Three fifty pound notes. Shane slipped the money in his pocket, with the rest. As he made his way down to the ground floor the splish, splash, of a new waterfall dogged his footsteps.

In the kitchen, a rack of stainless steel knives sat on the worktop, including a half-size Chinese cleaver. Shane emptied the snake on to the living room floor and threw the glass case on the couch. The creature was about four feet long and quite beautiful, all colours green, flecked with yellow and orange and a creamy white belly. Shane had thought it would give itself a shake and slither off sharpish, the way they did in nature films but the thing just lay there and looked at him. He prodded it with his foot and the snake slowly opened its mouth, in what seemed like a yawn. Shane sighed and said. "Who ate all the mice." A ripple of flesh, like a tic under the skin, ran the length of the creature's body. Shane placed the sharp edge of the cleaver in the centre of its skull. The snake closed its mouth and shuddered forward a foot or two. Escape? Fucker didn't know the meaning of freedom. Shane raised the blade, ready to split its head down the middle and then, no. Tossing the cleaver aside, he took hold of the snake by the tail and quickly dragged it through the house to the kitchen. It was writhing a bit, like the sudden rough treatment had livened it up and when Shane picked the thing up, it wound around his arm and he had to peal it away, to drop it out of the open window. Outside it lay on the path, slowly opening and shutting its mouth.

Drips of water were forming on the kitchen ceiling and dropping in clutches onto the tiled floor and the walls seemed to be sweating. A tinkling cascade was now running down the stairs and spreading like the incoming tide over the lower reaches of the house. Shane went back into the living room, ripped up the covers of the couch with the cleaver, trashed the telly and anything else that would break, pulled down a rack of free standing shelves and kicked in the glass of the snake tank. Everything looked just dandy. Before he left he found the electricity supply and with effort, pulled out the large, brown, mains fuse. The lights he'd turned on to do his work, all went out and he stood in the dark listening to the water.

The snake had disappeared by the time Shane climbed back out of the kitchen window. As he came down the front path, he looked across the street towards Lisa and Craig's. The lights were off in the lower part of the house and his own room was in darkness too. In Craig and Lisa's bedroom, the curtains were half drawn back and a night-light glimmered dully. Billy watched him from the window. Crossing the street, Shane asked himself again, what he was doing? Jeopardizing his own liberty, trying to make things right that could never be made right. He glanced around at the other houses. It was an estate and there were always plenty of curtain twitchers and loose tongues. How many had seen him going in or out of Dalrimple's?

Would there be any, like Stan, who recognised him from the past? He didn't care what anyone told Dalrimple, as he or Wilson would guess soon enough who their problem was. What he didn't want was some long nosed fucker calling the cops, not just yet and not because of some fake do-goody goody idea and a bit of a story to sell the papers. Billy waved and despite himself, Shane waved back and passing down the side of the house, to the back, vaulted the fence. He knew in the end, it didn't matter, nothing was fixed.

No more, that's what he'd told himself, the final knot cut in the ties that bind and he should already be back in Morocco but something had happened. It was strange to Shane, as if he was there despite himself. He liked it – he didn't like it. He unlocked the back door with the key Craig had given him and re-locked the door when he was inside. Craig and Lisa were cuddled in a sprawl on the couch and they looked cosy and comfortable. Craig said. "How did you get on? Saw you go past with matey and come over from that little cunt's." Lisa pulled herself off the couch, closed the curtains and turned on the lights. She looked at Shane, as though she thought he might have turned into some kind of were-wolf, she said. "You got blood on your shirt." Craig said. "What's happening? What did you find out?" Shane gave them the low-down about the expected attack. Craig reckoned he'd stand sentry outside, in front of the door, all night. Shane said. "At least three have got guns and these guys ain't shy." Craig laughed and gave Shane a sceptical stare, he said. "Come on, they wouldn't." Shane shrugged. Lisa said. "Doesn't matter. I'm not letting you stand out there!" They listened seriously to everything Shane had to say but managed to raise a laugh about Dalrimple's place and the state he'd be in, with the flood and the lack of lights, the snake.

Lisa told Shane to change his shirt and she would put it in the wash. He went upstairs but before he could get in the bedroom, Billy now came out of his own room, onto the landing, a finger against his lips. "Shhhhh." He had a hundred excited little expressions animating his face and probably a hundred questions to go with the expressions. Blinking his eyes, Billy took the finger from his lips and in a stage whisper, said. "Did you get him, Shane? I don't like him. Did you tell him to leave my mum alone? You were gone for ages and I saw you with him next door and that little girl – where they going? Will they leave us alone now, Shane, will they? Did you take your gun? Was he scared? I bet he was scared! I hate him! He's, he's, he's –." The boy stopped, his features screwed up as he realised he couldn't think of a word to describe Dalrimple, that wouldn't cost him ten pence. Taking pity on the overexcited boy, Shane put a finger to his lips and as he opened his bedroom door, beckoned Billy after him.

While he changed, he talked quietly to the kid. He told him owning or using a gun didn't make him anything big. Told him Dalrimple was out, so he'd left him a message. Told him he thought he'd seen a long snake, like a python, crossing the road. Billy shook his head slowly and sighed, as though to say do I look like a fool and replied. "You're such a liar." Shane held out his hands, palms up. "Come on, would I lie to you? And another thing, I don't want you telling your parents what I told you, 'specially about the snake." Shane hustled Billy out of the room, Billy whined. "But you didn't really tell me anything. Nobody ever really tells me anything." Opening the lad's bedroom door, Shane ushered him in and said. "If you think about what I said, maybe you'll see I did tell you things. Sometimes you don't see things 'till later, know what I mean?" Billy looked over his shoulder at Shane and said, cynically. "Oh, I know and now you pat me on the head and tell me to go to bed and be a good boy." Shane patted him on the head, gave him a little shove and as he closed the door, said. "Sleep well, see you tomorrow."

Back downstairs, Craig wanted to know more about the people next door, he asked. "Won't they call the police?" Shane shook his head. "Don't think so. You ever heard that country and western song, 'There's a hole in Daddie's arm where all the money goes?'" They looked at him with blank expressions then Craig twisted up his mouth like he'd swallowed a gob full of petrol. "Country and western! Do me a favour!" Lisa gave his shoulder a playful slap. Shane tried to croon a couple of lines. Craig laughed, Lisa giggled, Craig said. "Best keep the day job." Shane laughed too, he said. "Yeh, anyway, forget that. All I was trying to say was, there's a whole family like that over there." Both looked happy about that too and Craig shrugged and rubbed his hands together and grinning, said. "I was only wondering about the girl, you know, she's still a mother ain't she? She could wake up tomorrow and feel different." Getting off on Craig and Lisa's lightened mood and a happy glow from his own adrenalin glide down, Shane laughed again and said. "Some women take to motherhood, some don't. Anyway, with the smack she got and the money, she won't be coming up for air for a few days." It was Lisa's turn to rub her hands together and nodding at Craig, said. "See." Shane said. "What's with you two?" Craig hummed and rubbed his chin, dragging it out and Lisa said, excitedly. "Stop messing about Craig!" He pulled a, what me, kind of a face. Lisa beamed. "I've got an idea!"

She laid it out and it was quick and simple and would, with luck, at least stymie the attack for that night. She said. "We should set ourselves on fire."

Unable to help himself, Shane quipped. "You ain't Buddhists, are you?" Craig cracked-up and Lisa gave a bored, ho, ho, ho, then continued. "We need a diversion. Police, the lot. When the car was set on fire, a lot of people watched from their bedroom windows or came out and watched from their gardens, including that old bloke from next door. Seems to me, even Rowlands couldn't do much with so many witnesses about."

## ∞ 7 ∞

It was after eleven, by Shane's watch, when they went out into the back garden. They carried all the old newspapers they could find. The pub would close in the next half-hour, time was running short and as Craig pointed out. "It's a beautiful night for a fire." Shane told Lisa and Craig to stay back out of view. He didn't want any of the neighbours to chance seeing them setting the fire. The dismantled shed lay, as they had left it, in a great higgledy-piggledy heap in the middle of the garden. Shane skittered around the remains, screwing up paper and stuffing it into nooks and crannies and lighting it with a box of cooks matches, until there were a dozen little fires on the go. Lisa and Craig, arms around each other, stood and watched from the back door. When he happened to look up, Shane could see Billy looking down from his back bedroom window.

The almost friable planking, the tinder dry posts and flooring, the ply sheets covered in roofing felt were perfect and it took mere minutes for the fire to gather momentum. Craig went back in to phone the authorities. When he came outside again, Billy was with him, giving it the old innocent, about the noise waking him up and rubbing his eyes. He grinned at Shane. The four of them stood and watched for a few minutes. Craig was right, it was a beautiful night for a fire. There was no wind and the air was ambient. Apart from a rim of orange light thrown up by the town, the sky was deep and dark and clear. A great scattering of stars and a skinny silver moon twinkled far off in space. The fire gave a couple of loud cracks and pops. Flames whooshed up and sparks and smoke spiralled into the night sky. The heat was already uncomfortable on their faces and the fire seemed to have grown or the garden to have shrunk. Billy said. "Look at it." Lisa said. "Do you think it'll work, Shane?" He stepped back from the heat into the kitchen. "Maybe too well."

They could hear the fire engine coming up East Hill long before it entered the Estate. There was plenty of time for Shane to hide but he didn't bother much. He didn't want to be caught. He didn't mind running and he didn't mind fighting, but he wouldn't be a cat in a box. No cupboards, no attic, no squeezing under beds. Craig explained that, the last time they had all had to leave the house, while the firemen dealt with the blazing car. He said. "When we were outside, one of the firemen had a quick look through the house, just to make sure. Health and safety or something." Billy said. "Why don't you want them to find you?" Lisa said. "You should be in bed." Billy said. "I can't. The fire engine's coming." Lisa flipped the top of his head. Billy jerked about like he'd been hit with a brick and squawked like a parrot. "That's child abuse that is. Did you see that?" He looked from Craig to Shane and back again, hands held out in supplication. The two men looked at each other and gave him nothing. The boy nodded his head at this adult conspiracy. Amiably, Craig said. "Shut up a minute, Billy." Billy carried on nodding, but said nothing. Both Lisa and Craig started to speak and stopped. Craig shrugged and said. "What do you want to do, Shane?" Nothing was favourite. Shane said. "Just like we said, talk to the firemen and the cops, if they come, like it's the same thing as the car, you know?" Craig said. "You know what I mean, what about you!" Shane couldn't explain, he said. "They won't see me." Lisa said. "What. Like I can't see you now?" Billy, Craig and Shane tittered. Lisa said. Titter ye not." The three males tittered again. Shane said. "Don't worry. They won't be expecting to find anyone and they won't." Billy shifted around in his seat, cast a quick glance at his parents and said. "What you going to do, Shane? Where you going to go?" Laying a finger along the side of his nose, Shane winked. "What you don't know can't hurt you." Billy pulled half-a-dozen quick faces, from mock disbelief, through to a crumpled pretence of pain. Craig and Lisa shook their heads in a kind of hopeless acceptance of their parental fate. Shane said. "Billy, whatever you do, please don't tell anyone I'm here, will you?" The fire engine came along Circle Road like a bat out of hell. Shane went up to his room and the family went and stood outside the front door to welcome the brave men of the fire service.

The firemen all looked big even when they weren't big because of the boots and helmets and gloves and gear. They were quick and efficient. They unrolled hoses and ran them down the alley. They knocked on Stan's door and he came out and stood in the street with Craig, Lisa and Billy. One fireman went into Stan's to check it out and another did a swift run through of Lisa and Craig's place. Shane sat on the bed in his room until he heard the fireman on the stair and then stood and slid behind the open door. The fireman came to the doorway and flipped the light switch. The room was 60 watt bright and plain as a room could be, nothing showing. For that precise moment Shane did not exist. It was a moment he always looked for. The room in darkness again, the fireman down the stairs and Shane went into the main bedroom and watched through the crack in the curtains. By this time there were a few more heads on the street and people looking out of their windows. A car had stopped and another slowed down and passed at a crawl. Strangely, like moths drawn by the light or the noise or something, the two elder smack heads from across the alley, were out in the middle of the road arms around each other, rapt by the activity. Late like late was on time for them, the cops arrived. Two panda cars a pair in each car. They got out looking fat and encumbered by their equipment, giving it shoulder action like they could suddenly alter the run of events or take control. Two spoke into their radios and two went over to a fireman and he pointed out Craig and Lisa.

A couple more cars came along Circle Road, slowing as they saw the fire engine, only to be waved on by the police. On the pavements a couple of dozen bystanders were now gathered in small groups, smoking and talking and gawping. Some were swigging from beer cans, almost as though they were at some hastily convened, low rent, cocktail party and whatever was happening, it was better than the TV. Two of the policemen took Craig, Lisa and Billy to one side and began to take details and ask them questions. Craig shrugged and shook his head. Lisa said a few things and pointed to the burned out car in the front garden. Billy held Lisa's hand, said nothing and looked around. Most of the boy's attention was directed towards the firemen going about their business. He did look back at the house once, rubbing his nose with the back of his hand and, definitely not looking up at the bedroom windows. A guy walking a dog, stopped, nodded hello to a couple of people in the crowd. He had a blue plastic bag in his hand and after getting the dog to sit, he took out a can of cider, opened it, took a drink and began a conversation with the person nearest to him. It all seemed to be working out and by the look of it, Craig and Lisa were doing a double act on the police and if Shane hadn't known better he would have thought that they were enjoying it. Billy pulled away and stood near the alley, to get a better view of the action. Lisa went over to him and they stood watching together. A single policeman still talked to Craig, while the other three had a conference off to one side. Then after some radio chat, two drifted away, got into their patrol car and after a few minutes more, drove off.

Things went on and people came and went. The police, finished with Craig, mooched around the fire engine and looked disapprovingly over the gathered people. The guy with the dog offered them a can of cider, which they declined. The Mercedes cruised slowly by and the police barely noticed its passing. Inside were Wilson, Dalrimple, Dean (Rowlands son) and Rowlands himself. Behind them in another car, were five young blokes. Two were the mates of Dean from the corner, the other three Shane had not seen before. The two cars turned into the cul-de-sac and parked and all the men got out. They sat on the garden walls and leaned against the cars. Three guys from the crowd strolled over to join them. They joked and laughed and smoked and looked smug, as though what was happening was somehow of their doing and true or not, that was what the rumour on the estate would be.

It was the first time Shane had seen Rowlands and he studied him, now. Studied Wilson and Dalrimple, too. The rest of the group were just shit, bit of this bit of that men who played the dodgy card, ready to thug it for all they were worth for the glory that came from association. And Dean? He was like a skinny, strutting cock, fiddling with his cap and moving his head backwards and forwards, as though he was listening to some internal music and every movement he made was overblown. He lit his cigarettes by flicking them in the air and catching them on his extended lower lip, while firing up his zippo in one movement. He was the son of the fat man and everybody knew that.

Rowlands himself was a man in his mid-forties, maybe five-ten but height wasn't his thing, belly

was. Shane watched him, knowing with the Glock
he could down him and Dalrimple and Wilson and
probably walk out the front door and away down
Circle Road and he wouldn't exist like he didn't
exist but he was stuck with wanting something
physical. Stuck with the fact that he wanted someone to – to what? Living abroad, sometimes it was
as though he didn't have any real connection to
anything anymore, people, or the past. Was that
why he'd come here to see Gerry? But it wasn't
that definite, thoughts like that never were.
Rowlands looked like some of the English builder
types, he had seen in Spain. People who'd made
their money the hard way. Raw faced fat fucks on
bony legs. The fat man was pug ugly. A face made
up of jowls, little bow lips and stones for eyes. He
had that two legs good, pork dressed as man look.
Shaved head and tattoo's all up and down his arms,
a Lonsdale hooded top with the sleeves cut off,
baggy, calf length shorts, thick socks and a pair of
big, tan boots. He didn't put himself about like his
son, but there was no doubt he held power in his
little fiefdom and him and Wilson and Dalrimple
were tight. They stood a little away from the rest,
taking in the scene and judging it for their own
ends. What they made of it, what they thought of
the fire, didn't bother Shane. Sooner or later, like
the rest of the crowd, he hoped they would get
bored and itty off home. Maybe they would come

back to start their own fire, but he doubted it.

Suddenly animated, Dalrimple started talking to Wilson and then Rowlands. While he was talking he was pointing towards Lisa. With a leery grin, he exchanged low fives with the other two men and they were laughing and Dean came over. Wilson nodded over at the house and gave Dean a run down. Dean laughed so loud even Shane could hear him above the noise of the fire engine. Dalrimple set off looking well pleased and only glanced over his shoulder once just to make sure of his audience, as he nipped across the road. The police were near the rest of the watchers, who were spread over the road and pavement, by the front of the engine, where they could see what was going on down the alley. Dalrimple slid around the back of the fire engine and up behind Lisa, where she stood with Billy and Craig by the garden gate.

He moved quickly and it was hard to see exactly what he did but he seemed to run his hand up the inside of her thigh, over her bottom, up her back and as he did so, whispered something in her ear. Lisa jerked rigid, like she had been shot through with a quick couple of hundred volts and half-spinning to see where the assault had come from, dropped Billy's hand and staggered back into Craig. Dalrimple, who hadn't stopped moving, was a few feet away already. He looked pleased with himself. Casually back stepping near to one of the cops, he had both hands in his pockets as if they had rested there all night.

It was as though the family saw him all at once. There was an element of complete shock, a moment of hiatus, of double take. He lolled his tongue out of his mouth and waggled it at Lisa. All of an instant the family were all trying to do different things. Craig started shouting, as he tried to bustle past Lisa. "Bastard! Shithead! Fucker!" It took Billy seconds longer to realise something had happened to his mother, something unpleasant, and who was the culprit. Then Lisa struggled with them both. She shoved Craig in the chest with one hand, while trying to hold a suddenly determined, squirming Billy back by the scuff of the jumper he had over his pyjamas, going. "Craig, Craig, leave it! Remember what we said! Billy, Billy, please!" The bemused policeman, who had seen nothing, glanced at a butter wouldn't melt Dalrimple and began to amble towards the struggling Lisa, with a hello, hello, what's going on here type attitude.

Forget seconds and split seconds, never mind nano-seconds or shavings off time we can't comprehend, life just doesn't stop, it is never fixed by this or that moment, it is always fluid, always surfing the waves of chance. In the perfect moments, we too are fluid and surf those chance waves. Craig saw the cop coming and quieted down, knowing in his heart, Lisa must be right. Lisa saw the cop coming and saw the change happen in Craig's eyes, saw he was safe again. Billy didn't really see the cop at all. He was there on a peripheral level, but discounted by the boy's fast moving brain as not important, in the momentary scheme of things. And Billy was right. He sensed, rather than felt, the slight easing of pressure on the collar of his jumper, as Lisa saw the change in Craig's eyes and relaxed her muscles. It was only for the briefest moment. Billy shot from her grasp, a rat from a trap, gone on the crest of a wave. Lisa screamed. "Billy!" but it was already too late. See Billy moving too quick for the cop stretching out an arm, in a leisurely way, as though he had a chance of catching the boy. No chance. Billy's body swerved like he was born to it and dropped his head as he raced past the policeman and hurtled himself full tilt at Dalrimple. Billy drove his head into Dalrimple's midriff and the thug gave out a loud. "Oooff." They tumbled onto the tarmac, with Billy scratching and kicking and punching for all he was worth. Dalrimple fell heavily. Taken by surprise, he was unable to immediately free his hands from the pockets of his jeans and so gave a momentary advantage to the boy.

Everyone on the street was watching. And as Dalrimple tried to wriggle out from under the flailing boy and free his hands, everyone was laughing, even his mates. The cop grabbed Billy and pulled him off before Dalrimple could do any real damage and the other cop kept Lisa and Craig at arms length and there were hoots and hollers from the other thugs and would-be hard men. Dalrimple pulled himself up off the road, furiously dusting himself down and carrying on about how he'd been assaulted. The cop pointed out, that the boy was a minor. Lisa and Craig weighed in and told the cop how Dalrimple had spat at the boy but they didn't say when and Wilson and Rowlands, full of loud guffaws, shouted out from across the street how he should pick on people his own size. Locals were catcalling and making jokes and the cop was trying to find out why Billy had flattened our good man, all to no avail. Billy was still mad and spitting feathers and he didn't really know what had happened to his mum but he knew how he felt even if he could not explain and he knew well enough to say nothing, nothing at all. Dalrimple was gurning and chewing his cheeks and cursing Lisa and Craig and Billy tried to break free from the police and when he could not, he spat one at Dalrimple and it landed on his jeans.

Dalrimple lost it. He screamed and wildly swung a foot at the boy and only the cop dragging Billy backwards saved him. The other policeman left Lisa and Craig and stepped up to Dalrimple, who was swearing vengeance. Calmly, the policeman said. "Now, now, sir. Perhaps we should all calm down." Dalrimple took a handkerchief from his pocket and looked back to Rowlands and Wilson, who were no longer laughing. He caught their look and full of mean faced, short arsed indignity, ignored the cop and rubbed furiously at the spit. Lisa went over to the policeman holding Billy, who said. "Maybe you should all go back inside." The other cop said, to Dalrimple. "That sounds like good advice, sir. Why don't you go along home, the fun's over here." Dalrimple deliberately threw the handkerchief at the constable's feet and gave him his best sneer. "That's it, is it? I'm attacked by some little thug, spat on and now I should just go home, eh? That lot's trouble, they are. Was nice and quiet 'round here 'till they moved in." The cop said. "Oh really." He bent and with two fingers, delicately picked up the handkerchief and stuffed it into one of Dalrimple's hands. "Take your rubbish home with you, sir." Rowlands and Wilson began to cross the road towards Dalrimple.

Craig and Lisa took one of Billy's hands in each of their own and walked him back towards the house. Rowlands put his arm around Dalrimple's shoulder and said a couple of words in his ear. Wilson stood close but he looked about him, eyeballing anyone who still looked like they wanted to take the piss, even the cops. And Shane, hidden above, had the distinct impression Wilson expected to see him amongst the crowd. After a moment or two, the three men walked back across the road, towards the cars. Shane could see all the relationships simple from the bedroom window. Could see all the macho re-bonding going on amongst the guys. How they sympathised with the coked-up fool, built him up into something, so he could still be himself. Then when he was back to himself they, Rowlands taking the lead, took the piss until Dalrimple was forced to laugh at himself. Dalrimple didn't like it but he went along. It was a guy thing. And across the street it was a family thing. Once they were behind closed doors, Craig and Lisa tried to admonish Billy for his behaviour but couldn't help laughing at the sight of Dalrimple, with Billy on top of him, giving the thug hell. None of them quite knew, at that time what was right or wrong at that moment. And Billy, who'd acted on instinct, wanted to laugh and cry, so he did.

Meanwhile, at the back of the house, the firemen were doing their thing. They concentrated the hoses on the fire, while at times casually playing water over the back of the house and over Stan's shed and garden. They made it look easy. Perhaps it was an easy call for them. The fire was quite large and furnace hot but it was never going to cause any real damage. The firemen laughed and joked with each other as they toyed the water expertly, everywhere. An hour or so and they had it down to a smouldering, sodden, mess. Another half-an-hour and they had disconnected the hoses from the stopcock in the street and rolled them up. Shortly before that, the knot of men across the road started to break up and go their separate ways. Shane, still hidden, watched. Indicating his house with a nod of his head to his friends, Dalrimple ran an index finger under his nose. Rowlands, Wilson and Dean followed him up the garden path to the back door of his house.

Below in the road, things were breaking up as the excitement dwindled. With the firemen packing up their gear, most of the idlers went back to their telly's and the cops went back to sitting in their car. This was the moment Shane had been waiting for. The simple pleasure of seeing Dalrimple fucked up. Shane hadn't expected Billy's attack and so it would be even sweeter now, like indignity piled on the top of embarrassment. He didn't have long to wait. A great, inarticulate roar erupted from the back of Dalrimple's and reverberated through the night air. A chorus of expletives in various voices, of the fuck me, what the fuck type variety, followed. Then there was a silence. The cops in the car turned their heads in unison, as though the silence held the danger. The silence was brief.

Out of it came Dalrimple, behind him he dragged the much larger Wilson and Rowlands, who were grabbing and tearing at him and he was giving it everything, with elbows and knees and kicks. Lacking the trained restraint techniques of the social services, neither Rowlands bulk nor Wilson's strength could stop him. He was gone and they were scrabbling after him. He had it in the tight corner at back of the house but once he broke free, they had it over distance and managed to pull him down before he got to the end of the garden path. Once he was down, the full weight of their bodies smothered him. Dean, who had been hanging back, came running up now, giving it verbals like he was involved, instead of just an arm waver. Then the two policemen got out of the car.

Dean saw them first but by the time the two cops had hauled up their utility belts and trousers, all even Dalrimple, saw the danger. Dean offered his father a hand up and Wilson and Dalrimple helped each other to their feet. Before the police could cross the street, all four were laughing and brushing each other down. When the cops reached them and said. "What's going on?" They were all hugs and cuddles for each other and what for the cops. "What? What's up? What's that? What d'you mean? What's it to you? What were we doing?" When the police asked again, they took more of the same along with a few. "Nothing. Nothing. We weren't doing nothing. Just having a laugh. Yeh, a laugh, just having a laugh." They all put their arms around each other and laughed. The fire engine was packed and ready to go. It made a lot of noise and the cops left the men and went over to speak to the firemen. The four men let go of each other and their smiles. They stood in a huddle at the gate, dropping quiet words to each other and staring over at the family's house. They didn't look happy. After a few minutes they turned and trooped back to Dalrimple's.

8

The fire engine went away. The last of the gawpers left. The police knocked at the door and explained how they didn't know what was going on, but something didn't feel right – they were going to park up in the alley for a while. After that Shane came down and joined the others. They taped up the letterbox. They shut any open windows. They had the lights on everywhere and the curtains drawn but they were watchful. The police parked their car in the mouth of the alley and stayed over an hour, until they were called away. While the police were still parked up at the side of the house, Craig and Lisa took Billy, who was beyond sleep at this stage, out into the back garden to see the remains of the fire. Shane watched from the kitchen. Things were real now, for him and he didn't want to be seen by some dumb arsed cop, come down the back to do his family friendly, socially conscious, community policeman shtick and stumble on him like he was El Dorado or something.

They walked around out there hand in hand and it was sweet to see. With Billy and Lisa hopping around in the hot ashes and Craig laughing at them and then having to hop around himself and all three of them laughing like they were going to burst out crying. There were weird tensions rolling around and Shane could see as soon as he'd joined them downstairs, that the adults were in deep, scared but not backing down scared and they didn't know what to do with Billy. He was their son, their pride and joy. They wanted to protect him. But those kind of unreal expectations seemed to be sliding away into some kind of Neverland – worse still than when they had ended up in the bed and breakfast. Although they hadn't mentioned it to each other, both understood Billy's desire to strike out, as they both wanted to strike out too. Each was also doing the best they could to keep it together for the other two, each wanted to run away and each wanted to kill someone. It was only natural. What Shane saw was something he could never understand. A simple family thing. He liked to see it but he didn't understand it. It was like watching aliens. Prancing about out there in the hot ashes, like everything was cool.

When they came in, Craig rubbed his hands

together and said. "Get those little glasses, Lisa! What about it Shane? There's still a few shots in that whiskey bottle, eh?" Shane laughed and pointed to the bottle on the worktop. "Go for it." Craig and Shane had shots and beer chasers from the fridge, Lisa had a shot and made Billy a chocolate drink from cold milk and some kind of powder in a tin. They all had their own impressions of how the night had turned out and they took their drinks through into the living room for, what Lisa described as, a debriefing. Maybe it was for Billy's sake, Shane didn't know, but both Lisa and Craig seemed very upbeat. Confused alright, worried, but almost light headed, like the bonfire plan had been some kind of resounding success. And Shane had to admit, it mostly had.

Billy turned on the TV, drank the drink and ate a jam sandwich and watched some reality shit and although Lisa shook her head she let it be. Craig said. "Those old windows won't ever make cold frames now, the heat smashed all the glass." Lisa gave a snort of incredulity. "Cold frames! Do be brief! Mustard and Cress on the window ledge is about your limit. They would have lain out there 'till someone, no names mentioned, smashed them anyway." She raised her chin at Billy's back in front of the telly. But Billy was earwigging and without turning around, chipped in. "Not me, I wouldn't smash anything." Craig tried to look hurt and misunderstood but failed because he was grinning. "You can be very cruel. Here I am with great plans for a veggie paradise of squash, pumpkins, courgettes and cucumbers –." Billy turned his head, looked at his Dad and went. "Yuk!" Lisa shook her head despairingly. "I don't know who's worse out of you two." Craig and Billy looked at each other and then at Lisa as if to say, who us?

Lisa made sandwiches and they drank tea. It was gone three in the morning and everywhere was quiet. Some soft porn came on the telly and Craig switched it off. Billy still claimed not to be tired and Craig and Shane took turns to play him at draughts. Shane won the odd game but Craig had no chance and the boy battered him, despite the yawns and the tired eyes. By four thirty Billy was asleep in an armchair, where he sweated and twitched in his dreams like a dog. They talked then about what they could do next, about the consequences of confrontation, about the ifs and the maybes and there were many. None thought that chasing one little tosser back to his mammy or trashing Dalrimple's house was going to put a stop to the harassment. Shane didn't say much. He let them talk and answered questions where he wanted to. Agreed with them when he could. Not wanting a single word of his to affect their decisions, he told them. "We ain't in this together. I'll be gone soon but you'll still be here." Craig said. "That's too right. What about talking to Rowlands? You know, explain that we ain't about to move, we've been moved around enough but we don't want no more trouble. We won't give up the house though, trouble or not. Right Lisa?" She agreed and added. "When Billy came down with that gun I was almost sick, it was too real – but unbelievable – like something on the telly. I thought, is this what we've come too? All the struggles to shield Billy, to try to bring him up properly, then it's all there all around and there's a gun in the kitchen. I wanted to run away. But you can't can you, not always? I don't know if you being here's good or bad luck Shane but we will be grateful for any help you can give us but don't feel obliged." Shane smiled. "I don't feel obliged and it could turn out that you won't be grateful for my help."

Craig took Billy up to bed, carrying him in his arms like he was a toddler and Billy all snuggled down there and really liking it, waved a limp goodbye to Shane and his mum. Lisa said. "I know Craig wants to talk to Rowlands but wouldn't it be better to let them come to us. It takes a long time to get Craig really wound up but he's getting there and I want to be around if he –." With a shake of his head, Shane said. "No. I'm with Craig. We'll go to them." Lisa said. "But I –." Shane said. "No. You don't want these people in your house. Here's not the place to deal with it." They sat in silence for minute, then Lisa said. "You know it was me made Craig ask you to stay. I'm scared for him." She looked away, around the room at the cheap furniture, the fifty quid T.V., the council colour scheme and said. "Sometimes you wonder if anything's worth bothering with at all. Like you, you could be gone now. I expect you think I'm a bit of a cow for getting you involved." Shane said. "Do I?" She looked at him again, she wasn't crying but there was something fragile going on around her eyes. "Well we are using you, aren't we?" Now it was Shane who looked away, quietly he said. "You took in a stranger last night. You didn't take me in because of your problems, you took me in despite your problems." Proud and sad at the same time, Lisa said. "Yeh well, that's Craig that is." Eyes still on his shoes, Shane said. "Whatever. All I know is, this ain't over yet. All I've done is annoy them." Shane looked up and their eyes met. Lisa's mouth was all turned down, she said. "That's what I'm afraid of."

A few minutes later Craig came back down. He said. "Out like a light. Won't be hearing anything from Billy boy for a while." He yawned and stretched, looking at Lisa. "What about us, love?" Outside, engines could be heard on Circle Road, slowing down. Craig made a lunge for the curtains and Shane and Lisa were out of their seats and they were all wondering whether just to get the fuck out or what and they all looked through the gap in the curtains Craig had made. The sky was getting light and all the little clouds that make up a mackerel sky were backing up off towards the Thames. The streetlights were out and Circle Road and the cul-de-sac opposite the house, were touched with a bland greyness, like a snapshot from another age. In the silence after the engines were turned off, early birds were singing.

Two vans were parked outside Dalrimple's house. A plumber and an electrician, from some twenty four hour yellow pages job. The two trades-men left their vans and greeted each other, check-ing the time on their mobile phones as they strolled up Dalrimple's front path and knocked on the front door. Craig rubbed his hands together. "They'll cost him." Lisa said. "Little toerag can afford it." Dalrimple didn't use the front door but came up the side path. He couldn't help but stare over to where the source of his problems watched. Maybe it was the lack of sleep or just a silly notion but they couldn't help themselves, as one, they gave a cheery wave. With a scowl, Dalrimple spat on the path and herded the two men along to the back door. Craig liked that, he laughed. "I think you've upset the little man." Shane spread out his hands and gave Craig an appreciative nod of the head. "But don't thank me too soon. Dalrimples got to be mad as fuck." He stopped, glanced at Lisa and Craig. They looked back at him, nothing said. Shane licked his lips and went on. "So, we'll have to be a bit careful when we go and talk to these – cunts." Nothing. Shane laughed and said. "Lucky Billy's not here." Lisa waved her hand as though it had never really mattered, she said. "Well, under the circumstances, I reckon we can drop the no swearing rule."

# 9

For some reason, seeing the tradesmen at Dalrimple's and he like a normal person, smiling at them – the way you have to just so they don't get humpty and decide they have another job more urgent than your own – almost humanized him. Or humourized him. The three of them had a last laugh and a last cup of tea before the yawns got to Craig and Lisa, and Craig said. "We're off to bed." Shane nodded, but didn't rise. "I think I'll go for a bit of a walk." Craig said. "Still got that key, right?" Shane nodded again. "Is there still a café on the precinct?" Lisa said. "There's food in the fridge you know, just help yourself." Smiling at Lisa, Shane waved a hand backwards and forwards. "No, no, a good café breakfast is one of the things I miss about living abroad." Craig said. "There's a café there alright but I don't how good it is." There was a worried catch in Lisa's voice as she said. "Are you sure Shane? Aren't you tired?" Putting an arm around her shoulder, Craig said. "He's alright love, come on let's go to bed."

Locking the back door behind him, Shane nipped over the fence and up the alley. The morning was brighter now, more real. A few other people, daytime people were out and about doing their thing, going to work, to buy the paper, to get the milk. The one's who noticed him, looked at him as though they expected to know him. It was a small enough environment. When they passed they nodded as though they did, just in case they did. Shane nodded back. What the fuck! They weren't the problem. He went up the cul-de-sac, past Dalrimple's. Shadows could be seen moving around in the dim interior and Shane wondered where the snake had gone. Further up, Wilson's house was easy enough to see, with the car he'd come down the alley in, parked on the concrete front garden. The curtains were still drawn and a security light was still on. There was a wrought iron security gate over the front door and another protecting the side of the house. Immediately behind the side gate was a kid's bike. It was pink and had stabilisers.

Up at the end, in the bulb of the cul-de-sac, Rowlands had two houses knocked together. There were only two other houses in the bulb and they were boarded up, paint spattered and singed, front gardens a tangled mass of weeds and rubbish. Between these derelicts, Rowlands double fronted garden was like something out of a seed catalogue, with knobs on. The knobs being in the shape of two stone eagles rampant, set on high red brick plinths and a combination wrought iron and red brick front wall and gate. Foxgloves, lupins, hollyhocks, roses, chrysanthemum and another dozen flower types Shane didn't recognise, filled the space behind the wall. Most were blooming in a last mad end of summer rush, like some gross, overblown country plot and completely out of wack with its surroundings. Someone had spent a lot of time in that garden. The bulb of the cul-de-sac had Rowlands three vehicles, a four by four, a Merc' and a red Toyota sports car, parked over it as though it was his driveway. Shane had seen this sort of crap before and it was like people who had jam with their bread and thought they were kings when they were only kings in their own kitchen. He knew instinctively Rowlands had had it too easy for a while and it made him laugh inside. People get to thinking they can't be touched, but people disappear all the time.

Between the derelict to the left of Rowlands and Rowlands house was the alley that ran through to Bishops Avenue. Unlike the wide, truncated alleyways that separated the semi-detached houses on the outer circumference of Circle Road, these alleyways, more to the centre of the estate, were narrow, less than five feet wide. When the estate was built, few people had cars and the shopping precinct, almost at the centre of the estate, had originally been designed with that in mind. The alleyways were like spokes to the centre hub. Anybody who wanted to travel quickly used the alleys. By day the province of the housewife, the mother, the young kids, coming and going to the shops, pushing pushchairs and riding bikes. Old men off to the bookies, old bints going to the offie'. At night, when Shane had been young, these alleys had been safe, nothing more than the short cut home after the pub. These days after dark they were the rat runs. Could be okay, could be not okay, depends on luck and who you are. It was the same on this estate as anywhere.

Shane turned into the alley between the wrecked house to the left and Rowlands would-be manor house. He walked a few yards. Rowlands had erected a high, slatted wooden fence all down the length of his garden. Turning around, Shane went back out on to the cul-de-sac. In the front garden of the nearest derelict he rummaged around. Amongst the general detritus was a rusted length of steel pole about two inches in diameter and maybe two, three feet long. Shane went from car to car and smashed each windscreen. All the alarms kicked off. Sound bounced around off the houses and whined away demented in the early morning quiet and Shane walked back in to the alley.

There were other shortcuts to the precinct but there was no hurry and Shane walked along Bishops Avenue like he was inside a bubble that was all too familiar but changed. Like a photo of the past that is projected onto the 3D present. It threw memories up in his face. Not bad memories, just things with girls. Snogs and fumblings up dark passages. Or him and Gerry walking, walking when they couldn't go home and the first wrap of speed was running and they walked every road up and down and though they had to go to work in the morning they didn't care and who would? They were sixteen and had wanted to try everything. Shane didn't give a fuck then and he didn't give a fuck now. He'd tried most of everything and addicts were muppets. Drugs were for pleasure. When he reached the shops and the pub on the precinct, the café was closed.

In his youth there had been a range of shops on the precinct. A greengrocers, butchers, chemist, a post office, a drapers come wool shop, a newsagents, a shop that sold electrical goods like lamps and radios and all that nick nack stuff that people keep on shelves and in cabinets and ain't no use to no one. There had even been a model mak-ing shop, it's window full of Airfix box kits, with plastic and balsawood aircraft hanging from the ceiling by fishing line and aircraft carriers riding on painted seas. Some old guy who'd been a Japanese prisoner of war had run it. He never copped on why kids were always in buying modelling glue and never modelling kits. He died and the shop closed down but that was even before Shane had left school. A guy repairing and selling used washing machines and gas cookers took over. What happened to him?

Shane looked around. Something had happened. He'd seen it in other poorer parts of the country before and he'd seen it in other countries where an economic miracle had failed. The place was fucked. Some shop fronts were bricked up, others roller shuttered and graffitied over and over again until the original, "JUST BLUES", was gone for good. Okay, he hadn't been on this bit of the estate for a long time. He added time up and it looked close to twenty years. For some reason Shane had always thought that things had got better for most people, as they had for him, but really it didn't look like things had. From what Shane could see, all the place could muster now was a Happy Shopper mini-mart, a bookie's, a convenience store cum off-licence and the café. There was a light on in the back of the café. Shane peered though the window and then saw the sign in the door about the seven thirty opening.

Cutting across the car park, Shane kept walking.

He went down Kings Drive, a road similar to Bishops Avenue, which worked a slow curve through the half of the estate at the back of the shops. A left turn, right then and through a couple of connecting alleyways, onto Cloister Crescent and back onto Circle Road at the far side of the estate. Tracing a path he had followed probably from the age of eight, when he had first been allowed to come up to play with Gerry on his own. Gerry's parents had lived in Monks Crescent then, off Bishops Avenue. They were both dead now. His mother had had a heart attack when she was in her mid-fifties, sudden. Shane had come down from the city for the funeral. They were a very close knit family and Gerry was hard hit. A year later the father had turned up his toes. Died of a broken heart. Nothing to live for. Louise had told Shane, Gerry couldn't deal with it, couldn't function, not even to organize the funeral. Lay on the couch and drank, while she did what was needed. It was the first and only time Shane ever saw Louise disappointed in Gerry.

Shane hated to go back to the day or the day before the day or whenever it was because it was all only an illusion of something he could not change and he just could not be arsed with blame or with guilt. He thought about the future and he thought about the past but there wasn't an answer in either. Every little thing, all the small choices he made everyday, much more than the big ideas he had, made him what he was. But like most people, the past pulled at him. Like coming to visit Gerry and Louise. Like the way he was walking the estate. Like the guys he'd killed in Manchester. Irrelevant and relevant all at the same time. Now he walked along Circle Road thinking, fuck it, I'm here. When he was a kid, the far end of the estate had backed up on to a stretch of waste ground and beyond that, the canal which ran down to the Thames. Back then the other side of the canal was the arse end of the town. Like a place time had forgotten. Run down repair shops, dodgy garages, cheapskate printers, crumbling rented housing, smelly bedsits, small engineering firms, a couple of rough boozers and his dad's scrapyard. Adjacent to the scrapyard and almost a part of it, was the ramshakle house he'd grown up in. The front door opened directly onto the street, with three foot of pavement separating the house from the lorries and trucks that used the road as a short cut. Outside the back door there had been a barren, fenced in area of packed earth, Shane's parents had laughingly called a garden. Nothing ever grew there but dust in the summer and mud in the winter. Out the back gate was the scrapyard. Stacks of rusting mashed up cars and twisted metal, an old crane on rubber tyres for shifting the shit around. A greasy, dirty, noisy, perfect place.

When Shane was a kid it had been easy to get from his house onto the estate. Through a hole in the fence at the back of the scrapyard, onto the canal towpath, over a set of lock gates, which were usually closed and then about a hundred yards of waste ground and the estate. Early on, the gardens of the houses on this section of Circle Road had backed directly onto the waste ground. Later, the council or somebody had erected a six-foot high wire fence. People ignored it. They went over it, under it, through it. Every time it was repaired, some fucker would just cut another hole. The fence was now nearer twenty feet high and the waste ground was some kind of Business Park. Beyond the Business Park, the arse end of town had become regenerated. The scrapyard was now an upmarket, apartment block, one of the pubs a restaurant and the other completely redesigned into a French style café bar. Most of the old businesses had been levelled to make way for new, expensive housing. The canal had been tarted up, trees planted, turf laid, few memorial benches and the area was now called Bankside. Twenty feet high or not, a fence was still a fence and somewhere along it's length people would still be going though it. Shane reconnoitred the alleyways between the houses, until he found the gap he was looking for.

By the time he'd walked back to the shops, the café was open. There was a sweet smell of frying tomatoes and bacon. Shane ordered liver and bacon, fried tomatoes and chips, toast and tea. The only other customers were a couple of builder types, with mobile phones clamped to their ears. Shane sat at an empty table facing the door. The food came steaming on a big oval plate and the tea in a thick white mug. Yeh, the place had been redecorated, there was a new counter and new owners but the food was pure café. It tickled Shane to think that of all England is made up of, a café breakfast was up there. He went at the food with intent because there was a lot of it and faint heart never cleared the plate and even that was more history shit, more memory. When Gerry and he would sit here after some teen all night session brains still half fried, egging each other on to order huge breakfasts they could never eat and laughing, laughing.

Shane saw the guy clock him as he came though the door. A stiffness in his shoulders as their eyes slid over each other. He had on a wool hat and paint covered overalls. Shane pegged him at forty odd. He ordered from the counter and came back to Shane's table carrying his tea, he said. "Mind if I sit here?" Shane took an exaggerated look around the café. The man said. "Yeh I know. I could sit anywhere but I saw you earlier." Shane looked down at his plate. He'd eaten two thirds of his meal and was about full. He could have just left. Instead he sighed, looked up and nodded. Pulling out a chair and sitting down, the man drank tea and said. "Thanks." Shane stared at him, waiting.

The woman behind the counter, brought over an egg and bacon sandwich. As he put brown sauce on it, he said. "I take it you don't work for the Fatman, then?" He chewed at a mouthful of sandwich, sauce dripped onto his fingers and he licked it off, he said. "Scum. All of 'em." Shane looked at the guy's work-a-day hands and his washed out blue eyes and said. "I don't work for anyone." The guy raised an eyebrow, spread a flat grin over his face and without enthusiasm said. "Who does anymore, we're all self-employed these days." He raised the other eyebrow, his eyes were wide and cynical but they didn't say anything. He said. "But by the cut of you, I'd say we follow different trades. You ain't a cop, are you?" Shane gave a short laugh. "Don't think so." Then he dropped his voice and said, without inflection. "What did you see? What the fuck do you want?"

The guy was on the second half of the sandwich and had already almost finished his tea. He held his hand up and nodded at Shane's empty cup as he caught the waitress's eye. A strange ennui came over Shane and he thought, briefly, about the boat waiting near Plymouth and how long it would be before the bloke opposite would recognise him and say hey, didn't you used to be somebody? He would try to remember Shane's name and maybe he would. Shane didn't like to think about that. He nodded and the bloke held up two fingers to the waitress. The builder guys, still yakking on their phones, waddled past and out the front door. The woman came over, slid their teas onto the table and picked up Shane's plate, she said, happily. "Alright, love?" Shane smiled up at her, he had done the dog on the fry up and there were only scraps of tomato skins and a few bits of chips left. "Perfect." Two lads came into the café, laughing, looking like they had been up all night. All tight tops and baggy trousers, eyes like saucers and floppy hand movements. Almost on the heels of the guys, came a couple of pensioners. A crusty old guy and a blue haired bint pulling a shopping trolley. The old lady sat at a table and sparked up a fag. The old man went to the counter and waited behind the young guys, to order. Shane recognised the old couple. Couldn't remember their name but they had lived a couple of doors up from Gerry's parents. It was about time to leave. He didn't care if he was being paranoid, paranoia had a place and he had a life to lead.

"Well?" Shane swallowed several mouthfuls of tea and reaching across the table took one of the bloke's hands in his own as gently as if they were lovers and looking into his eyes, said. "Thanks for the tea but I've got to go in a minute. Tell me whatever it is, I don't give a fuck but tell me anyway. Get it off your chest or I'm going to hurt you. Now hurry up." The bloke quickly pulled his hand out of Shane's grasp and pressed back in his chair. Shane stared at him. The man stared back and without a trace of fear in his voice, said. "There's no need for that." Shane looked around the café at nothing and sighed. "Okay. I'm –." The guy came forward in his chair again and half raised the hand Shane had gripped, to show the palm. "Don't bother saying your sorry because you ain't. I saw you do the cars. Upset you has he?"

Shane was starting to feel that old ennui now as tiredness, a desire for bed. Nerves in the corner of his eyes were twitching. He looked over at the two young dudes, who were stuffing buttered toast into their mouths like there was no tomorrow, while talking nonsense and sending text messages on their phones, all at the same time. At that moment he envied them. He hated feeling weary. A table away the old couple were sat in a world of their own doing a crossword in a newspaper and enjoying each other's company like they were still teenagers. He didn't know where people got that shit from! How did anyone manage to make anything last that long? It mystified him.

The guy said. "You don't have to threaten me. That cunt Rowlands has done more to hurt me than you ever could. I ain't even against drugs, I'm a painter and decorator, if you didn't smoke dope you'd go barmy. But that's not it." Shane said. "No?" The painter and decorator came down now resting his elbows on the Formica topped table, hands swivelling about, head bobbing. "There's always been drugs on the estate, know what I mean? Dealing between friends, that sort of thing." Shane knew exactly, he nodded. "But Rowlands just took over. It was easy. Him and his 'oppo's just battered anybody who was doing a bit and told them, if they wanted to do business it was through him." Shane yawned and said. "Fuck it mate, it's progress ain't it. Global markets, and all that. Big business. That post hippie shit is dead in the water. There's a couple of million kids drop little fella's and go clubbing every weekend, what do you expect?"

The man pulled at his hat and flared his nostrils. Speaking fast and low, he said. "My boy went to school with Dean. They were always together. Disappearing for whole weekends. Teen shit, raving and stuff and like, you know what you were like yourself, so you let them go. Maybe we were too easy and fuck it, anyway he got into smack. Dean was smart enough though, he didn't." The tiredness started to crawl out from the back of Shane's eyes into his brain to roll down his spine, to spread across his shoulders, he said. "Look mate –." But the painter was on a roll, and he rolled straight over Shane's mild attempt to leave. Shane sighed and the man continued. "Apart from the thieving, there are worse things than him being a smack addict." Despite his weariness Shane couldn't help laughing. The guy said. "No, really. At least he'd just end up nodding out. Since he got out of the young offenders unit about a year ago, he's been on that crack." He shook his head and gave out a defeated little chuckle. "I tell you, that shit makes me wish he was back on smack. It's like having a squirrel in the fucking roof. A fucking nuisance. They don't sleep and they won't let you sleep neither. It's fucked his brain up."

Shane stopped him then. After all what was the point? A sob story was a sob story and everyone had one, especially about their kids. He said. "So what do you expect me to do?" The abruptness of the question took the guy by surprise. He squinted at Shane and at his cup and then up at the big menu painted up on the wall. His mouth was partly open and he took a couple of short breaths and scratched his scalp through his woolly hat. Shane cocked his head and raised an eyebrow. "Well?" Slowly, he said. "I don't know. Nothing I suppose." He paused. "Look, I don't really want anything. It just cheered me to see you smashing up the cars." He paused again. "I saw you sitting here and I wanted to say something." He chewed his bottom lip and without making eye contact with Shane, said. "I don't know, maybe I just wanted to unload. I can't do anything about my Jake. I can't do anything about anything. But –." He slumped a bit, got control of himself and squared his shoulders. "But it's all shit ain't it? If you got your nose above it, things are alright. Like forget it, know what I mean? Sorry." The painter and decorator pushed back his chair and rose to leave. Shane reached out and took his hand again but in a different way, he said. "Hang on." Punters were beginning to come into the café in dribs and drabs now and Shane knew he had to get away before any trouble came in, because the way he felt he just didn't want it. But tired as he was, there was something he wanted. The man sat back down again. Shane said. "Tell me about Rowlands." And the painter and decorator did. It was all he had to offer.

∾ **10** ᔓ

Billy was making a fuss about something. By the rise and fall of their voices, Lisa and Craig were attempting to be semi-rational parents. Trying to cajole him on one hand and showing signs of impending madness on the other. Explaining whatever it was carefully several times, before threatening mutilation and murder. Although he couldn't hear their words, he couldn't miss Billy's shrill tones. The inevitable. "It's not fair!" The obligatory. "You always say that!" Followed by the age old cry of the chancer. "But why!" And of course. "No! No! No!" Still in bed, relaxed and rested now, Shane couldn't help smiling. Billy was a natural born scallywag. Loudly, the boy said. "Anyway –." But Lisa wasn't having it. Exasperated, her own voice rising to match Billy's, she snapped. "Anyway! Anyway what? You're a ten year old boy!" Smart as, Billy came back. "Exactly!" Shane was sure he heard Craig banging his head against a wall and Lisa stifle a scream. Billy on the other hand was nonchalant. "I heard you telling Dad, if he went to that pub with Shane, you were going too. But you told me before, that parents couldn't leave kids on their own at home alone until they were twelve. Remember in the bed and breakfast place, when that lady used to go out and leave that little girl and come back drunk and you said –." Lisa sounded like she was choking and Craig gave an astonished, admiring laugh. Lisa said. "Craig!" Craig coughed and Lisa continued. "Don't get too smart with me, Billy, I've about had enough!" Billy spoke again but it was low, beneath Shane's hearing. Lisa's response wasn't. "What was that!" Audible now, Billy said. "Maybe we should ask Shane."

Shane flinched and decided it was time to rise. There were words, some he heard even though he didn't want to and some dropped way below his auditory senses. Sure, he heard all of Billy's buts and knew that the new devil always looked better than the devils that reared you. He would have liked to put the boy straight but there ain't no putting anyone straight. Old or young other peoples realities are just that. He got out of bed and had a wash and a crap and a shave. It was going to be a long day. He changed into whatever bits of clean clothes he had left in the bag and marvelled at the fact Billy hadn't either seen or mentioned the fat wad in the bag with the gun. It was strange but guns had an effect on people, especially a kid. It was like the gun evened out the score in an uneven world. Any ten yearold could become the man he was desperate to be. Shane rarely used guns. For him there was no joy in it, no fun. The exhilaration, the adrenaline rush he got from the physical just wasn't there. Like the difference between a porno movie and sex. For Shane the weapon was nothing more than the tool it was. A wank job but it had its uses. Before he went downstairs, he slipped in the clip, checked the safety and put the gun under the mattress out of sight.

Lisa was in the kitchen by herself when Shane went down. She looked embarrassed but just raised her eyebrows and shrugged her shoulders as if to say kids, what can you do, eh? The back door was open and outside in the garden, Billy had his head down and his hands in his pockets and was kicking dejectedly around in the ashes at the edge of the dead fire. Craig was sitting on the back step, his head in his hands, watching the boy. Lisa put the kettle on, she said. "Tea?" Craig came in and sitting himself at the table, said to Shane. " I suppose you heard all that?" Shane nodded and said. "Sounded funny from where I was but." The couple exchanged glances and Craig said. "Yeh, well." Lisa added. "They're all the same these days, think they know everything, too damn smart for their own good." Gently Craig said. "Alright love. He's just a kid. We're all a bit tense." The kettle boiled and Lisa huffed at Craig and he got up, told her to sit down and made the tea. Before the tea could mash, Billy's yelling broke into their silence. "Dad, dad, mum!" He was in at the back door eyes wild with fear, stopping suddenly short when he saw Shane. "Shane! Shane! Quick Shane! There's a man in the garden!" Everybody was up on their feet, Craig grabbed Billy and Lisa grabbed them both.

The guy was huge. They could see him crossing the garden. Shane sighed and looked quickly around the kitchen for a weapon. It was all clean and shipshape. Shane went to the back door. The guy was six four at the min' and built like Desperate Dan. Shane took several slow, deep, breaths through his nose. He held himself casual, poised. On the step, the guy held out a mitt. "You probably don't remember me, I'm Rodney, Stan's son." Shane looked up and over this brick shit-house on legs and shook his head. "No mate, I don't." He took the proffered hand and watched Rodney. He had clear blue eyes and a mad stack of blond hair and he was tanned from a summer of working outside. With a smile on his mug he looked like a huge child but Shane had had runnins with guys like this before. Their sheer bulk could take most of what anyone could deal up. Lisa said.

"Stan next door? Come in, Craig just made tea."

The adults sat at the table and Billy wandered around taking in everything with a suspicious eye. Lisa tried to get the boy to go and watch T.V. but he wasn't having it. Instead he stood by the side of Shane's chair, a moody puss on him, almost daring them to make a fuss. Like Rowlands, Rodney was in his mid-forties and Shane could see that together they would have made a formidable pair. Shane said. "Stan alright?" Rodney nodded and looked around the table, a little shamefaced, he said. "Dad's dad, know what I mean? He's always been a bit of a cantankerous sod. But he don't like what's happening." Speaking directly to Shane then, he added. "And neither of us liked what happened to Gerry and Louise." A breath of anger in his voice, Craig said. "I heard it was Rowlands and you in the beginning." Rodney didn't like that and he swung his head around and looked at Craig, blue eyes suddenly not so sunny. Shane said. "Stan told me yesterday, you helped set Rowlands up." Still staring at Craig, Rodney said, gruffly. "That was years ago, seven, eight." Sounding like a sour old man, Billy chipped in double quick. "You all better leave my mum alone." Shane put an arm around Billy's shoulder and looked him straight in the eye. "Be quiet, Billy." Lifting his eyebrows and shoulders, as if joined by the same muscle, Craig eased back on Rodney. "Sorry, we're a bit wound up."

Tea was drunk and Billy walked around the kitchen again, an executioner's gob on him, eyeing Rodney like he was next for the scaffold. Maybe Billy's disapproval touched the roofer's conscience because he began to explain. "Look, things have changed." With a nod towards the circling Billy, he went on with. "I've got kids of my own now. Hopefully they won't, you know have to, well you know, whatever." He looked at Shane like they were somehow fellow travellers and said. "We all need a start in the world. The fat man, well he's Terry to me. We went to the same school. When he first moved up here we became good mates. Then he needed muscle and I'm a big bloke. He knew some people and we both put up money to buy the bulk. The rest was easy. Threats and a few slaps. I'd been labouring since I left school. I was fed up breaking my back. Wanted to start up my own roofing firm." Walking like the living dead, Billy staggered over to his mother and flung his arms across her shoulders as she sat in the chair and yawned into her ear. Lisa gave out a big sigh and looked askance at the lad.

Shane couldn't help liking Craig and Lisa and Billy and liking the fact that they could sit now and not give anything much away. Liked the way they took Rodney at face value and gave him space for his explanation, when they were the ones under threat. Holding all the stuff back because at that moment there wasn't anything else to do with it. And when Rodney was done and gone, it would be time to take some kind of family outing to the pub and what? It was crazy! Just the idea of it made him want to laugh out loud, it was all out of wack but he knew he would go along. What else was there? The painter and decorator had told Shane that Rowlands and a few of his cronies spent most of the afternoon in The Temple Bell. And that before five was the best time to do it because the little bar he used as an office wasn't all his through the afternoon, the customers being more mixed. In the night the snug changed character. Became more territorial. So Shane would go family style, in the afternoon and something would happen. If you lived as close to the moment as you could, it was like time travel. Knowing you didn't know what was next was as close to the truth as you get. It was why he lived. Then everything else was down to chance. When he looked in the mirror, sometimes he felt like a mug. Wanting to be in the moment. Maybe he was a mug. Everybody had to be a mug sometimes. He wondered if he was beginning to enjoy it – as a feeling.

Rodney said. "I got out because while I'm a big bloke, that don't mean I like hurting people. They reckon that drugs are the mother business, don't they?" Nobody answered him. Maybe they'd all read different books. "Well anyway, it was to me.

Soon as I'd got enough to set myself up, I pulled out." He looked pointedly at Shane but Lisa jumped in. "Look." Her voice had that nice ameliorating female edge and the three men were happy to look to her and hear what she had to say. She got hold of Billy's wrist and gave him a Chinese burn until he squealed. She said. "I don't really know you or Stan. We don't really know anyone. While I'm listening to what you're saying it doesn't really mean anything to me. My reality is waiting for tonight when those animals come to burn us out." Billy tried unsuccessfully to give Lisa a Chinese burn and found himself in a headlock. Lisa said. "As Craig pointed out, we're a bit tense, so please don't be offended if I ask you why you're here?" Now Shane did almost laugh out loud and Craig got hold of Billy and buried his face into the boy's neck and made animal noises and Billy tried to give Craig Chinese burns but they didn't hurt and Lisa said, smilingly. "Well?"

Rodney looked about him as though everything was a bit surreal but he didn't let on. Instead he stood up because being big you can always do that and fuck you. But none of them even seemed to notice, so he said. "Yeh, well just wanted to have my say, while I was here. Anyway, dad asked me to come over. He said, if there's any trouble to pop over the fence and come in with him, the back door's always open. Okay?" The adults looked at

Rodney and Billy extricated himself from his father's grip and came back over to Shane and tried the Chinese burns on him, Craig said. "Tell him thanks. You never know we may take him up on it." In a resigned voice, Lisa added. "Don't suppose you want to have a word with your mate Terry, do you? Ask him to leave us alone." Eyeing the door now, hands in his pockets, feet shuffling here and there, Rodney looked embarrassed for the first time, he said. "He might owe me, but not that much. We ain't such good mates any more. You know, he wasn't always a cunt." He quickly made to apologise for swearing but Billy was already on it. There in front of Rod with his hand out and although Craig and Lisa, said. "Billy!" He wouldn't shift until the roofer had crossed his palm with silver.

When he'd gone, Lisa blew air between her teeth, she said. "Don't need him easing his bad conscience on us. Mother trade! People have got excuses for everything. Does he think we care! Does he think we want to know? Why are people always going on about all the bad things they did in the past? Like nobody tells you all the good things they did in the past, do they! The bloody world's obsessed! What's wrong with being decent? We can't all be gangsters!" Nobody was arguing but Shane wondered if this was at him too. If she was showing she wasn't letting him off, even if he was on their side. But even as she spoke, she waved a few fingers at him, the way people do when they accept your personal strangeness. She stood up and carried on. "Why not just come over and say, Stan said, blah, blah, bloody blah and have done with it. I don't even have to know he mends bloody roofs! Why are people always telling you what they do? Mostly it's totally tedious. I can't believe people." In one swoop she grabbed the cups up off the table and dumped the lot in the sink. In another swing by she grabbed the milk and stowed it in the fridge. Billy said. "Mum." So next on her list was Billy. Lisa grabbed hold of Billy by the wrists and squatted down in front of him. She said. "I know I said bloody, three times, so don't even think what you're thinking. Just don't, alright!" Billy gave her a butter wouldn't melt look. But Lisa wouldn't have it. She eyeballed him until he blinked and then stood up and said. "So, are we going or what?"

## ∽ 11 ∽

They left the house like family, like they were tight with each other and knew the score. Like they were a happy family who didn't need to shop yellow pack. Like they weren't shit scared. And Shane went with them. Billy wanted to walk with Shane.The afternoon was fine again, with the sun pouring itself all over the south lands and the Temple Estate especially. The sky was bleached white and cloudless and the air was dry and full. Grass cuttings, overblown roses, dusty earth, cleaning fluid, dog shit, warm car and as they passed Dalrimple's, the smell of the wet rugs and furniture dumped all over the front garden. Billy couldn't contain himself. He demanded high fives off Shane right in front of the window, with Dalrimple looking out. But even Lisa had to laugh after they'd gone by. Billy said. "I wonder where the snake's gone? Do they come home when they're hungry like dogs and cats?" None of the adults knew. Or cared. Billy said. "Dad did you tell Shane about him going next door and all that yelling and that woman screaming to come and save her. Did you?"

Lisa took hold of the boy's hand and dragged him up alongside her and Craig dropped back to walk with Shane. As they strolled up the cul-de-sac like loopers on day release, with silly grins and everything, Shane pointed out Wilson's house. The security gate to the side of the house was open and the car was gone from the front. A blond little girl was on the pink bike. She was riding it around the space where the car had been and her mother was sitting on the front step, smoking a cigarette. The front door was open and music was playing. Wilson's mott watched them as they went by. She flicked the ash off her fag and nodded amiably at them. Maybe she knew who they were. Maybe she didn't.

Others were out and about and doing things to their cars or their gardens, sitting, standing, watching, wondering. Some kids, near Billy's age, had got hold of a length of plywood and propped it up on a few bricks, to make a ramp. There were four of them, three boys and a girl. They were coming down the slight incline one at a time on their skateboards and firing themselves off the ramp with

great hoots and hollers. A little black and white terrier ran down after each kid, barking like it was part
of the game. When they saw Billy and the rest coming up, they had a quick confab and the girl took
hold of the dog. She stood it on one of the skateboards and the dog lolloped out it's tongue and
panted, looking at the girl like she was the saviour
of dog kind and this sort of manoeuvre was it's
heart's desire. She carefully positioned each of the
critter's paws on the board like it was a four-legged
land surfer, then all the kids got behind and gave it
a shove. Dog and board hurtled down the road and
flew off the ramp. For a heartbeat, the little dog and
the board parted company and the kids all yelled
and the terrier barked as it and the skateboard landed and rattled past Billy and his family.

Like an eel gone from the grasp, Billy was gone
down the road after the dog. When the skateboard
was going slow enough for the dog to abandon
ship, Billy scooped up the board and after petting
the dog, walked back up to where the other kids
were standing. He dropped the skateboard to the
tarmac and pushed it towards the bunch of kids.
They looked at each other and the dog rambled up
and looked at the lot of them. One of the boys
picked up the skateboard. Billy looked over his
shoulder at the adults approaching and bent down
to pet the dog like they were nothing to do with
him. He said. "What's his name?" The girl said.

"Flatpat." All the others laughed and Billy said. "Flatpat?" Giggling herself, she said. "Yeh, he was called Pat but got run over by a bread van when he was little." Billy and the whole lot of them laughed. One of the boys said. "You from that house down there?" Billy had his hands in his pockets, the toe of one of his trainers was digging at the tarmac but his chin was out. "Yeh." Another boy said. "They got rid of them." He pointed behind him to the wrecked houses each side of Rowlands own little Pondarosa. The girl pulled a sour face and said. "We don't like them up there." Lisa called over and all the children looked. The boy carrying the skateboard held it out to Billy. "Want a go?" Looking over at Lisa but reaching for the board, Billy grinned a complicit grin. Lisa called again, despite Craig's hand on her arm. Anyway it was too late because Billy was already on the move. With a holding wave at the adults, he was on the board and pushing off with his foot. As he gathered momentum the dog trotted beside him making little jumps and barking. Bending his knees and spreading his arms like a tightrope walker, he took the jump yelling, like the others before him and landed foursquare, cruising to a halt like he was born to it.

As Billy handed back the skateboard, Craig called. "Come on, Billy!" All the children did a jaw drop and looked at each other as though something nasty this way comes and Billy in the slowest of motions, turned his head to look at his father. He wanted to be left. The tilt of his head, the way he folded his arms over his chest said it all. But despite his silent pleading, deep down even Billy knew Lisa wouldn't have it. Craig was sharper now. "Billy!" And Billy gave his new acquaintances a duty calls turn down of the mouth and with a little upward lift of the chin, sauntered back over to the others. Lisa went for his hand but too quick for her, he skirted around both his parents and ended up walking beside Shane. Shane said. "Alright?" Billy nodded and shoved his hands in his pockets. They were nearing the top of the street and in a quiet voice, Billy said to Shane. "They made those people leave, didn't they." Shane glanced at the wrecked houses and down at the boy. "Yeh." Over his shoulder to Shane, Craig said. "Gives me the creeps every time I come past here." Lisa added. "Makes you wonder what goes on in people's heads. It's like they can't enjoy life without hurting other people." Billy said to Shane. "Will they make us leave, Shane?" Craig said. "Come on Billy, he can't answer a question like that."

It was true he didn't have an answer and shrugged. "I don't know Billy. Depends." With a withering look, the boy said. "Onnnnn?" Shane laughed. "On some kind of luck." Billy thought about it and eyed up Shane. "Alright, what kind of luck?" Shane couldn't help giggling as he said. "The lucky kind of course." Lisa and Craig groaned, while Billy held his hands over his ears and shook his head like a robot gone wrong. He kept saying over and over. "That was useless, that was really useless." The three vehicles were there and as they passed, Craig stopped and whistled. They all stopped and admired the smashed windscreens. Craig said. "Well, that's a turn up. Maybe there's someone else don't like him." Shane said. "No, I did that this morning." Nervously Lisa laughed and said. "He won't like that. You really are a dangerous man, aren't you?" Lisa was scared and Shane knew she had reason to be. He said. "Not to you or Craig or Billy." They started walking again and entered the alley. Billy held out his hand, he said. "I trust you Shane." He slapped the boy's palm in a low five and said. "Thanks Billy."

As they walked along Bishops Avenue towards the shops and pub, Craig told Shane what he'd seen and heard earlier. "I saw Wilson coming down from his house talking on his phone and go into Dalrimple's. Few minutes later they came out and headed across the road. I thought they were coming to us but they swung off down the alley. I went out to the back door, just in case but they didn't even look my way." He laughed. "You'd think after you going in there last night, someone would have locked the back door. No. Those two walked straight in." Billy said. "That's when the screaming and shouting started, didn't it Dad!" Craig shook his head at the boy and sighed. "Yeh more or less. Went all quiet after about five minutes." Shane said. "How long were they in there?" Craig shrugged. "Maybe ten minutes. They didn't look any happier when they came out than when they went in." Shane said. "She can't tell 'em much they don't already know so fuck them. Damn, I mean fiddle-sticks, I mean sorry Billy." He got the phone he'd taken the night before out of his pocket, turned it on and poked in the mini-cab man's number. When he answered, Shane said. "It's that bloke up on the estate. – Yeh. – That go all right last night? – Right, good. What you doing now? – Oh right. What time you due back on then? – Right. – Do you fancy a little job now? – Okay, meet me by the car park at the shops up on the estate. – That's right. – Ten minutes? – Great. See you there."

They went into the mini-mart and Lisa bought baked beans and frozen chips and some weird look-ing things in batter that claimed to be the most ten-der parts of the Turkey, for Billy's tea. Rubbing his hands together gleefully, Billy said. "Yes!" Craig and Lisa exchanged glances and Lisa shrugged and said, to Shane. "Bit of comfort food for old Billy boy." She reached out and ruffled his hair and Billy went. "Mum!" Shane put four of those very large bottles of Stella in the basket. In the newsagents he got a couple of comics that Billy wanted and a copy of Carp Masters, the angling magazine. The magazine was glossy and thick and full of pictures of carp the size of small pigs and smiling men struggling to hold the fish for the photograph. Craig shot him a quizzical look and said. "You into fishing?" With a laugh, Shane said. "No."

When they finished the bit of shopping they walked over to the car park. Ten minutes is a weird amount of time in any language and can come out long or short, depending. They waited another long, uncomfortable ten minutes, thinking that ten minutes was an hour and that they were on show and that anyone passing was watching them, marking them out as victims. Shane rolled up the carp magazine and stuck it into the back pocket of his trousers the way working men did, when they were off to the bookies. Craig was jumpy, knowing they still had the confrontation to come and that waiting only made it harder. Lisa was like she didn't want to let go of him and took his hand or put her arm around his waist whenever she could. Billy seemed to be watching them all. He mooched around with his hands in his pockets or stood beside Shane looking up at him and asking questions like why he didn't bring his gun and what was he going to do in the pub and would there be a fight and could he watch. Shane said nothing and Billy said. "But." And Shane saw the cab coming and pointed and said. "Here comes the cab."

The driver's name was Frank. He said. "Getting to be quite a regular, ain't you. In case you're interested my name's Frank." When Shane didn't answer, Lisa shook his hand through the car window and said. "Hello Frank, I'm Lisa and this is Billy and Craig." Cutting the introductions short, Shane said. "Right Frank look, will you wait here with Lisa and Billy? Me and Craig, we'll be back in a minute." He opened the door of the mini-cab. Craig kissed Lisa and ruffled Billy's hair. Lisa made to speak but Craig gave a little shake of his head. Instead, taking Billy by the shoulders she propelled him before her into the back of the vehicle. Shane shut the door and slipped Frank a handful of crumpled banknotes. "We may need to leave in a hurry." It didn't seem to bother Frank, he nodded and stuffed the money away, uncounted. Shane said. "You got a spare petrol can in the car?" Frank said. "Yeh, in the boot." Shane said. "Full?" The driver nodded.

## 12

The Temple Bell was redbrick, squat and solid looking, with that late 1950's tilt towards the mock
Tudor. When Shane had drunk there in his teens, it
had been an ordinary working man's pub but the
painter he'd met over breakfast, had told him the
place had been opened up into two big bars, with a
snug at each end. The snug Rowlands liked to think
of as his "office" could be entered via either of the
main bars or from a door to the side of the pub.
There were a couple of CCTV cameras overlooking
the car park and a couple more over by the shops,
plus two more angled over the front of the pub. It
didn't worry Shane. Half the time the cameras in
places like this either didn't have film or had
already been vandalised. Anyway he'd already
noticed there were none covering the side entrance
or the expanse of pavement between the pub and

the car park. As they got to the door, Craig looked back over his shoulder at Lisa and Billy in the back of the cab. Shane put a hand on his arm and said. "We don't have to do this." Craig pulled a face and in a resigned voice, said. "What else is there." With a shrug Shane said. "I don't know." They looked at each other for a moment then Craig put a hand on the door and pushed it open.

The snug was maybe ten metres by five. There were eight men in it and they all looked as Craig and Shane entered. The place was smartly decorated in greens and pale yellow, with rattan, colonial style chairs and tables topped with fake marble. At the far end three working types were sat on high stools, drinking pints at the bar. A fake stained glass and wood partition wall separated the snug from the main room. There was a connecting door at the end near the bar. One of the drinkers on the stools was the painter and decorator. The lighting was subtle and the music was piped crap. Neither he nor Shane acknowledged each other. Rowlands, Dean and Wilson were sprawled around one of the tables, playing cards with a couple of other blokes.

A kind of silence fell. Rowlands took a mobile from his pocket and speed dialled. Wilson began to rise but Rowlands put a hand out to stay him and whispered something in his ear. Dean threw his cards down on the table. The other two shifted their shoulders nervously. Shane took a look at the bunch of them as he and Craig walked towards the bar. Rowlands had a smug, vicious tilt to his mouth as he spoke a couple of words into the phone, flipped it shut and dropped it back into his shirt pocket. To Wilson he said. "Well, well, well look what's wandered in." Loud enough to be heard, just, Dean said. "Cunts." Shane winked at him and in a voice not quite his own, Craig said. "Let's get a drink."

At the bar the painter and decorator raised an eyebrow in greeting and to nobody in particular, Shane said. "Where's the barman?" One of the drinkers raised himself up off the stool and leaning across the bar, said loudly. "Barry!" Barry came through from the other side. He was young and big and Eastern European and peeved. In a harsh, choked kind of English, he spluttered. "I tolt choo moy noimes nok Bawee! Dunt cull moy Bawee!" The drinker who called him Barry gave it the innocent. "Yeh, sorry, but the last barman was an Aussie and we called him Barry. His name weren't Barry neither." The barman screwed his face up in exasperation. "Arrg! Choo Inglich!" He put a finger to his temple and made like he was screwing in a screw. "Efry day der same yoke!" The drinker licked his lips in satisfaction. Job done. With a sneer on his face, the barman scanned Craig and Shane and said, sharply. "Vat!"

Shane looked at Craig, who drew in a deep,

slow breath and compressed his lips over it. In a voice the whole snug could hear, Shane said. "Two bitter lemons." The barman studied them momentarily like he was waiting for another crap joke, like he was waiting for the other shoe to drop. Someone at Rowlands' table gave vent to a loud, sarcastic guffaw and in a mincing voice, Dean said. "Ooo, bitter lemons." There was more laughter. The barman looked down the bar at their table like they were shit on the end of his shoe, mumbled a few words under his breath in his own tongue and reaching up took two glasses from the overhead rack and served Craig and Shane. Four guys in their mid-twenties came in, nodded at Rowlands and sat at a table near the door. The barman took Craig's money, rung it up and with his arms folded, stood with his back to the till, surveying the room. Pushing back his chair, Wilson sauntered over to the connecting door into the other bar and leaning against it, addressed Shane, like Craig didn't exist. "I told you, whoever the fuck you think you are, you're on the wrong side." From the safety of his seat near his father, Dean called. "Yeh, you should walk while you still can. When Dal's finished with you you'll be crawling off the Estate like 'is snake." He giggled and made a half-hearted attempt to rise but his father laid a hand on his forearm and said. "Leave it." But Dean, sinking back into his seat, still wanted to show he was in the game and said.

"You shouldn't have fucked with his snake, man!"

Shane looked down the bar and wondered how it was he never quite managed to get away from the past. And how come the last thing was never the last thing and didn't ever quite lead to a new beginning, either. He didn't believe in redemption yet here he was. Nothing changes the past, people just learn to live with the things they've done, learn to put the hateful things to the back of their minds but sometimes those hidden things just jump up and bite you. Looking down the bar was like looking at history from the other side with no chance of changing it or it seemed, of altering the future. Here he was, again. He took a sip from his drink. It was foul. Suddenly Rowlands stood up and coming around the table perched his bulk on its edge. He jabbed a fat finger at Craig. "You, you cunt. You're costing me money." Holding up a hand, Craig tried to remonstrate but Rowlands wasn't the sort of man who liked to listen and so rolled straight over him in his loud cracked voice. "Shut the fuck up!" Craig looked sideways at Shane but if Shane saw him he didn't acknowledge it. Instead he pushed his glass towards the barman and said. "Put a bit of ice in there, mate." The barman complied and went back to his station at the till. The way Shane saw it was, you didn't argue or bother to try to negotiate with the likes of Rowlands because they didn't see themselves as having to negotiate. They had their little fiefdoms sown up or so they thought. They didn't see themselves as little but their little estate as the whole world. For Shane it was simple. Who to go for first.

Rowlands stood up and beckoned the guys up from near the door. Dean and the two at Rowlands table rose as well. To the other three drinkers at the bar, Rowlands barked. "Fuck off!" Wilson shifted enough to push open the connecting door to the other bar and smile as two took their drinks and slid past him. When the painter and decorator didn't move, Wilson leaned over him and said, threateningly. "What's up Kevin? These prats are standing next to you but they ain't your friends, know what I mean?" Kevin had his hand on his pint and his eyes on the floor, with a tremble in his voice, he said. "It's a free country." Rowlands laughed, Wilson laughed and the rest of the pack around Rowlands laughed. Suddenly the pub seemed very crowded to Craig. He couldn't remember how he thought it was going to be but it wasn't this way. Like most men he hadn't had a physical fight since his school days and was shit scared. Shane was beside him alright but he wasn't doing or saying anything. For a paranoid moment Craig thought it was all a trap. Shane's arrival out of the blue, everything he'd done and said, was it all to get him here, alone? Could he really be with Rowlands? And Lisa and Billy sitting in a stranger's car. He wanted to get out, out of the pub now but knew that was impossible. The group of men came in closer. Wilson let his arm drop and the door through to the other bar swung shut. Shane could smell the sweat of fear coming off of Craig but he couldn't do anything about it.

As they came closer, Rowlands said. "It ain't a free country. Nothing's free." With a sneer, Dean said. "Maybe ol' Kevin's been smoking that crack with 'is son — makes you stupid, that stuff." The painter and decorator finished his pint but kept the glass in his hand. Craig was beside Shane and the two men looked at each other. Shane smiled soft and contented, as though he didn't have a worry in the world. It made Craig want to laugh. It settled him. It gave him back the sense that he wasn't alone. He straightened himself up, squared his shoulders and wiped the sweat from his brow. He sighed. To Rowlands, he said. "So, you don't want to talk about our problem, right?" Rowlands reached into his trouser pocket and pulled out a set of knuckles and as he pushed them onto his fat fingers, said. "You stupid cunt! You think I'm about to discuss anything with you after what your cuntin' mate done to my cars. No fuckin' way! You got to find out who the fuck runs this estate." And then, to Shane. "And you, you cunt. When I've finished with you, I'm giving you to Dal'. Dean's right, you'll be happy if you manage to crawl off this fucking estate."

The painter and decorator, Kevin, still sat on the stool between Shane and Wilson. Wilson was leaning in on him and talking at the same time as Rowlands. "And you Kev' me old mate. Why are you getting so aggressive with your close neighbours? Something tells me you need a bit of a slap, just to remind you who your real friends are, know what I mean." It was close. It was getting closer by the nano-second. Shane could smell the collective tang of all the after-shave and deodorant, the sweat and fags. The painter and decorator stepped down off his stool and stood beside Shane and Craig, glass still in his hand. The three men had their backs to the bar. There was no place to go. This was Shane's place. He took the carp magazine out of his back pocket and rolled it into a tight tube.

The great smack of noise as the barman smashed the baseball bat down onto the bar top, cut through the mounting tension like a clap of thunder and Barry the barman was shouting at them in his mangled English. Everyone stopped, everyone looked. Even the three men with their backs to the bar, swivelled their heads. Some around Rowlands actually took a step back. Barry was raging. "Stop! Stop! Choodunt do dat! Choo fuckars! Choo, choo, choo bin tolt! Bifor choo bin tolt bifor!" He smashed the bat back down on the bar and pointed it at Rowlands. "I dunt like choo!" A sneer of contempt wriggled across Rowlands' face but before he could say a word, Dean stepped out from behind his father, adrenaline and coke working on him better than bad judgement ever could. He pulled a taped-up Stanley knife from his pocket. There was about half an inch of blade showing and he waggled it at Barry. "You, you stupid fucker. You're just a fucking barman. You talk to my dad like that and we'll 'av' you, you cunt!" As he spoke, the barman reached under the counter and a bell could be heard somewhere back off in the building. Reaching out a hand Rowlands tried to take his son by the shoulder but Dean shook it off. "Na, fuck it I've 'ad it. Lets do these cunts." Nodding the knife blade at Barry, he said. "Fuck him!" Grunts of approval came from most of the men but Shane saw Wilson and Rowlands exchange uneasy looks and Rowlands said, sharply. "Dean. Leave it!" Nothing moved. Everybody waited. Barry shook his head slowly at Dean and two guys pushed open the connecting door to the other bar, almost knocking Wilson off his feet. Barry looked happy for the first time.

They had baseball bats and maybe it was their haircuts but to Shane they looked like Barry's brothers. There were a few confused fuck this and fuck that's from the hard men and everybody else, including Shane was wondering what the fuck was going on. Barry pointed the baseball bat at the two men and said, proudly. "Moy brozzers." He thought a moment and said. "Yust call 'em Bawee." He looked around the crowd as though he expected a round of applause. When it didn't come he waved the bat around at the various men. "Sit, sit, go sit or go. Okay. Trouble finish. Over." The men with Rowlands looked at each other, they shrugged and looked to Wilson, who was staring at Shane with a see you later look on his face. They looked to Rowlands but things weren't going his way. The odds were way too even now. He just waved a furious hand at them and they milled around and began to drift back towards their seats. Rowlands tried to point out to Barry that maybe he was making a mistake but Barry didn't seem to give a fuck that he was making a mistake. Barry stretched his arm over the bar and shoved the business end of the bat towards Dean, who, even though he was already out of range, jumped back a step. Barry laughed. "Fuck Bawee, eh? Choo Inglich! Choo all tink choo ist gangsta'. Moy country, ist real gangsta'. Eh? Vat choo tink ve do to bring family here? Get money for owning pub? What choo tink?" He saw the surprise on Dean and his father's face and smiling said. "Yes, Bawee own. Now sit, shut up."

Realising they were on the verge of being banned from what they considered their own bar, Wilson tried to pour a little oil on troubled water and moving away from the brothers, he said. "Nice speech Barry. Maybe you're right and we shouldn't sort out our problems in public. Anyway, got time to serve a customer?" Barry cocked his head. Business was business. Wilson ordered for himself, Rowlands and Dean. As he served them Barry said, to Rowlands. "I dunt like choo but I serve choo, okay." Rowlands and Dean were chewing their cheeks in frustration and trying to evil-eyeball the three men still backed up against the bar but it wasn't working. The fear factor had evaporated. Craig and Kevin had the silly, irrepressible grins of reprieved men all over their faces. Kevin was looking at his glass again and licking his lips as though he was thinking of a refill. Craig had one eye on Shane and one eye on the door. Shane waited. He had his elbows resting on the bar and was staring back at the father and son with the same, see you later, smile on his gob as Wilson had given him. He'd seen this lot up close and he already knew he'd be coming back to fuck them up. As Barry had pointed out, every half-arsed fuckwit in the country thought because they thugged it around their poxy estates and sold a few drugs they were gangsters. Muppets. The painter and decorator put his glass on the counter and tried to get Barry to fill it but the barman wasn't having it. He pulled his mouth down and shook his head. "No' choo. No." He waved a dismissive hand at Shane, Craig and the Kevin. "No trouble. Go now." They made to move and Barry pointed to the door into the other bar. "Zat vay."

After they exited the pub, Craig stopped dead and said. "What the fuck?" Kevin shook his head, pulled a face and started giggling like a schoolgirl. Shane looked around, half-expecting a covey of Rowlands thugs to come barrelling around the corner, he said. "Come on, let's get the fuck out of here." As they walked away Kevin stuck out a hand towards Craig and said. "How do. I'm Kevin." Craig shook his hand and said. "Yeh, Thanks for that in there. I'm Craig." Shane walked ahead but could hear the two men bonding behind him. Craig said. "Fucking strange or what!" Kevin still had the breath of a giggle in his voice, as he said. "Talk about living in a gangsta's paradise! Even the barman turns out to be a gangsta!" Craig started to laugh a little bit now, he said. "What about that Bawee! And his brothers!" They both got the giggles and Shane said, to Kevin. "We've got a cab over there, do you want a lift?" With a shake of his head, Kevin said. "Think I'll walk. Get myself together. Wait for my slaps." Craig said. "What?" Kevin didn't feel sorry for himself, as it was he'd made a stand and in some ways it made him happy but he was no fool, he said, matter-of-factly. "You don't juggle with those cunts like I did and get off scot free." They were near the taxi now and turning, he waved a hand and walked away.

## ❧ 13 ❧

Shane sat in the front seat of the cab and Craig sat in the back with Lisa and Billy. Billy wanted to know the gory details and why Shane hadn't taken his gun with him and just blasted everybody. Shane gave him a hard look and said. "What gun." Billy looked at the back of the driver's head and mouthed a silent sorry to Shane. Lisa treated Craig like a hero just back from the war. She petted and kissed him, touched his cheek with the palm of her hand as though he was precious, while her eyes searched his features for any mark or blemish. Craig accepted the attention with big round eyes and not much to say, knowing as he did, just how close all that physical violence had been. When she questioned him, he told her there wasn't anything to be gained by talking to Rowlands and that they had been lucky to get out unharmed. He told her about the barman and the gangsta's paradise joke. He told her about the threats and said. "It ain't over yet, is it Shane?" Shane looked over his shoulder at the family and curling his top lip back off his teeth, said. "It will be tonight." His voice had a cold finality to it that cast a pall over the inside of the car and nobody spoke for what remained of the short journey back to the house.

As they unloaded the shopping Billy sidled up to Shane and in an excited whisper, said. "You'll kill 'em all won't you, Shane?" Shane looked down at the boy, he sighed, he said laughingly. "Billy, Billy, Billy, lets not be silly." As he spoke, he mischievously poked Billy here and there with his index finger, until a giggling, indignant Billy launched himself at Shane. For the next few minutes they dodged around the taxi and every once in a while Shane would let Billy get a few shots in and the taxi driver banged his hand on the side of the door and told Billy. "Go for his nuts, kid!" And Shane almost fell over laughing and Billy pulling grotesque faces managed to catch him with a neat little tolchock to the kidneys. The boy was overjoyed. He ran around the other side of the taxi, so Shane couldn't get him and punched the air like a winner and ran around in a little circle, going. "Yes! Yes!" Lisa came to the front door and called Billy to get off the street. In a no-nonsense voice, she said. "If you want to watch telly or me to cook your tea, you

better get inside and get cleaned up. Now." Billy
was a smirker as he nipped around Shane and
speaking through the corner of his mouth like
movie convict, said. "I bet you'll kill some of
them." As he back peddled into the front garden,
he made his hand into the shape of a gun and raised
his arm so it pointed at Dalrimple's house, he said.
"Pow!"

After she had ushered Billy past her into the
house Lisa stayed in the doorway, leaning against
the jam, her arms folded. Shane took some cash
from his pocket and gave it to the driver, who
glanced at it and put it away, Shane said. "How
would it be if you didn't go to work tonight?" The
driver sucked his teeth, raised his shoulders and up
and under eyed Shane through the open window.
He swallowed and said. "I'm mister ordinary. Like
I told you before, I don't see or hear nothin'."
Shane went to speak, he needed this man, needed a
way out of town. The driver waved his hand. "No,
listen. I don't want to be involved. I don't know
what you got going on here and I don't care."
Shane looked over his shoulder. Lisa was still standing, arms folded, at the front door. At her feet was
the gallon of petrol Shane had taken into the house
with the shopping. The driver said. "I drive, that's
what I do." It occurred to Shane that perhaps Lisa
was waiting for him. He checked behind him again.
She was still there in the same position.

To the driver, Shane said. "I don't want you to do anything. I just need you to be available." The driver said. "I don't know." Shane could feel Lisa's eyes on him and it made him nervous, like he'd done something and it made him wonder what that something was. He said. "I'd make it worth your while. How much do you usually make?" Frank pulled a couple of faces and it was obvious he wasn't all that happy about being put on the spot. With a sigh, he opened the car door and got out. It was the first time Shane had seen him standing. He was broad shouldered and barrel-chested and about five-six. He leaned back against the car and put his hands in his pockets, he said. "A night like tonight, about two hundred plus but it's not just me. I still have to pay the rental on the radio and the boss won't be that happy." Despite himself, Shane couldn't help glancing over his shoulder once again. She was still there. He said. "Would a grand cover it?" Cash was the least of Shane's worries. There was over fifteen thousand, that he'd taken from the dead muppets in Manchester, in his bag. Now Frank was stunned, he straightened up and gave Shane a sharp stare and said. "Don't tell me you don't want me to do nothing. In the words of the prophet, a grand don't come for free." Shane wanted to close, wanted to see what was eating Lisa, he said. "Five hundred now and the rest when we meet. Don't worry it won't be on the estate."

The driver nodded and Shane couldn't help smiling. Money had a language all it's own. Shane knew the man could take the cash and never be seen again but so what? There was a chance he himself wouldn't make it off the estate at all, he said. "Hang on a minute."

Lisa watched him coming up the garden path, she unfolded her arms as he got to the door, she said. "Shane I need a word with you." He was going to go past her and said. "I'll just get rid of the driver, alright?" Tapping the container of petrol with her foot, she said. "No, before." Shane stopped and Lisa rolled her head from side to side the way Indians do, like she wasn't quite sure if she was right or not and she spoke quietly, so neither Craig or Billy, who were both in the kitchen, would hear. "Is that what I think it's for?" She nodded down at the petrol. He shrugged, there wasn't anything much Shane could say. As far as he was concerned, from the moment they had decided to front out Rowlands at the pub, there were no limits. Almost apologetically, Lisa said. "I – I don't think – that woman, you know, the one we passed this afternoon, the one with the little girl in Wilson's front garden? I don't think she deserves that. I don't think even Rowlands wife deserves that. If we burn down their homes that makes us the same as them. I couldn't live with myself if that child was hurt." It wasn't worth Shane's while to explain that, so far in life, he'd been able to live with everything he'd done, instead he said. "Alright." Then as an after-thought, he smiled and said. "You're a decent person, Lisa." Lisa eyed him like he was laughing at her but he said. "I'm serious, both you and Craig are good people, but I'm not. One way or another this business will be finished tonight, I'm going to fin-ish it. If you don't want me to, tell me and I'll go now. Just get in the taxi and disappear."

All the tension she'd been living under for the last weeks became manifest in Lisa's face. Her fea-tures crunched up, her lips trembled, eyes had a lost look and Shane thought she was going to cry. He took one of her hands in one of his own and said, gently. "Lisa?" Taking a couple of deep breaths, she pulled her mouth down unhappily and in a tremulous voice, said. "I'm scared. I don't know. I'm scared for Craig. I don't want him to get hurt. I'm scared for us all. I don't want you to leave. I want you to help us, please. It just all seems like it's got out of control. I – I don't –." Her shoulders slumped. Shane said. "Don't worry Lisa, take care of your family and I'll take care of the shit-heads." She looked him in the eye and said, sadly. "But no fires, please." Shane said. "No fires."

In the bedroom Shane pulled his bag from under the bed and took out the thick wad of cash, which he split roughly in half, putting one pile under the pillow of the bed. From what was left he stripped off five hundred and shoved it in his pocket, for Frank. The rest went back in the bag with his few belongings. He left the nine, with the spare clip, under the mattress. He took the bag down with him and picking up the petrol at the front door, put both into the boot of the taxi. Frank was already back sitting back at the wheel and as he handed the money to him through the window, Shane said. "My bag's in the boot, so when we meet we'll be able to itty off, no-problem. Look, I'll phone later and tell you where, alright?"

## ∽ 14 ∽

When Shane went back in the house, Lisa seemed to have regained her composure and was in the kitchen preparing food. She smiled a wane little smile at Shane and said. "I'm sorry Shane, I suppose my moral qualms must seem pathetic to you." Shane sat down at the kitchen table and looked out of the kitchen door. Across the garden, Craig was standing at the dividing fence with Billy, talking to Stan, from next door. Shane said. "There's nothing to be sorry about. Anyway we've all got our opinions, don't mean any of us are right." Lisa looked at him, eyebrows knitted and sighed, she said. "You're different from anyone I've ever met before. You seem so sure and self-contained." With a grimace and a shrug, Shane said. "I'm not sure of anything. I'm a stranger that's all." Out in the garden Stan and Craig parted company and Billy came into the kitchen like a bat out of hell. Screeching to a halt beside Shane, he exclaimed. "That man wants us to go to his house after tea." Lisa said. "What?" Craig came in then and added. "Seems we ain't the only ones who've had enough of Rowlands and his mates."

When Billy realised Shane would be going that night, it was like he didn't seem to want to leave Shane alone for a minute and moved a chair so he could sit right beside him at the table. There, he regaled his hero with a string of groaning jokes and boyish nonsense until Lisa snapped. "Get in the other room and watch telly like a normal child!" Billy scraped back his chair and moped out of the room, only to reappear immediately, and cheekily ask Shane if he wanted to watch with him. Both Lisa and Craig looked goggled eyed and were about to read the riot act to the boy but Shane flapped a hand at them as though accepting the inevitable and followed Billy through.

The TV was all news round-ups and early evening rubbish and it seemed to Shane that Billy didn't want to watch anything at all. As soon as they were comfortable on the couch, Billy copped the remote and flicked aimlessly from channel to channel. Finally he settled for a moronic show which featured two midget Geordies with absolutely no discernible talent competing in stupid tasks against each other. In Morocco Shane didn't even own a TV and now whenever he saw it he could not figure out what had happened. Billy wanted to talk. He started off on easy stuff and Shane told him what he could, like his parents names and that they lived on an island in the Atlantic Ocean and all manner of other small bits and pieces. It got harder when Billy asked if Shane believed in God and Shane said. "No." Billy replied. "My mum does but my dad say's he'll wait and see." Shane said. "What about you?" The boy watched the two idiots on the telly for a few moments and said. "What would you do if some kids said things and stuff to you, you know, like." Without moving Shane tried to look at Billy's eyes but he had already turned back towards the TV instead he said. "I don't know, like what?" Without turning back to look at Shane, Billy shrugged. "Just stuff."

Shane put a hand on Billy's shoulder and said. "Hey Billy." The boy turned to face him and flopped back in the couch, Shane said. "You can tell me, I'm no one." Billy made to say something and stopped, then he said. "At school some kids would make fun of me like, the bed and breakfast and that." He eyed Shane uncomfortably but carried on. "Anyway one kid started pushing me around, he did it to a few kids." Shane said. "Did you tell your parents?" The boy's face made a tight little movement before he said. "Yeh. My mum just wanted to go to the school." Shane said. "That no good?" Billy pulled a face and shook his head. Shane said. "What did your Dad say?" He took in a deep breath and let it out in an exasperated blow out of the cheeks. "He told me to ignore it and it would go away and make friends with other kids but it used to make me so mad." Shane said. "Did you do anything?" Billy shook his head. Shane said. "What happened?" Billy said. "We moved here. I'll be at a different school after the summer holiday."

Shane said. "So what's the problem?" Billy came forward again now and like he was determined but shy all at the same time, asked. "Would you Shane?" Not knowing what was coming next, Shane just pulled a face. Billy said. "You're not like my dad, you know things, you're – you're scary." The boy paused, hesitated and said, sincerely. "But I really like you." Shane said. "Now hang on, Billy." But Billy didn't hang on, he said. "Please Shane, please show me how to, you know, I – I don't want –." Shane stopped him there and said. "Don't upset yourself Billy boy, they ain't worth it." Billy said doggedly. "He lets people push him around but I don't like it. He's not like you. I want –." Interrupting the boy, Shane said. "Your dad's a really good man and you're lucky he's not like me. And he's brave. It takes a lot to walk into a place like that pub." Chastened, Billy said. "Yeh, alright." Then pausing, he said. "But." Shane, exasperated at last, said. "Alright, what? What do you want?"

Just on the edge of eagerness, he said. "Would you show me, you know?" Shane didn't help him. Billy finally said. "You know how to – stop someone, hurt someone." Shane just looked at the boy. From what he remembered school was pretty much a dog eat dog affair and you had to learn how to keep the bullies away. Rubbing his nose, Shane stood up, he said. "Is that what you really want me to do?" The boy nodded. Knowing how much bigger he was than Billy, Shane made more of himself by his stance, so to Billy he appeared huge and then, held out his hand. Almost shyly, Billy allowed himself to be pulled up from the couch. After turning off the TV Shane knelt down in front of Billy, so they were on a level, he said. "This is something my dad showed me when I was about your age, maybe younger." Taking a handful of the boy's hair as gently as could be in one hand, with his other he softly took hold of a wrist and raised it ringed in his fore finger and thumb, he said. "Find whoever it is on their own. What they think doesn't matter. Jump straight in on them and grab a hank of the guy's hair so, but tight. Grab one arm at the wrist with your free hand so, but hard." Bringing his forehead down so it brushed Billy's nose, Shane said. "You smash your forehead down on his nose as hard as you can. Then dump the fool and run. Don't hang around, get away. And don't say nothing. There'll be loads of blood and snot and every-thing. Don't matter, just go. It always worked for me." Billy looked shocked and said nothing. Shane stood up and stretched, he said. "The thing about violence is, almost everybody's frightened. You just have to make yourself less frightened." Flopping back down on the couch, Billy said, quietly. "I don't think I could do that. I don't know if I could –." Flopping down on the couch beside him, Shane said. "Good. I'm glad."

Over supper Craig wanted to talk about a strat-egy for when they went back to the pub that night and Lisa wasn't happy. When Shane spoke he com-mitted himself to nothing involving Craig. He agreed he was going back there, that was all. Lisa tried to remonstrate with her husband but Craig wasn't having any of it, he said. "What do you think I am? I'm going to let him go back up there by him-self? Is that how you see me?" Lisa said. "No!" Billy said. "No!" Shane forked up his food without looking at anyone. But Craig felt justified, he eyed Shane like it was all a forgone conclusion and said. "So, there you go!" Lisa threw up her arms in exas-peration and Billy just sat there looking glum. Craig said. "Look I was just talking to that Stan from next door, if there's any trouble tonight you can go into him." Lisa said. "Thanks."

After eating, Shane went up to his room and lay on the bed. The family sat down in the living room and watched the telly, with one eye on the street outside. As time moved the family watched the three young men take possession of their corner and business commence. They watched Dalrimple come out and greet the lads with Dean and him giving it the big mate's bollocks. They watched the way everything the group did or said seemed to be directed towards their house and wondered what the coming night would bring. Lisa and Craig held hands and under his breath, Billy said. "Shane."

Dusk was coming down and Shane watched them too as he checked the Glock and got himself together. It heartened him that Dalrimple was out on the street with Dean and his two boys. Saved looking for anyone. But after half an hour or so, he went back into the house. Shane thought of the snake and wondered where the creature was. Probably making itself a cosy little home under someone's garden shed. He waited until darkness had fallen and then went down the stairs quickly, through the house and out the back door, almost before the three in the living room had noticed. Outside he hid the gun and the spare clip in a clump of grass by the fence. In one pocket he had the rolled up Carp Masters magazine and in a back pocket the Chinese cleaver he'd taken when he'd trashed Dalrimple's house. He heard Craig and Billy shout his name but he was already striding up the alley and he didn't want to talk to them anyway.

Dean and his two mates saw Shane crossing the road towards them and they didn't even have the sense to be scared. In a way it was what Dean wanted. He pulled the baseball cap into a more jaunty angle on his head and giving his shoulders a little shake, like he'd seen movie actors do, he slipped the taped up Stanley out of his pocket. One of the other guys was astride one of those little bikes and as Shane got close, he circled round behind. Shane didn't give a fuck. He walked straight up to Dean and without stopping hit him so hard in the kidneys he didn't even have time to raise his blade and dropped it, as Shane shoved him into his mate, swung around and as the guy on the bike swooped in, smashed his foot into the youth's knee and boy and bike went down screaming. Dean was puking and staggering about but had somehow managed to upend his mate, who was trying to get to his feet, until Shane kicked him in the head. Grabbing Dean, he dragged him over to the low wall on which he usually sat. Forcing Dean's head down and twisting it, until his nose was resting on the brickwork, Shane took the little chopper out of his back pocket and chopped off Dean's nose and put the chopper back in his pocket. There was gouts of blood and snot and puke and it was all coming at the same time, in convulsions, with the piss he couldn't hold and Shane gave him a savage blow under the heart that killed him and turned away. He kicked the screamer, who was still tangled up in his bike, in the head and it all went quiet. Dragging him by the arms over to the curb, Shane broke all of his fingers over the curbstone and then he did the same to the other guy's hands, whose whole body shook.

Quickly, Shane went through their pockets and took all the money worth having and smashed their phones. Then he went to the brick under the bush in Dalrimple's hedge and threw their stash down the drain at the curb. Everything was out in the open, people would be watching but as far as he was concerned, what they did was up to them. Even in the midst of his business, Shane had been aware that a car had passed, slowed down and then driven on. He didn't care, it was ultra-violence, everything was moving and he loved the flow. Down the side of Dalrimple's house, Shane took the chopper out of his back pocket and stepped gingerly to the back door, which was half open. The back garden was full of ruined household effects, while inside, Dalrimple could be heard crooning to himself like he was his own favourite Hip-Hop star and it made Shane want to laugh. He slipped through the door into the damp, unlit kitchen and was less than three metres away from him in the living room, before Dalrimple noticed he'd got company. The room was empty, down to the floorboards. Half the ceiling had been ripped down and the place was illuminated by long, yellow, temporary lights on stands. Dalrimple was sitting in a green canvas camping chair with a mirror on his knees, chopping lines.

Maybe he was expecting Dean because he looked up from the mirror, a silver coke straw hanging from one nostril and he was smiling. Shane threw the little chopper and it spun end over end and landed twanging, in Dalrimple's forehead. It stuck in the bone like some stupid party hat but it didn't stop the mad little fucker. Spilling coke and mirror he launched himself at Shane, bellowing something about his snake. He landed on him like a baby monkey and legs gripping Shane around the waist, the smaller man grabbed him by the ears and tried to butt him in the face with the cleaver still in his forehead. Shane managed to get a forearm in Dalrimple's throat and locked together they staggered about, bouncing off walls and knocking over the light stands. Nearly choking Dalrimple let go of one ear and started trying to gouge Shane's eyes out with his free hand, but all of his effort was lost because Shane was bigger and better. Forcing his head back with his forearm Shane gave Dalrimple two stiff fingers into the armpit of the hand that was still gripping his ear. Half of Dalrimple's body went numb and limp and Shane spun him hard into a wall and the rest of the air in his lungs came out in a great oof and his legs unwrapped and Shane threw him down on the floor. A person can be as mad as they like but when Shane tossed Dalrimple on the floor, pulled the chopper out of his forehead and laid it to one side, Dalrimple knew he was dead and it was a time not to be mad anymore. Dalrimple begged, promised, weaselled and whined. Picking up the silver straw from amongst the shards of broken mirror, Shane shoved it up Dalrimple's nostril into his brain. Dalrimple went all gaga, with little trembles in his arms and legs and Shane kept pushing. Dalrimple shit himself and it wasn't very nice for Shane to go through his trouser pockets but he did anyway and pocketed the money he found. In a jacket hung over the back of the canvas chair, Shane found about three grammes of coke in a cling film twist, all neat and tidy, so he took that as well.

Although it had taken less than a couple of minutes to deal with Dalrimple, Stan was already standing in his doorway smoking a fag, when Shane came back out on to the road. He had his hands in his pockets and he took one out and keeping it low, by his thigh, gave Shane a little thumb's up. From the house opposite Dalrimple's, at the mouth of the cul-de-sac, a middle aged couple had come out and were standing at their garden gate. The man had his arm protectively around the woman's shoulder. They had serious heads on them and although they watched Shane cross the road, they didn't do or say anything. A glance here and there and he could see other curtains twitching too. Dean was a lifeless bag of bones, crumpled on the ground where Shane had left him. His two mates were crying and crawling around the pavement on their elbows, like blind men. The one with the broken leg fell into a heap and began keening like a whipped dog.

Lisa, Craig and Billy were stood in the front garden next to the burnt out car and as he approached, they all tried talking to him at once but he wasn't listening. He went straight past them and down the alley, where he picked up the Glock and the spare clip from beside the fence. When he turned around all three of them were coming down the alley towards him. Craig was excited. "I've never seen anything like that, you were –. Wait! Wait! I'm coming with you!" Lisa had hold of his arm and there was a sick look on her face. Billy was beaming, looking at Shane like he'd come down out of the sky on a golden chariot and going. "Wow! Shane! Wow!" Craig wouldn't listen to Lisa and insisted he go along. Almost as he went by, Shane clipped Craig on the chin with a short little tolchock and he fell comatose back into Lisa's arms. Then Shane was gone across the street and up the cul-de-sac. He could hear Billy's plaintive cry of. "Shane. Shane." As he passed the couple at their gate he gave them a smile. Without changing their expressions, they both acknowledged him with tight little nods, before turning their eyes back to the pleasurable spectacle of suffering youths on the pavement opposite. A couple of times he heard Lisa shout. "Billy!" But he didn't look back.

## ∽ 15 ∽

He dialled up the taxi driver, he said. "Do you remember a pub called The Oddfellows Arms?" The driver said. "Yeh but it ain't there anymore, it's a restaurant." Shane said. "Wait for me down near where it was." At the top of the cul-de-sac he noticed that the windscreens on the cars had been replaced. He picked up the short length of steel tubing out of the garden again, smashed the lot and threw the pipe down. Fuckers wouldn't be getting nothing fixed tomorrow. The alarms wailed away and Shane thought of the painter and decorator and how people can always surprise you. He moved as quickly as he could through the estate, knowing he had only just started and already wanted to be gone and knowing it could go wrong but the adrenaline buzz made it all so smooth, like cruise control and he just wanted to get about his business.

Before he entered the pub, Shane took the Carp Masters magazine out of his pocket and rolled it tight. In his other hand he had the Glock. Although Shane didn't own up to believing in anything, he always looked for the luck, took even the narrowest window of opportunity if it would give him a moments advantage. He waited. Not long. The door swung open and a guy with a slack mouth, like he'd just finished laughing, came stepping out into the night the way men do. He wasn't anyone. The blow to the throat from the rolled end of the carp magazine crushed his voice box, sending him reeling back into the pub and crashing into the nearest table, where he thrashed about like an epileptic on ecstasy. People tried to get out of his way and drinks went flying and people started shouting. They shoved the guy away and he convulsed on other people and the table fell over and a woman got Guinness all down her jeans and started screaming.

Shane didn't stop moving, everything he did became something else and something happened and he did something else and something else and something else. Inside, two of Rowlands thugs were near the door almost like security. Shane killed them both with the Carp Masters Monthly. Head butted the next person he saw and stabbed at anyone within reach with the magazine. People fell away from him clutching eyes, nose, throat and groin. He shot the screaming woman and the man next to her. The noise from the gun in the small bar was so extreme it seemed to stop the world turning for a moment and that was all the time needed. Space opened up in the shock of that moment and Shane stepped into it. Rowlands was exactly where he'd been sitting earlier in the day and was only just pulling himself upright when Shane shot him twice in the head. There wasn't much left of his brain to think with, so the fat fuck fell over and his two mates in the seats beside him didn't even get to raise themselves up before they died. Blokes were coming at him now and he smacked one down with the gun butt and broke another's ankle. All Shane really wanted now was Wilson but he couldn't see him anywhere and it was already time to leave.

Shane was fighting to get back out of the door. It was really that simple. He fought with every part of his body. He kicked out, smashed down and gouged. He hit, he bit and blocked and took the shots and the smacks, the fists and punches, the bottles, glasses and everything else that was being thrown at him. He didn't count the men coming at him but dealt with every moment presented to him. It was like being at the centre of a riot. He could hear the shouts and screams, the grunts and moans and even 'Bawee's' voice booming. The carp magazine was gone, replaced by a glass ashtray. Two more went down and it shattered in some other fool's face. He didn't know how it got there but at one moment he had a little blue bookies pen in his fist and he stuck it in some fool's eye. The guy reeled away from him, hands thrown in the air like some modern day King Harold. He shot the two men nearest to him and people backed off again. The door was right behind him and he was almost out of it, when Wilson came bursting in through the connecting door to the main bar. His piece was already in his hand and he fired twice. One bullet seared Shane's arm like a skid mark. The other smacked into the wall above his head. The last thing he saw as he fled through the door was Wilson powering down the bar towards him, shoving aside the maimed and trampling over the dead and anyone else in his way.

Shane wasn't feeling that good. He'd taken everything in the pub but at the moment the door had shut behind him and he had started to run, he knew he was a tired man. Blood was seeping from several wounds. He'd been gouged and punched, sliced and cut and obviously if he tried to out run Wilson, he was on a loser. The gun was still in his hand, so he turned. Billy was stood a few feet from the pub door. He had something in his hands. Shane couldn't fit Billy into his brain at that moment, the boy was like a hallucination and he didn't have time to think about it. Wilson came barrelling out of the pub at full force with the gun already levelled. Billy smashed Wilson on the shins with the length of steel tubing and Wilson went down. Billy dropped the pipe and jumped back, shocked at what he'd done. Wilson made a move to pull himself up and Shane shot him in the head. He saw Billy's body give an involuntary jump at the explosion and his big space cadet eyes when he saw the blood and brains. Somewhere sirens were already spinning around the estate. There wasn't time for counselling, Shane took the boy by the hand and said. "Come on." As they ran away, Shane said. "Where did you learn a trick like that?" Billy said. "In a film on the telly."

In a narrow, dark alley, between two houses, Shane squatted down and took the boy by the shoulders, he said. "What are you doing here, Billy? Are you alright? I'm sorry boy, you should never have to see something like that but it was him or me, I'm sorry." Billy started to cry and Shane put his arms around him and Billy cried into his shoulder. After a bit, Billy told Shane that he wasn't crying because he'd seen that horrible man shot but because now Shane would go away. He said. "But you shouldn't have hit my Dad. I was mad you did that." After a second or two he added. "Mum shouted after me but I didn't go back. I wanted to –. I saw you smash the windows in those cars. I was going to hit you with that bit of pipe. Then I saw you in the pub. I saw what you did. My Dad, he won't mind when I tell him." Shane hugged Billy and said. "I tell you something Billy boy, I like you. Believe me I would stay if I could."

The way that Shane was bashed up, the speed that Billy moved at was a good speed and they stumbled along, down alleys and short cuts that Shane dredged up from his memories and anywhere else that kept them off the main estate streets. They could hear the sirens but they didn't see any patrol cars. If they encountered any other people, they held hands and pretended to be father and son. When they reached the alley on Circle Road where Shane had found the gap in the fence earlier in the day, they had to say goodbye. He told Billy about the money he'd left under the pillow and told Billy to tell his parents to hide it until all the fuss had died down. They hugged and Billy on the edge of tears again, said. "Do you have to go?" Shane nodded and in a sad, plaintive voice, Billy said. "I love you." The boy's simple words hit Shane in the heart like a physical blow and his voice caught in his throat as he tried to reply. He said. "Love your mum and dad, they're good people." Then, as an afterthought, Shane said. "Fuck it, oops!" He pulled a handful of cash out of his pocket and stuffed it into Billy's hands. "Here, that's for your swear box. Now get home."

Shane pushed himself through the hole in the fence, flitted across the businesspark and sure enough there was another hole in the opposite fence and he was on the canal side. He waited there in the darkness. Waited for all the sounds, small as they were, to settle in his head. Across the lock gates, the muted, ambient orange lights, of all the new properties, made what had been the arse-end of town look quite seductive. But despite it's upgrade since he was a youth, there were no lovers on the canal bank, nor dog walkers, or muggers, or perverts, child molesters, or rapists, or anyone and he was glad. Shane threw the Glock and the spare clip in the canal as he went over the lock gates. He didn't care if they found it, he'd be gone. On the other side was a wooden stile and gate leading out onto a silent, narrow road with all the cars parked on one side. Shane tried to walk along looking as normal as could be and knowing he wasn't quite making it. A car engine mumbled and lights went on. The taxi driver pushed open the passenger side door and said. "You look a bit rough."

Shane sat up front with Frank and they went out of town nice and steady and when they were clear, the driver pulled into a lay-by. From under the seat he took out a grubby looking first aid kit and passed it to Shane. "Here, there's some antiseptic in there somewhere." Shane held the box on his knees for a few seconds. He tapped the sides with the tips of his fingers and smiled. Frank gave him a quizzical look and Shane fiddled in his pocket until he pulled out the twist of coke. He plopped it on top of the first aid box and said. "Fancy a little line?" Licking his lips the driver said. "Where am I taking you?" Shane said. "Southwest, near Plymouth." Frank grinned and said. "Yeh, nice one."

*fiction direct*

If you enjoyed **Shane** or would like to make
any comments or have any enquiries
regarding **Fiction Direct**, please go to the
comments page on our website at

**www.fictiondirect.com**

*Coming Soon*

# SHANE DOS

Adrenaline is a powerful drug
and one Shane cannot live without –
well, not forever, anyway.
It is six years earlier and Shane
has a problem –

Boredom.

The quiet life in rural Spain may have
helped to keep him a free man –
but now it was getting to be too quiet.
He wanted something to give him a kick.

After all, what is life without kicks?

# Cnegwarth
# o Had Maip

**JOHN IDRIS OWEN**

Gwasg
Gwynedd

*Argraffiad Cyntaf — Ebrill 2005*

ISBN 0 86074 214 8

*Cyhoeddwyd ac argraffwyd
gan Wasg Gwynedd, Caernarfon*

I

EINIR, DYLAN, MARIAN AC OWEN

# Cynnwys

# *Cyflwyniad*

Enillodd rhan o'r gyfrol hon Fedal Ryddiaith Eisteddfod Môn o dan y teitl 'Atgofion', pan oedd yr Eisteddfod honno ym Mro Goronwy, ardal fy mebyd. Fe gyhoeddwyd detholiad o'r gwaith yn ail rifyn y cylchgrawn *Mabon* – rhifyn gaeaf 1969-70 – dan olygyddiaeth Alun R. Jones a Gwyn Thomas.

Pan oedd yr Eisteddfod Genedlaethol yma yn Ninbych yn 2001, fe ddewiswyd darn o 'Atgofion' yn destun cystadleuaeth lefaru. Yn dilyn y Steddfod, gofynnodd amryw (wel, dau o leiaf!) ble roedd cael gafael ar y darn. Eglurais ei fod allan o brint ers blynyddoedd. Fisoedd yn ddiweddarach, es ati i'w ddiweddaru gyda'r bwriad o'i gyhoeddi. Ychwanegais at y gwreiddiol ac ailysgrifennu rhannau ohono i greu darlun llawnach o gyfnod fy mhlentyndod. Nid oedd bwriad o gwbl i ysgrifennu hunangofiant!

Hoffwn ddiolch i'r Athro Hywel Wyn Owen am ei eglurhad ar y gair 'Olgra' ac i'm cyfaill William Lloyd Gruffydd am ddarllen drwy'r gwaith a chysoni a chywiro sawl peth. Diolch hefyd i Nan Elis o Wasg Gwynedd am drefnu a thocio'r cruglwyth o atgofion yn benodau trefnus, ac am amryw o argymhellion adeiladol ganddi wrth iddi lywio'r gyfrol drwy'r wasg.

JOHN IDRIS OWEN

## Hel Meddyliau...

Erstalwm, pan oedd y Beibl yn wir bob gair a Mam yn hollwybodol, roedd haul yn yr haf ac afalau yn y berllan a thonnau diog yn llyfu aur Traeth Llugwy.

Bryd hynny, roedd y byd crwn cyfan yn troi o amgylch capel, cartref ac ysgol, a'i ffiniau yn ymestyn o Lanbedrgoch i Farian-glas ac o'r Califfornia i'r môr. Oddi mewn i'r ffiniau, roedd y pethau cyfarwydd: Capel y Tabernacl yn balas o adeilad aruthrol ei faint ac yn llawn dop o Gristionogion a saint y Sêt Fawr; Eisteddfod Gadeiriol Marian-glas yn glod i Ddewi, ac yn orlawn o blant iau nas dihidlwyd gan ragbrofion – ac o famau. Ac roedd yno ddau gôr, Côr Bro Goronwy a Chôr Mathafarn, a fu'n cythraul ganu eu ffordd drwy genedlaethau o eisteddfodau.

Ond ai felly roedd hi mewn gwirionedd? Mae amser yn gallu rhoi rhyw wawr gynnes ar atgofion, ac wrth iddyn nhw bellhau i fwrllwch y gorffennol mae hi'n mynd yn anodd iawn dweud y gwahaniaeth rhwng y gau a'r gwir. Yn sicr ddigon, mae tuedd ym mhawb ohonom i ramantu cyfnod bore oes – pan na fyddai hi byth yn bwrw glaw yng Ngorffennaf ac Awst, pan oedd eira gwyn glân bob bore Nadolig, a phan oedd ennill di-ben-draw mewn eisteddfod ac arholiad heb fod y fath beth â cholli. Ac wrth gwrs mae 'na rai pethau briw yn ddwfn yn yr ymwybod – ac islaw hwnnw, hyd yn oed, yn ôl seicolegwyr – nad ydi rhywun ddim yn dewis nac yn dymuno rhoi llwyfan cyhoeddus iddyn nhw.

Felly ffeithiau dethol – hanesyddol, fwy neu lai – ac argraffiadau sydd ar brydiau 'yn gelwydd oll' (neu o leiaf wedi eu gwyrdroi a'u lliwio gan amser, pall ar y cof a pharchusrwydd) ydi atgofion y rhan fwyaf ohonom ni.

Nid pethau twt bwriadol y gellir eu dosbarthu fel mewn catalog yw atgofion chwaith. Tryblith ydyn nhw, a thryblith oriog ar y naw hefyd. Weithiau fe ddônt yn ribidirês fel petaent wedi eu clymu gynffon wrth gynffon ym mhlygion y cof: atgof yn galw atgof o 'fwynder trist y pellter', fel ceiliog R. Williams Parry! Dro arall, fe drônt yn ystyfnig, nes bod rhywun yn teimlo fel pysgotwr aflwyddiannus sydd wedi treulio oriau ofer bwygilydd wrth bwll ar lan afon, eto yn sicr ynddo'i hun bod pysgod yn llechu yno yn rhywle. Ambell waith fe ddônt heb eu galw – weithiau'n ddieisiau – wedi eu symbylu gan arogl neu sŵn neu lun sy'n rhoi sbardun sydyn i'r meddwl a'i gychwyn ar drywydd arbennig. Ond mae *rhai* profiadau, profiadau dwys ac ingol neu rai eithriadol o bleserus, nad oes eisiau unrhyw ymdrech i'w galw i gof.

Does gan f'atgofion i fawr o barch i drefn amser ac efallai nad yw rheswm yn chwarae rhan bwysig iawn yn eu byd hwy chwaith. Gan amlaf, bodlonais iddyn nhw ddilyn eu mympwy eu hunain – ond weithiau bu'n rhaid eu ffrwyno fymryn yma ac acw i geisio parchu trefnusrwydd!

# Cysgod y Capel

Mae'n rhaid i mi ddechrau yn rhywle, felly waeth i mi ddechrau yn y dechrau ddim – fel y dechreuodd y bydysawd. Fe ddechreuodd hwnnw yn ôl pob sôn efo clec enfawr. Hyd y gwn i, fu'r un glec fawr pan gefais i fy ngeni ym Marian-glas ym 1937, yn fab i saer coed a gwraig tŷ ac yn frawd bach i Marian oedd ddwy flynedd yn hŷn na mi.

Symudodd y teulu mewn byr o dro o Bencraig, Marian-glas i fyw i Dŷ Capel y Tabernacl ym mhlwy Llanfair Mathafarn Eithaf. Ches i ddim siawns i fynegi barn ar y mudo hwnnw, ond does fawr o syndod am hynny gan fy mod i'n rhy ifanc ar y pryd i siarad heb sôn am fynegi barn ar unrhyw beth. Mae 'na rai pobl sy'n honni cofio pob dim o'r groth bron – nid felly fi. O'r herwydd, braidd yn niwlog ydi tair neu bedair blynedd cyntaf fy oes. (Mae'n wir bod rhieni a theulu a chydnabod wedi llenwi rhai o'r bylchau, ond nid atgofion go iawn ydi profiadau ail-law felly.)

Ond ni chaf unrhyw drafferth o gwbl mewn dwyn i gof lu o atgofion am Dŷ Capel y Tabernacl. Hen hongo o dŷ mawr y galwai Mam o. Wyddwn i ddim beth oedd union ystyr y gair 'hongo' bryd hynny, a dydi Geiriadur Prifysgol Cymru ddim wedi taflu unrhyw oleuni ar y mater. Ond roedd 'hongo' Mam yn gweddu rywsut. Efallai mai gair technegol ydoedd i ddisgrifio anferthedd daearyddiaeth a chynllun anhylaw y tŷ, oedd dalcen wrth dalcen â'r capel.

Roedd y tŷ ei hun yn adeilad helaeth – a pha ryfedd? O dan yr unto yr oedd parlwr, cegin, dwy lofft a math o siambr, festri, ysgoldy'r capel, coetsiws a stabl. Fe gysylltid y cyfan gan rwydwaith o lobïau tywyll hirion, dwy res o risiau a drysau dirifedi. I gymhlethu pethau, fe'i hadeiladwyd fel bod ysgoldy'r capel uwchben yr ystafelloedd byw a'r llofftydd cysgu ar bwys y capel uwchben y festri.

Tan ddechrau'r pumdegau, nwy carbaid, lampau paraffîn a chanhwyllau oedd yn goleuo'r amryfal adeiladau. O ganlyniad, roedd hi'n daith hir a brawychus yng ngolau cannwyll i'r gwely gan fod tywyllwch dudew'r lobïau yn llyncu golau fflam y gannwyll, a'i fflam hithau yn ei thro yn taflu cysgodion dieithr a bygythiol o wrthrychau cyfarwydd lliw dydd. Ac yn goron ar y cyfan, roedd drws y festri'n wynebu grisiau'r llofftydd a'r drws cefn yn arwain bron yn syth i'r fynwent! Yno, gyferbyn â'r drws bron, roedd 'cwt y gais' – cartref y tanc diwydiannol lle, ar un adeg, y cynhyrchid y nwy i oleuo adeiladau'r capel.

Ar waelod talcen y tŷ ar bwys y ffordd yr oedd carreg farch. Dyfais oedd hon ar lun grisiau carreg, grisiau o'r ddwy ochr gyda chopa gwastad a adeiladwyd i gynorthwyo gweinidogion nad oeddynt ystwyth o gorff i ddringo i gyfrwy eu ceffylau. Welais i neb erioed yn ei defnyddio hi, mwy nag a welais i gert yn y coetsiws na cheffyl yn y stabl. Adlais yn unig oeddynt bellach o oes aur y gweinidogion pan oedd ceffylau'n brif gyfrwng cludiant. Mae'n drist nodi bod y ceffylau a gweinidogion wedi prinhau a cholli eu statws mewn cymdeithas tua'r un adeg – ond am resymau gwahanol, gobeithio!

Fyddwn i byth wedi bod yn fab tŷ capel o ddewis. Doedd mab tŷ capel ddim yn union yr un fath â phlant eraill. Nid ei fod o'n *hollol* ar wahân – fel mab gweinidog, dyweder – eto roedd o'n ddigon agos at ddaioni i gael ei wahardd ar brydiau rhag ymuno ym mywyd llawn y byd mawr y tu allan, hynny o'r byd mawr oedd 'na yn Sir Fôn ar y pryd.

Doedd mab tŷ capel, felly, ddim yn cael ei fesur efo'r un llathen â phlant eraill. Roedd disgwyliadau oedolion crefyddol honedig cynulleidfa'r capel yn rhai uchel. Fe ddisgwylid iddo fo fynychu holl wasanaethau'r capel fore, pnawn a nos a bod yn bresennol ym mhob gŵyl, seiat a chyfarfod gweddi. Fe ddylai fod yn seren yr Ysgol Sul, ac yn barod – yn wir, yn hael ac yn gywir – ei adnodau ar bob achlysur. Ni wnâi ailadrodd 'Duw cariad yw' Sul ar ôl Sul mo'r tro iddo fo. Fe ddylai fod yn weddus a chwrtais a pheidio byth â chael ei ddal yn rhegi na gwneud drygau. Rhaid oedd iddo fod mor barchus, ffurfiol a di-fflach ei ymateb â'r *Rhodd Mam* ei hun.

Dydd Sul oedd diwrnod hiraf yr wythnos ac roedd deuddeg a deugain ohonynt mewn blwyddyn! Bob dydd Sul mi fyddai pobman yn anghysurus, angladdol o daclus. Doedd dim sôn am na thegan na chomig yn unman ac roedd pawb yn gwisgo dillad parch. Yn amlach na pheidio, byddai gweinidog i ginio nes bod y capel yn ymestyn ei grafangau hyd yn oed o amgylch y bwrdd bwyd.

'Pobol hen' oedd yn arfer galw cyn ac ar ôl y gwasanaeth. Hen gan mwyaf oedd y blaenoriaid, hen oedd y bobl a alwai i mewn i dwymo eu hunain ar dywydd oer wrth dân y gegin, a hen bobl a arhosai ar ôl oedfa i ddisgwyl am i gerbyd un o'r blaenoriaid ddod i'w cludo adref. Sgwrs gwynfanllyd, ystrydebol, anhyblyg hen bobl oedd ganddynt – y tywydd yn oer, y gwynt yn fain, rhy sych i'r ardd, rhy wlyb i'r anifeiliaid – a hynny'n rhagarweiniad di-feth i ddisgrifiadau o boenau arteithiol ac afiechydon y corff dynol. Hyn oll a marwolaethau a phrofedigaethau oedd testun pob sgwrs bron.

Ond efallai fy mod braidd yn annheg wrth wthio pawb i'r un blwch cenhadol, fel petai. Roedd yna o leiaf *un* hen gymeriad yn byrlymu o hiwmor a direidi. Ambell waith, mi fyddwn i'n cael gadael sêt y teulu yn y capel a mynd i eistedd gyda fo, ac mi syrthiais i gysgu fwy nag unwaith yn ei gesail. Fe ddysgodd adnod i mi unwaith a phan ddaeth y gorchymyn i ni'r plant ddweud ein hadnodau, mi gerddais i'n dalog i'r Sêt Fawr i adrodd:

> How-di-dw a how-di-dan,
> Sut mae dy dad a sut mae dy fam?
> Gwelais dy dad yn un porchell tew!
> Sut mae dy fam – ydi hi'n o lew?

a pheri i gynulleidfa gyfan, ar wahân i Mam, chwerthin.

Ond yr argraff sy'n aros yw mai tŷ pawb oedd tŷ capel ac mai gweision bach y gynulleidfa oedd yn byw ynddo fo. Ystafell aros ar blatfform gorsaf oedd cegin tŷ capel, ac fe brynwyd yr hawl i'w defnyddio gyda cheiniog ar blât y casgliad.

# Y Teiliwr

Mi fyddai Mam yn arfer gwneud mat rhacs, yn bennaf oherwydd prinder nwyddau yn gyffredinol yn ystod ac ar ôl y rhyfel. Y cyfan oedden nhw oedd clytiau o wahanol ddarnau o frethyn, yn siwmperi gwlân, darnau o hen sgert neu gôt ac ati, wedi eu torri'n stribedi a'u gwnïo at ei gilydd mewn cynllun heb iddo gynllun i wneud gorchudd digon lliwgar a chynnes ar loriau carreg y tŷ. Rhyw orchest ddigon tebyg, am wn i, ydi pwytho clytiau o atgofion at ei gilydd!

Rhan annatod o fywyd cymdeithasol y capel a'r gymdeithas ehangach oedd yr elfen gystadleuol. Yn y capel, yr oedd hyd yn oed dweud adnodau'n glir a chywir yn rhyw lun ar gystadlu, ac fe gynhelid hefyd 'Y Gylchwyl' flynyddol, deithiol (math o eisteddfod oedd honno) – yn ogystal, wrth gwrs, â'r Arholiad Sirol oedd wedi ei sylfaenu i raddau helaeth ar gynnwys *Y Rhodd Mam* i'r plant iau a'r ysgrythurau i'r rhai hŷn. Y tu allan i'r capel roedd nifer helaeth o fân eisteddfodau a gyrhaeddai eu hanterth yn Eisteddfod Môn.

All rhywun ddim llai na theimlo na roddai'r holl gystadlu yma gyfle i famau lenwi rhyw wacter yn eu bywydau beunyddiol, drwy baredio'n ail-law dalentau eu plant mewn eisteddfod a chylchwyl a chymanfa...

Roedd teulu fy mam yn dipyn o adroddwrs a bu Mam

yn ei dydd yn cynhyrfu cynulleidfaoedd gyda darnau dramatig a melodramatig y cyfnod. Roedd fy chwaer er pan oedd hi'n ddim o beth wedi bod yn ennill yn rheolaidd mewn gornestau adrodd barddoniaeth. Siom enbyd i deulu ochr fy mam oedd darganfod bod y ddawn draddodi, fel yr offeiriad hwnnw rhwng Jerico a Jeriwsalem gynt, wedi mynd 'o'r tu arall heibio' i mi. Roedd barddoniaeth, am ryw reswm, yn troi'n rhyddiaith garpiog ar fy ngwefusau. Doedd gen i mo'r ddawn na'r hyder i wthio mynegiant i na llais na wyneb. Roedd fy safiad a'm goslefu yn ddiffygiol, a'r cymhelliant i lafarganu rhi-bi-di-res o linellau o flaen cynulleidfa, a bod yn gwbl onest, yn isel iawn.

Ond nid oedd Mam am fy ngadael ar fin y ffordd nac ar dir caregog, ac ni bu'n hir cyn darganfod bod gen i lais canu 'digon o ryfeddod'. Ar wahân i Nhad, nid oedd gan yr un aelod o'r teulu unrhyw grap ar na sol-ffa na hen nodiant, a braidd yn gyfyng oedd gallu lleisiol fy nhad. Doedd o'n sicr ddim yn cyrraedd safon fyddai'n rhyngu bodd beirniaid eisteddfodol. Yn anffodus i mi, nid oedd angen chwilio 'mhell am arbenigwr i feithrin y ddawn newydd.

O fewn tafliad carreg i'n tŷ ni roedd Siop y Tabernacl, cartref un o'n cymdogion agosaf. Yno y trigai J. C. Parry (John Charles Parry, a rhoi iddo'i enw llawn), efo'i ddwy chwaer, Leusa a Maggi Parry. Teiliwr oedd 'JC' – fel yr adwaenid ef – wrth ei alwedigaeth, ond roedd o'n adnabyddus drwy'r sir a thu hwnt fel unawdydd, canwr deuawdau ac, yn fwy diweddar, fel arweinydd Côr Bro Goronwy. Adeg fy mhlentyndod i roedd o'n ŵr gweddw; yn ogystal â'r ddwy chwaer, roedd ganddo hefyd un mab, Iolo.

Roedd JC yn *dipyn* o gymeriad. Roedd o a minnau'n

ffrindiau mawr – fo oedd yr unig un fyddai'n fy ngalw i'n 'Sionyn', neu 'yr hen Sionyn'. Yn ystod misoedd yr haf mi fyddai'n galw amdanaf i fynd efo fo i Ffynnon Bwlch i nôl dŵr yfed. Mi gerddai JC â phwced ym mhob llaw a minnau wrth ei ochr yn mân gamu ac yn ei efelychu yn ddyn i gyd drwy gario piser. Erbyn i ni gyrraedd adref, byddai fy mhiser i'n hanner gwag a minnau'n llawn balchder pum mlwydd oed.

Mi fyddai rhai pobl llai ystyriol na'i gilydd yn ei alw'n ddyn celwyddog. Yr oedd rhyw elfen o wir yn hyn; roedd o wrth natur yn dipyn o froliwr ac roedd o bob amser yn ceisio creu argraff dda ar gydnabod a dieithriaid. Yn ddieithriad, i'r perwyl yma, mi fyddai'n ymestyn ychydig ar y gwir gan orliwio sefyllfa a gwneud y cyffredin yn ddramatig. Hyd y gwn i, wnaeth ei ymestyniadau ar y gwir erioed ddrwg i neb. Na, rhyw straeon celwydd golau oedd ganddo ac roedd y rhain yn fwy tebyg o wneud drwg iddo fo'i hun nag i neb arall.

Mi oedd rhyw ddigwyddiadau tebyg i hyn yn eithaf cyffredin:

'Yn deyn' – ei hoff gyfarchiad – 'sut ydach chi, Mari Jones, ers tro byd?'

'Gweddol, JC; gweddol, diolch.'

'Mi dwi wedi bod yn meddwl llawar amdanoch chi ers i mi weld Edith eich chwaer ym Marchnad Llangefni pwy ddiwrnod.'

'Edith fy chwaer?'

'Ia'n tad, yn llond 'i chroen ac yn anfon ei chofion at y teulu.'

'Ond JC bach, mi fuo Edith druan farw chydig cyn y Dolig y llynedd.'

'Wel, be haru fi deudwch, a finna'n gwybod yn iawn. Cymysgu'n lân rhwng dwy Edith wnes i…'

Rywsut neu'i gilydd, mi fyddai'n medru'i 'siarad ei hun' allan o bob sefyllfa anffodus.

Pam bydda fo'n gwneud hyn? Dyn a ŵyr, ond rhan yn unig oedd hyn o gymeriad cymhleth y teiliwr, y blaenor, yr unawdydd a'r arweinydd côr.

Ond nid JC oedd yr unig gantwr yn Siop y Tabernacl. Roeddent yn berchen poli parot lliwgar a oedd yn lleisiwr, yn chwibanwr ac yn ddynwaredwr hynod. Yn ystod misoedd yr haf roedd hi'n arferiad gosod y parot yn ei gawell wrth y drws ffrynt er mwyn iddo gael ychydig o awyr iach a mwynhau peth o haul tebyg i haul gwlad ei febyd. Roedd hi'n arferiad yn ystod misoedd yr haf hefyd i ddyn o'r enw Hewitt o'r Benllech logi ceffylau march-ogaeth i Saeson dŵad, a digwyddiad digon cyffredin oedd gweld mintai o farchogion tindrwm yn cael eu harwain ar gefn ceffylau hynafol ar hyd ffyrdd cefn troellog yr ardal. Yr oedd un o'r gorymdeithiau hyn yn mynd heibio i'n tŷ ni a Siop y Tabernacl cyn amled â dwywaith yr wythnos.

Cofiaf yn dda gerdded heibio i Siop y Tabernacl pan ddeuthum wyneb yn wyneb â chryn hanner dwsin o geffylau, yn cael eu marchogaeth gan ferched o wahanol faintioli. Pan oedden nhw gyferbyn â mi a drws ffrynt Siop y Tabernacl, daeth chwibaniad clir o du'r parot, y math o chwibaniad deunod y bydd 'hogia lancia' yn ei defnyddio i ddangos eu gwerthfawrogiad o ferched siapus. Y fi gafodd y bai. Trodd arweinydd y fintai ataf a rhoi llond ceg i mi am fod mor bowld. Rhag c'wilydd i hogyn bach feiddio bod mor eofn! Doedd gen i ddim digon o Saesneg ar y pryd i achub fy ngham.

Dro arall, roedd Seth Owen, Olgra Fawr, yn aredig efo pâr o geffylau gwedd mewn cae cyfagos. Pan fyddai'n dod i ddiwedd cwys fe fyddai'n gweiddi cyfarwyddiadau a gorchmynion i'r ceffylau – pethau fel 'We' a 'We Back'. Ar ganol cwys fe benderfynodd y parot roi ei big i mewn a gweiddi rhibi-di-res o gyfarwyddiadau nes ffwndro'r ceffylau a chynddeiriogi Seth Owen. Fel arfer, fe fyddai cwysi'r Olgra Fawr yn union syth, ond y prynhawn hwnnw fe ddirywiodd y grefft o aredig yn arw.

Un prynhawn cefais fy hun, â chopi o 'Y Rhosyn Rhudd' yn fy llaw, yn dringo'r ysgol bren a arweiniai at 'ddrws-yn-llawr' gweithdy'r teiliwr (gweithdy oedd yn llenwi un talcen o Siop y Tabernacl). Mawr oedd y croeso gefais i gan JC a chan Mr Howells, y teiliwr oedd yn cydweithio ag o, wrth i mi esgyn o'u blaenau trwy'r drws yn y llawr. Fe eisteddai'r ddau fel dau Fwda â'u coesau wedi eu plethu ar lwyfan o goed oedd fel bwrdd isel anferth, ac yn ymestyn dros dri chwarter llawr y gweithdy. Roedd gwisgo blynyddoedd wedi rhoi sglein ar wyneb y pren. O'u cwmpas yr oedd llathenni o frethyn siwtiau a leinin, rîls, sisyrnau o bob maint, nodwyddau a sialc main marcio defnydd, a math o sebon i gasglu darnau o edafedd afradlon. Roeddwn i wastad yn destun eiddigedd fy ffrindiau gan y byddai gen i bob amser gyflenwad di-ball o rîls anferth i wneud 'tractor rîl' efo darn o lastig, darn o bren, dwy hoelen a phwt o gannwyll wêr. Ar bwys y wal roedd stôf fechan a thri hetar smwddio anferth yn twymo eu penolau arni. Ar y llawr roedd darnau o frethyn, pinnau ac edafedd. Roedd arogl brethyn yn pereiddio'r ystafell.

'Hylô, 'rhen Sionyn, be ga i wneud i ti 'ngwas i?'

JC oedd y cyfarchwr. Wincio'n garedig arna i wnaeth Mr Howells. Un da oedd o am wincio.

'Mae Mam wedi deud bod yn rhaid i mi ganu yn Steddfod Marian-glas, ac mae hi'n gofyn plîs wnewch chi fynd dros y darn efo mi.'

'Wel ia, fachgen, mi soniodd dy fam fod 'na ddeunydd canwr ynot ti. Gad i mi weld rŵan. Safa'n y fan yna i mi gael golwg arnat ti.'

Cymerais gam yn ôl, a bu bron i mi â baglu dros y stôf.

'Rŵan, safa'n syth a sticia dy frest allan.'

Edrychodd arnaf fel pe bai'n mesur siwt â'i lygaid. Yna trodd at Mr Howells a gofyn:

'Ydach chi'n meddwl y gwnawn ni ganwr ohono fo, Mr Howells?'

'Siŵr o fod,' atebodd hwnnw'n gadarnhaol, a thaflu winc a gwên arall ata i.

'Oes gin ti gopi?'

'Oes,' atebais, a rhoi copi newydd sbon danlli yn ei law.

'Copi sol-ffa! I'r dim.'

Edrychodd arno am eiliad neu ddwy heb ddeud dim. Yna dechreuodd hymian yn ddistaw o dan ei wynt. Aeth ei law i boced ei wasgod – roedd o'n ddyn gwasgod – a thynnu *pitchfork* allan a'i tharo'n ysgafn ar gornel y bwrdd cyn ei chodi at ei glust.

'Doh. Doh me soh doh'.' Llanwodd ei lais clir yr ystafell. 'Doh. Doh me soh doh',' meddai'r parot o'r gegin islaw. Gwenodd JC ac yna aeth ati i droi'r sol-ffa yn felodi hyfryd mor rhwydd â phe bai'n darllen pennod mewn cyfarfod gweddi. Euthum oddi yno â'r diwn yn troi yn fy mhen a 'mhocedi yn llawn o rîls.

Ond dim ond y dechrau oedd hyn. Fel y dynesai'r

eisteddfod awn i'r gweithdy'n amlach ac yn amlach ac, o dipyn i beth, fe ddaeth y nodau a'r geiriau yn nes at ei gilydd. Unwaith y digwyddodd hyn, ceisiwyd rhoi lliw a mynegiant i'm canu. 'Sionyn! Mae hi'n mynd fel rhuban' fyddai ei eiriau pan fyddwn i'n canu'n dda, a winciai Mr Howells ei gymeradwyaeth yntau yn egnïol fel petai ganddo bry yn ei lygaid.

Noson cyn yr eisteddfod fe gefais fy ngalw i gael 'y ffeinal polish', chwedl yntau. Curais wrth ddrws y ffrynt gan fod drws y gweithdy ar gau. Daeth JC i'r drws toc, a'm harwain i'n syth i'r parlwr ffrynt. Yno'n eistedd fel brenhines o flaen y piano roedd ei chwaer, Maggi Parry. I'r sawl nad oedd yn ei hadnabod yn dda, dynes fechan gron, braidd yn fawreddog oedd Maggi Parry, ond yn llechu tu ôl i'r gragen gyhoeddus yr oedd cywirdeb ac anwyldeb. Dynes dim lol oedd hi. Yr oedd pen ucha'r piano wedi ei orchuddio â chwpanau arian a medalau, a'r rheiny'n sgleinio fel swllt newydd – gwobrau JC yr unawdydd, y deuawdwr a'r arweinydd côr.

Doedd dim amheuaeth o gwbl pwy oedd y bòs tra oedd hi y tu ôl i'r piano, ac roedd y teiliwr am unwaith yn hynod o dawedog. Heb yngan gair, fe chwaraeodd y darn yn urddasol gan ddisgwyl i mi ddod i mewn ar ôl y cyflwyniad. Fe sefais inna'n stond heb agor fy ngheg. Roeddwn i'n 'nabod yr alaw yn iawn – sut gallwn i beidio, a honno wedi bod yn canu yn fy mhen i ers wythnosau – ond roedd y cyfeiliant yn wahanol i'r alaw.

'Wel cana, John bach,' medda hi.

'Dydw i rioed wedi canu efo'r piano o'r blaen, Miss Parry.'

'Yli, mi fydda i'n chwarae'r cyflwyniad; tyrd titha i mewn pan nodia i fy mhen.'

Mi roddwyd cais arall arni ac mi ddois inna i mewn yn rhy hwyr o beth mwdral.

'Na, na, na, John! Tyrd i mewn yn *syth* pan nodia i fy mhen!'

'Mae'r hogyn yn trio'i ora,' medda'r teiliwr yn llawn cydymdeimlad.

'Ond tydi'i ora fo ddim digon da. Ar fy ôl i – *one, two, three.*'

Wn i ddim ai'r cyfrif yn Saesneg wnaeth y gwahaniaeth ond mi ddaethon ni'n dau, y piano a minnau, i mewn efo'n gilydd a llwyddo i gadw efo'n gilydd fwy neu lai tan ddiwedd y pennill.

'*Well done* ti. Eto rŵan, efo mi.'

Cefais fy nrilio'n ddidrugaredd am awr gyfan, nes ei bod hi'n edifar gen i imi rioed glywed sôn am y rhosyn rhudd.

Ar ddiwedd yr awr, dyma hi'n cau caead y piano a gwenu arna i.

'Wel, os cani di felna, fydd 'na neb yn Steddfod Marianglas fedr dy guro di.'

Ar noson oer yn nechrau mis Mawrth, yn fuan ar ôl te, fe gychwynnodd Mam, Nhad, fy chwaer a minnau gerdded y ddwy filltir a hanner i Farian-glas. Ar y ffordd, deuem ar draws cymdogion a chyfeillion a chydnabod fesul dau a thri, hwythau ar eu ffordd i'r eisteddfod. Erbyn i ni gyrraedd yr hen ysgol ym Marian-glas, roedd mintai dda ohonom. Wn i ddim pryd y peidiodd yr hen ysgol â bod yn ysgol, ond ers blynyddoedd maith hi oedd cartref eisteddfod yr ardal ac mi fyddai dan ei sang bob blwyddyn.

Bryd hynny, fe edrychai'r adeilad yn anferth a'r gynulleidfa'n dorf enfawr.

Pan gyrhaeddon ni, roedd yr ysgol yn bur lawn ac o fewn rhai munudau roedd hi'n orlawn. Yn orlawn o blant mân, mamau a neiniau yn gymysg ag eisteddfodwyr proffesiynol a fyddai'n eistedd yn ddeallus drwy eisteddfod ar ôl eisteddfod bron tan doriad gwawr. Er oered y noson roedd chwys gwres y gynulleidfa eisoes yn dechrau rhedeg i lawr y waliau. Yna, dechreuodd y gweithgareddau gyda chanu emyn.

Daeth yr arweinydd i'r llwyfan a chyhoeddi: 'Cystadleuaeth adrodd i blant dan chwech oed: "Mae Gennyf Adnod Fechan". Ddaw'r rhai canlynol i'r llwyfan, os gwelwch chi'n dda – Gwen, Heulwen, Meirianwen, Dilys...' – ac aeth yn ei flaen i restru tua phymtheg o enwau, pob un ond dau ohonynt yn enethod. Ar ôl peth annibendod, fe gasglwyd y criw yn rhes ddestlus ar flaen y llwyfan, rhai ohonynt yn eofn, rhai'n ceisio dal llygaid eu mamau, a'r gweddill yn gryndod ofnus.

Roedd hi'n gynulleidfa garedig – yn hael ei chymeradwyaeth a pharod ei chydymdeimlad os digwyddai i rywun anghofio. Erbyn y bumed 'adnod fechan' roeddwn i wedi colli pob diddordeb, ac mi ddechreuodd fy stumog i droi wrth feddwl yn hunanol am yr artaith oedd yn fy wynebu i.

Oriau a dwy gystadleuaeth yn ddiweddarach fe ddaeth fy nhro innau.

'Rŵan 'ta. Unawd i fechgyn: "Y Rhosyn Rhudd". Ddaw'r canlynol i'r llwyfan, os gwelwch chi'n dda – Elwyn, Elfed o'r Llan, Cledwyn, John...'

Pan alwodd yr arweinydd fy enw i, rhoddodd Mam

bwniad i mi yn fy ochr nes i mi godi'n anfoddog i ymuno â'r trueiniaid eraill oedd eisoes ar y llwyfan. Na, doedd y gair 'trueiniaid' ddim yn gweddu i bawb – roedd Elfed o'r Llan yn geiliog i gyd, ac mi gafodd gymeradwyaeth fyddarol. Wedi i mi sefyll am hylltod fe ddaeth fy nhwrn inna. Clywais y piano'n dechrau canu, aeth fy ngwddw'n sych grimp ac, am foment, aeth y geiriau'n glir o'm cof. Yna mi gofiais am gyngor JC: 'Dewisa di wyneb yn y gynulleidfa a chana iddo fo a neb arall.' Chwiliais y môr wynebau a gweld wyneb Mam. Dechreuais ganu'n grynedig – a chwarae teg iddi hi, mi ganodd hi bob gair efo mi!

Dydw i ddim yn cofio'r feirniadaeth ond enillais i ddim. Fodd bynnag, mi wnes i'n ddigon da i gadw ffydd fy mam ynof ac i sicrhau digon o rîls am weddill fy nyddiau ysgol. Ac mi ddeuthum i'n ffrindia penna efo JC, un o'r cymeriadau prin a diddorol hynny a oedd yn dewis torri ei gŵys ei hun a herio cyffredinedd confensiwn, dyn a oedd yn mentro breuddwydio breuddwydion gan greu cerddoriaeth a gwneud bywyd yn bêr i eraill.

# Y Crydd

Anodd yw sôn am J. C. Parry heb sôn ar yr un gwynt bron am gymeriad arall, sef Robert Matthews, Lleiniau Llwydion. Yr unig debygrwydd rhwng y ddau oedd eu bod tua'r un oed a bod y naill a'r llall yn ennill eu bywoliaeth trwy ymarfer crefft draddodiadol.

Crydd oedd Robert Matthews, blaenor yng Nghapel y Bedyddwyr ac un o golofnau Eisteddfod Gadeiriol Marian-glas. Gŵr hynaws a rhadlon, ac yntau fel J. C. Parry yn gymeriad. Fe ellid dadlau am y ddau mai dau bysgodyn mawr yn nofio mewn pwll bach oedden nhw, ond gwell hynny na phwll mawr heb bysgod o gwbl fel yr oedd hi ac fel y mae hi mewn ambell ardal.

Roedd gweithdy'r crydd yn union ar draws y ffordd i Ysgol Gynradd Tyn-y-gongl, ond na feiddiai yr un creadur ohonom ni'r plant groesi'r ffordd tuag yno adeg oriau'r ysgol. Cwt sinc digon diaddurn oedd y gweithdy, a byddai dieithryn yn mynd heibio iddo fo heb dalu fawr o sylw iddo. A pha ryfedd – roedd y cwt (yn enwedig ei ddrws) yn crefu am baent, a'r paent oedd arno wedi crasu a chwyddo'n swigod yng ngwres haul haf a chrebachu'n graciau mân yn rhew y gaeaf, ac amser wedi pylu'r lliw gwreiddiol yn rhyw fath o wyrdd llwydaidd.

Roedd y gweithdy ei hun yn gyfleus ddigon, hanner ffordd rhwng y Benllech a Bryn-teg ac yn ddigon agos at

Farian-glas a Llanbedr-goch. Pe bai'r gymdogaeth yn olwyn, yma yng ngweithdy'r crydd – am sawl rheswm – y byddai ei both. Oherwydd bod pawb yn y gymdogaeth gyfan yn berchen pâr o draed, yr oedd yn anochel eu bod, yn hwyr neu'n hwyrach, yn galw yma.

Mi dreuliais i lawer iawn o oriau fy mhlentyndod yng ngweithdy'r crydd, nid am fod gen i dyllau yn fy esgidiau ond am fod Robert Matthews yn gwmnïwr mor ddifyr. O lusgo'r drws yn agored (a llusgo oedd raid), trewid dyn yn syth gan arogl a oedd yn rhan annatod o'r lle. Anodd yw disgrifio'r arogl yn union – cymysgedd o arogl lledr, mwg stôf baraffîn a fu'n duo'r nenfwd ers blynyddoedd wrth wresogi'r cwt, arogl paent o'r ddau bot ar y fainc a hen, hen chwys traed ardal gyfan.

Byddai tu mewn y gweithdy yn ddieithriad yn baradwys o anhrefn – darnau trwchus o ledr anferth eu maint yn bolio yn erbyn y wal ac ar fin syrthio; sgidiau o bob rhywogaeth, lliw a maint ar silff, ar lawr ac ar ambell gadair heb gefn nes bod y lle'n edrych, fel y byddai Mam yn dweud, 'ar gychwyn'. Yr un diffyg trefn bwriadol oedd ar fainc y crydd o flaen y ffenest. Roedd ar honno forthwylion, gefeiliau, cyllyll miniog, ebillion, dau ful, hoelion o bob cenedl a maint, pot o ddŵr, a dau bot jam efo paent du yn y naill a phaent brown yn y llall.

Tu ôl i'r fainc, yn wynebu'r ffenestr ac mewn safle i weld pawb a fyddai'n digwydd pasio heibio, fe eisteddai'r crydd. Dyn mawr cryf, llydan ei gorff, er gwaetha'r ffaith ei fod yn siŵr o fod ymhell dros ei drigain. Yn ei ddydd fe fu'n bencampwr tynnu torch nodedig, ac er bod ei ysgwyddau'n dechrau crymu erbyn hynny nid oedd amheuaeth am nerth ei freichiau a'i ddwylo. Gallai dorri â'i gyllell drwy'r lledr gwytnaf fel drwy fenyn, ond fe allai'r un dwylo mawr drin celfi bychain fel ebill a nodwydd yn gelfydd gain. Fel ambell ddyn arall mawr o gorff, roedd ganddo natur annwyl a llygaid bachgennaidd direidus. Fe fyddem ni'r plant yn gwneud unrhyw esgus i alw yn y gweithdy ar ôl yr ysgol i brynu cnegwarth o sbarblis neu holi hynt pâr o sgidiau. Byddai'n ein diddori drwy wneud i geiniogau ddiflannu trwy ei fysedd neu wasgu coes morthwyl nes bod dŵr yn rhedeg ohono. Flynyddoedd yn ddiweddarach y sylweddolais i fod ganddo ddarn o wlân cotwm gwlyb rhwng ei fysedd, ac nad o goes y morthwyl yr oedd y dŵr yn dod!

Doedd o fawr o ddyn busnes ac ni fyddai byth yn taro nac addewid na chyfrifon ar bapur. Fe ddibynnai'n gyfan gwbl ar air ac addewid llafar ac ar ei gof. Roedd o'n un da iawn am addo, ond nid oedd lawn cystal am gyflawni ei addewidion. Gan hynny bu'n rhaid iddo fo fod yn ddyfeisgar dros ben er mwyn lliniaru llid cwsmeriaid dicllon. 'Dyn stimrwg' y galwai Mam o, nid yn gyhuddgar o gwbl, ond gyda rhyw wên wybodus ar ei gwefusau. Dros y blynyddoedd fe ddyfeisiodd y crydd nifer o amryfal ddulliau i liniaru cwsmeriaid a gawsant eu siomi. Er enghraifft, dyma un o'r dulliau mwyaf cyffredin oedd ganddo i oresgyn sefyllfa pan ofynnid iddo: 'Ydi fy 'sgidia fi'n barod, Robat Matthews? Roeddech chi wedi addo'n bendant y byddan nhw'n barod erbyn heddiw a finna'n mynd i angladd ddiwadd yr wythnos.' Atebai'r crydd yn syth: 'Ydyn, 'n tad, newydd 'u gorffan nhw. Mi ro' i ddarn o bapur llwyd amdanyn nhw ichi rŵan.'

Daliai'r sgidiau yn ei law gan eu rhwbio'n garuaidd efo darn o glwt.

'Ond nid fy sgidia i ydi'r rheina.'

Yn dilyn, fe geid darn gwych o actio. Dros ei wyneb fe redai anghrediniaeth lwyr, siom, amheuaeth a hunanfeirniadaeth lem.

'Ydach chi'n *siŵr?*'

'Yn berffaith siŵr. Sgidia duon oedd fy rhai i i fynd i'r angladd. Fyddwn i byth yn *meddwl* mynd i angladd mewn sgidia brown.'

'Wel, dyna hen dro a finnau wedi bod wrthi'n un swydd drwy'r bora 'ma i'w cael nhw'n barod erbyn i chi gyrradd.'

Doedd dim y gallai neb ei wneud yn wyneb y fath ddiffuantrwydd ond bodloni i'r drefn.

Dro arall mi fyddai'n gweld rhywun yn troi am ddrws y gweithdy, drwy gil ei lygaid. Byddai ennyd o brysurdeb mawr tra byddai'n cael gwared o'r esgid oedd ar y mul, a rhoi esgid gwbl wahanol arno o dwmpath oedd ar y silff ar y chwith iddo. Pan ddeuai'r cwsmer i mewn mi fyddai'r crydd yn barod amdano.

'Ydi sgidia Megan fy chwaer yn barod, Robat Mathews? Mi ddeudsoch chi y byddan nhw'n barod ganol dydd.'

'*Yn* dechra arnyn nhw oeddwn i rŵan.'

'Ond mi roeddach chi wedi addo…'

'Do, mi wn i hynny, ond ma' hi wedi bod yn andros o brysur. Os leiciwch chi aros, mi ddylwn i eu gorffen nhw mewn llai nag awr.'

'Na, fedra i ddim aros. Mi alwa i ben bora fory.'

A dyna gwsmer arall, os nad wedi ei fodloni, wedi cael tynnu'r gwynt o'i hwyliau.

Rhaid bod y 'stimrwgrwydd' yma'n nodweddiadol o'r teulu. Mae gen i frith gof am stori gan Robert Matthews a ddigwyddodd yng nghyfnod ei dad. Roedd 'na ŵr o Fryn-teg angen prynu het ar gyfer achlysur go arbennig, ac ar ei ffordd i Siop Tyn-y-gongl mi alwodd yn y gweithdy i dorri ei siwrnai, gan fod hwnnw, fwy neu lai, hanner y ffordd rhwng Bryn-teg a'r Siop. Ar ôl rhoi'r byd yn ei le a datgan ei fwriad, i ffwrdd â fo ar duth i brynu ei het newydd.

Bryd hynny, roedd Siop Tyn-y-gongl yn swyddfa bost ac yn siop-gwerthu-pob-peth, o baraffîn i ffisig, o sgidiau i hetiau a dilladau. Cyn pen dim roedd y gŵr yn berchen het barchus ddu a oedd yn addas ar gyfer priodas neu angladd ac, yn ôl geiriau braidd yn gamarweiniol y perchennog, J.P. Williams, roedd hi'n ffitio fel maneg. Dyma osod yr het newydd yn barchus mewn bocs crwn pwrpasol, ac anfon y cwsmer bodlon ar ei daith yn ôl i Fryn-teg.

Ar ei ffordd adref fe benderfynodd dorri ei siwrnai yng ngweithdy'r crydd. Tra oedd yn disgrifio'i bwrcasiad newydd, fe lwyddwyd i dynnu ei sylw, agor y bocs, a chyfnewid yr het newydd am hen gap budr. Ymhen peth amser ailgychwynnodd y gŵr ar ei siwrnai, â'i focs dan ei gesail.

Cyn pen yr awr yr oedd yn ei ôl yn bytheirio am J. P. Williams, Siop Tyn-y-gongl, ac yn ei alw'n ddyn twyllodrus – a gwaeth. Fe gafodd bob cydymdeimlad gan gynulleidfa'r gweithdy, a thra oedd o'n rhefru fe lwyddwyd i gyfnewid y cap yn ôl am yr het unwaith yn rhagor, heb iddo sylweddoli dim.

Wedi hynny, i ffwrdd â fo am y siop gan dyngu y byddai'n 'sortio' J. P. Williams un waith ac am byth. Brasgamodd i mewn i'r siop ac anelu'n syth at y perchennog:

'J. P. Williams, mi ddois i yma bob cam i brynu het, a thalu pres del amdani. A be gefais i?'

'Wel het siŵr iawn…'

31

'Het gythraul. Pan agorais i'r bocs, hen gap budr oedd ynddo fo. Drychwch!'

Agorodd J. P. y bocs a thynnu'r het allan.

'Wel diawch, Mr Williams bach, mae hi'n het ac yn gap bob yn ail,' meddai, gan syllu'n llawn syndod ar yr het.

Mae'n debyg i mi dreulio oriau bwygilydd yn gwrando ar y crydd ac, ambell waith, yn dadlau efo fo o fewn fy ngallu ar bynciau crefyddol fel Arminiaeth, bedydd drwy drochiad (roedd o'n flaenor efo'r Bedyddwyr), gras, cyfiawnhad drwy ffydd, ac anfarwoldeb yr enaid – a mynd i ddyfroedd dyfnion iawn ein dau.

Mi ddysgodd hefyd imi rigymu barddoniaeth. Roedd o'n dipyn o fardd gwlad, ac yn unol â'r traddodiad hwnnw mi fyddai'n llunio penillion coffa a cherddi i achlysuron arbennig a'u cyhoeddi yn y *Clorianydd* neu *Herald Môn*. Roedd ganddo fo grap ar y cynganeddion, ac roedd ganddo stôr o straeon ar ei gof. Mi fyddwn i wrth fy modd yn ei ganfod o yno ar ei ben ei hun, heb fod neb arall i ymyrryd yn ein sgyrsiau ni.

Ond nid felly y byddai hi bob amser. Roedd y gweithdy'n gyrchfan ddeniadol i lawer. Yn wir, yr oedd o'n rhyw fath o ganolfan gymdeithasol i'r hen, y segur a'r di-waith. Yno ar eu rhawd fe ddeuai llond dwrn o ddynion lleol ac eistedd yn rhes ar y cadeiriau heb gefn. Hon oedd ystafell bwyllgor y cynghorwyr nas etholwyd, seiat y blaenoriaid nas dewiswyd, cyffesgell y di-gapel, ysgol farddol y beirdd talcen slip, a llwyfan ambell storïwr go amheus. Byddai'r crydd yntau – er ei fod â'i gefn atynt – yn arwain y fintai frith. Byddai'n gadeirydd, yn offeiriad, yn athro ac yn gynulleidfa yn ôl y gofyn. Ac er fy mod i'n llawdrwm ar yr ymwelwyr eraill am eu bod yn fy rhwystro rhag cael y crydd i mi fy hun, os cofia i'n iawn roedd seiadau cwt y crydd yn fwy diddorol na seiadau uniongred Capel y Tabernacl.

Roedd Robert Mathews hefyd yn gynhyrchydd drama, a chynhelid y dramâu yn Ysgol Marian-glas i godi arian at Seion, Capel y Bedyddwyr. Fe wnaeth y cynhyrchydd gawl iawn o bethau mewn un perfformiad nodedig. Chofia i ddim be oedd teitl y ddrama er fy mod i yn y gynulleidfa, ond un o'r uchafbwyntiau oedd llofruddiaeth, pan saethwyd un o'r cymeriadau efo gwn llaw.

Y crydd, fel cynhyrchydd, oedd yn gyfrifol am greu effaith sŵn yr ergyd. Yr oedd wedi datrys y broblem drwy fynd â mul a morthwyl o'r gweithdy i gefn y llwyfan a tharo capsen i greu clec ar yr eiliad dyngedfennol. Ond roedd hi'n dywyll yng nghefn y llwyfan, a methodd y crydd gyda'i ergyd, a bu'r actor yn tynnu ar y taniwr sawl gwaith heb greu ergyd. Ar ôl peth oedi fe waeddwyd 'Bang' o gefn y llwyfan, ac aeth y ddrama yn ei blaen tan ddiwedd yr olygfa. Yn ystod yr egwyl daeth clec anferth o gefn y llwyfan nes bod y gynulleidfa'n neidio. Roedd y crydd wedi dod o hyd i'r gapsen.

## Cocos Traeth Coch

Mae'n sicr bod byw yn y wlad yn gwneud rhywun yn fwy ymwybodol o'r tymhorau. Nid gwanwyn, haf, hydref a gaeaf y calendr sydd gen i mewn golwg, ond adegau a digwyddiadau oedd yn cael eu pennu gan fyd natur oedd yn fwy caeth i haul a gwynt a glaw nag i ddyddiadau neilltuol. Pethau i bobl hŷn oedd tymor torri gwair neu godi tatws, pethau ymylol plentyndod. Ond yr oedd hel madarch (neu fysharŵms, gyda'r acen ar yr 'w'), a hel mwyar duon a chnau yn sicr ddigon yn nheyrnas nefoedd plant. Achlysur go debyg oedd mynd i hel cocos i Draeth Coch.

Fe benderfynodd Mam a Mrs Jones, Tan Bryn, un diwrnod y byddem ni'n mynd i hel cocos drannoeth, os byddai'r tywydd yn braf. Y *ni* oedd Marian fy chwaer, Richard Tan Bryn, Mam, Mrs Jones a minnau. Ac yn wir mi oedd hi'n braf – diwrnod tanbaid ym mis Gorffennaf, heb gwmwl yn yr awyr. Ar ôl cinio cynnar am un ar ddeg, dyma gychwyn wedi'n llwytho efo brechdanau, diodydd, llwyau a phwcedi, a chroesi croesffordd y Tabernacl am Lôn Bwlch. Roedd Mam a Mrs Jones yn gwisgo het wellt yr un a bu'n rhaid i minnau, yn groes i bob graen, wisgo cap. Roedd hi'n llethol – y pyllau tar ar y ffordd yn ffrwtian yn araf fel uwd du yn llygad yr haul, a'r ffordd yn y pellter yn troi'n llynnoedd disglair o gryndod gloyw, byw.

Wrth i ni gerdded yn wasgarog i lawr Lôn Bwlch roedd ychydig o gysgod dan frigau coed, ac fel yr oeddem ni'n cerdded ymlaen, ac i Lôn Bwlch newid ei henw yn Lôn Coed Glyn, roedd mwy fyth o gysgod. Roedd Richard a minnau'n cerdded y tu ôl i'r lleill gan lusgo'n traed yn y ffosydd ar naill ochr y ffordd.

'Cerddwch yn iawn, chi'ch dau,' medda Mam.

'Ia wir,' ategodd Mrs Jones. 'Gwyliwch chi rhag nadroedd yn yr hen ffos 'na – ma' Coed y Glyn yn llawn ohonyn nhw, gwiberod gwenwynig...'

Roedd hynny'n fwy na digon i'n cael ni i gerdded ar ganol y ffordd a chau'r bwlch oedd wedi tyfu rhyngom ni a nhw.

Cyn hir, daethom allan o gysgod Coed y Glyn yn ymyl gweddillion hen stesion y Benllech, a oedd bron i ddwy filltir o'r pentref glan môr hwnnw. Yna troi i gyfeiriad Capel Saron a dechrau mynd ar i waered i lawr yr allt serth at y môr. Hyd heddiw, mi fydd fy nghalon i'n rhoi llam bob tro y bydda i'n gweld y môr. Rhaid bod Richard yr un fath â mi achos mi ddechreuodd y ddau ohonom ni redeg fel dau filgi am y tywod.

'Arhoswch, y trychfilod bach,' gwaeddodd Mrs Jones. 'Peidiwch chi â meiddio mynd yn agos i'r tywod 'na. Mae 'na siglen berig iawn fan'cw, ac mi ellwch chi'ch dau gael eich llyncu a diflannu i grombil y ddaear.'

Dyma hi'n ein gosod ni'n drefnus ar bwys wal tafarn Min y Don i ddiosg ein sgidia a rhannu'r pwcedi: dwy bwced fawr i Mrs Jones a Mam, a phwcedi llai yr un i ni'n tri. Fe gawsom ni lwy bob un – hen lwyau pwdin pyglyd – a'n cyfarwyddo i ddilyn yn ôl traed Mrs Jones ar draws ffrwd fechan at y gwelyau cocos, gan osgoi'r siglen. Roedd y môr allan yn bell, bell y tu hwnt i Landdona, bron at Benmon.

'Cadwch chi lygad ar y môr, blant.'

'Ond mae o'n bell allan...'

'Hidia di befo hynny, mi ddaw i mewn mewn chwinciad, ac yna mi fydd y tipyn afon 'ma'n llenwi a'r môr mawr yn rhuthro amdanom ni, fatha'r dyn Cantra'r Gwaelod hwnnw erstalwm.'

Wnaeth neb ddadlau efo hi. Roedd hi'n siarad fel un ag awdurdod ganddi. Felly dyma ddilyn Mrs Jones at y gwely cocos yn ufudd. Heb hel dail dyma hi'n stwffio gwaelodion ei ffrog i'w blwmars a dechrau crafu efo'i llwy, fodfedd neu ddwy o dan wyneb y tywod gwlyb.

'Dowch, dechreuwch hel fatha fi, ne' mi fydd y llanw i mewn cyn i ni gael mwy na chnegwarth.'

Roedd y tywod yn feddal dan draed ac mewn ambell lecyn roedd rhywun yn suddo dros ei fferau. Roeddwn i ofn aros yn f'unfan yn hir rhag i'r siglen fy llyncu i grombil y ddaear. Mi ddechreuais i grafu efo'r llwy a tharo cocosen yn syth bìn.

'Mae'r lle 'ma'n *fyw* ohonyn nhw,' gwaeddais.

'Wel ydi, 'ngwas gwyn i,' atebodd Mrs Jones, a gwên fawr ar ei wyneb hi.

Mi fuon ni'n crafu ac yn tyrchu am ymron i awr, pawb yn ei gwman a'n cefnau ni'n bynafyd nes i'r pwcedi lenwi at yr ymylon. Bob yn hyn a hyn mi fyddai Mrs Jones yn mynd â'n pwcedi ni at bwll o ddŵr ac yn golchi'r tywod oddi ar y cregyn.

'Waeth i ni heb â chario tywod y Traeth Coch yr holl ffordd adref,' medda hi.

Roedd y tyrchu anghyfarwydd yn boenus i gefn, ond

ymhell cyn i ni ddiflasu mi sylwodd Mrs Jones fod y llanw wedi troi a bod dŵr yr afon yn codi.

'Dowch, dyna ddigon; dydi pwced ond yn dal 'i llond. Mi fyddan nhw'n drwm iawn i'w cario'r holl ffordd adref, ond mi gawn ni sgram i swper.'

'Drychwch, Mrs Jones! Mae fy llwy i'n sgleinio fel newydd.'

'Dyna pam y daethon ni â hen lwya, 'sti. Mae tywod yn llnau llwya'n well na dim.'

A dyma droi am adref. Croesi'r ffrwd a gwisgo'n sanau a'n sgidiau ar wal Min y Don, a chychwyn y daith o ddwy filltir a mwy yn ôl am Dŷ Capel y Tabernacl a Than y Bryn. Fel y cerddem fe âi'r pwcedi'n drymach, ein breichiau'n hirach a'r ffordd yn feithach. Braf oedd cyrraedd croeslon y Tabernacl a gwybod mai dim ond prin hanner canllath oedd ar ôl i'w gerdded.

Rhoddodd Mam y cocos mewn dwy sosban anferth a'u berwi cyn gynted bron â'n bod ni wedi croesi stepen y drws.

'Y peth gwaetha am gocos,' medda hi, 'ydi bod yn rhaid eu bwyta ar unwaith cyn iddyn nhw fynd yn ddrwg, ac mi ân' nhw'n ddrwg mewn byr amser yn yr holl wres 'ma'.

A dyna gawsom ni i swper, platiad o gocos ffres yn eu cregyn efo ychydig o bupur a halen a dogn go dda o finegr. Siomedig oeddwn i ynddyn nhw – roedd rhyw ansawdd lledr gwlyb iddyn nhw, ac oni bai am y finegr a'r pupur a'r halen, pethau digon di-flas fuasen nhw hefyd. Yn waeth na dim, wrth i mi eu cnoi, roedd gronyn neu ddau o dywod yn crinsian yn atgas rhwng fy nannedd.

Beth amser yn ddiweddarach, fe fu llofruddiaeth yn Nhraeth Coch a fu'n destun siarad ardal gyfan am wythnosau lawer. Roedd 'na ddyn dŵad o Sais o'r enw Nettleton wedi lladd ei wraig a chuddio'r corff yn yr union siglen y rhybuddiodd Mrs Jones, Tan y Bryn, ni rhag mynd yn agos ati. Rhaid ei fod o wedi meddwl y bydda hi'n 'diflannu i grombil y ddaear'. Ond wnaeth hi ddim. Y farn leol oedd nad oedd Nettleton yn adnabod y traeth a'r llanw'n ddigon da, ac nad oedd wedi deall dirgelion y siglen.

Pan ddaethpwyd o hyd i'r corff doedd dim modd dweud pwy oedd hi nac o ble yr oedd hi wedi dod. Yna fe sylwodd plismon lleol fod deilen ar y corff, ac fe fu'n ddigon craff i gyfateb y ddeilen â gardd Nettleton a darganfod bod gwraig y gŵr hwnnw wedi mynd ar goll. A dyna sut, yn ôl y si lleol, y llwyddwyd i adnabod y corff a dal y llofrudd.

Mi gododd y llofruddiaeth fraw drwy'r ardal gyfan, ac mi fyddai Marian fy chwaer yn edrych o dan y gwely bob nos cyn mynd i gysgu am fisoedd lawer.

## Ysgolion Dyddiol

Taith bum munud oedd hi o'm cartref i'r ysgol gynradd. Bryd hynny, yn Nhyn-y-gongl yr oedd ysgol ein pentref ni ac nid yn y Benllech fel y mae hi'n awr. Ysgol dri athro oedd hi – Miss Laura Jones yn 'fam ni oll' ar y babanod; Miss Jinnie Owen (Mrs Williams wedi hynny) â gofal canol yr ysgol, a'r prifathro, H. Emrys Jones, yn dysgu'r gweddill. Yn wahanol i drefn heddiw, roedd y prifathro'n dysgu drwy'r amser, a does gen i ddim cof am nag ysgrifenyddes na gweinyddesau meithrin. Cymry Cymraeg naturiol oedd naw deg pump y cant o'r disgyblion, o'r Benllech a Thyn-y-gongl gan mwyaf, er bod ambell un yn dod o Fryn-teg a Llanbedr-goch. Roedd rhyw lond dwrn o'r disgyblion yn dod o gartrefi Saesneg neu gartrefi cymysg yn y Benllech, ond roedd pob un yn deall os nad oeddynt yn gallu siarad Cymraeg.

Doeddwn i fawr o 'sglaig. Welodd neb rhyw addewid mawr ynof yn yr ysgol – yn wir, roedd Mam yn rhyw fud boeni na fyddwn i'n pasio'r Sgolarship a dilyn fy chwaer, oedd yn dangos llawer mwy o addewid, i'r ysgol sir. Doeddwn i ddim yn cael trafferthion darllen nac ysgrifennu a gallwn gyfrif yn gymedrol, ond doedd fawr ddim yn fy nghymell i at ddysg nac yn fy nenu i ddarllen yn wirfoddol. 'Dipyn o freuddwydiwr ydi John' – dyna oedd barn  yr athrawon ysgol gynradd amdanaf. Nid rhyfedd, felly, nad oes gen i atgofion byw am lafarganu tablau rhifo na gornestau sillafu. Ond mae gen i atgofion cynnes am y tri athro fel pobol, ac am rai digwyddiadau nad oes a wnelont ddim oll ag addysg ffurfiol.

Diddordeb mawr Emrys Jones oedd y ddrama. Enillodd yn Eisteddfod Genedlaethol Pen-y-bont ar Ogwr, 1948, am gyfieithu i'r Gymraeg y ddrama un-act hanesyddol, *Campbell of Kilmohr* gan J. A Ferguson. Roedd Emrys Jones yn gynhyrchydd ac yn actor medrus a chofiaf yn dda ei gynhyrchiad o *Campbell o Kilmohr* gyda chwmni o actorion lleol. Roedd hon yn ddrama gwbl wahanol i'r comedïau arferol, ac roedd graen ar y cynhyrchu a'r actio. Ef ei hun gymerai ran Campbell, y prif gymeriad – gŵr creulon a oedd â'i fryd ar ddal 'Bonnie Prince Charlie' yn ucheldir yr Alban – a chodai arswyd arnom ni'r plant.

Bu bron i'w ddawn actio achosi rhyfel cartref ar fuarth yr ysgol un waith. Y diwrnod dan sylw roeddem ni, blant canol yr ysgol, wedi cael ymuno efo'r plant mawr yn nosbarth Mr Jones. Gwers hanes oedd hi am fyddinoedd Llywelyn yn ymladd yng nghadarnleoedd Eryri yn erbyn grym y Saeson. Adroddodd fel yr oedd Môn ffrwythlon yn ffynhonnell fwyd i'r milwyr ac mai dyna pam y gelwid yr ynys yn 'Môn Mam Cymru'. Soniodd am dactegau'r Cymru yn defnyddio'r tir mynydd i ymosod ac encilio ar yn ail nes ffwndro'r gelyn, a ninnau'r bechgyn yn cymeradwyo pob ystryw o eiddo'r Cymry gan fendithio'r glaw a'r tywydd garw a oedd yn torri calonnau'r milwyr Seisnig. Roedd Saeson y Benllech yn hollol fud. Ond fe dawelodd y bonllefau pan ddechreuodd y prifathro sôn am Edward y Cyntaf a'i gestyll, a oedd yn ymestyn ar hyd yr arfordir o Fflint i Gaernarfon a Harlech. Soniodd sut y bu i sefydlu Castell Biwmares roi terfyn ar Fôn fel ysgubor i borthi byddinoedd y Cymry ac am farwolaeth greulon Llywelyn ei hun.

Amser chwarae fe ymosodon ni fel un gŵr ar Saeson yr ysgol, a chael a chael fu hi ar ambell un i gyrraedd adref yn ddianaf!

Drama arall a gafodd effaith fawr ar blant y pentref oedd *Canwyllbrennau'r Esgob* – drama a sylfaenwyd ar ran o *Les Misérables* gan Victor Hugo. Emrys Jones oedd yn chwarae rhan y lleidr a ddygodd ganwyllbrennau aur yr esgob, er i hwnnw roi lloches i'r lleidr yn ei gartref. Fe gafodd y ddrama ddylanwad mawr ar ardal gyfan, yn gymaint felly nes i griw o'r plant roi perfformiad ohoni yn eu geiriau eu hunain yn stabl Olgra Fawr. Idris yr Erw oedd y lleidr; John Quarry Banc oedd yr esgob, a Marian, fy chwaer, yn forwyn y tŷ. Er fy mod i'n rhy ifanc i fod yn y cast mi gofiaf y cynnwrf yn dda gan fy mod i fel nifer o blant iau eraill yn rhan o'r gynulleidfa. Rywsut neu'i gilydd fe glywodd Emrys Jones am y perfformiadau stabl a galwodd ar y cwmni i roi perfformiad o flaen yr ysgol. Swil oedd yr actorion ac amharod iawn i arddangos eu doniau o flaen y prifathro, a buan iawn y daeth y chwarae arbennig hwnnw i ben.

Er gwaethaf pryderon Mam, mi lwyddais i basio'r Sgolarship. Roedd newid ysgol yn newid byd. Ddechrau Medi 1948, fe ymunais â fy chwaer ar y groesffordd ym mhen y lôn i ddal y 'bỳs ysgol' am Langefni. Doedd honno ddim yn daith uniongyrchol o bell ffordd. Yn lle mynd yn syth drwy Fryn-teg am Langefni, byddai'r bỳs yn troi i'r chwith ym Mhenchwintan ac yn dilyn ffyrdd cefn troellog ac anwastad drwy Lanbedr-goch, gan osgoi Cefniwrch a throi i'r chwith am y Talwrn, ac ymuno â ffordd Penmynydd heb fod nepell o Theatr Fach Llangefni.

Ysgol Ramadeg weddol fechan oedd Ysgol Sir Llangefni pan ddechreuais i ar fy addysg uwchradd. Pan adewais i saith mlynedd yn ddiweddarach roedd hi mewn cartref newydd ac yn un o'r ysgolion cyfun cyntaf ym Mhrydain. Ysgol Brydeinig oedd hi ar yr wyneb a oedd yn credu mai Saesneg oedd iaith dysg. Ar wahân i rai eithriadau gloyw nid oedd llawer o'r athrawon yn arddel eu Cymraeg yn gyhoeddus, ac fe es i drwy'r ysgol heb wybod bod Llywelyn Jones, yr athro Hanes, yn siaradwr Cymraeg rhugl. Roedd elfennau digon gwrth-Gymreig ymysg rhai o aelodau'r staff, yn enwedig Mr Young, y gŵr sarcastig oedd yn dysgu Daearyddiaeth a Mr Cameron, y gŵr creulon oedd yn dysgu Lladin ac yn rhoi gwersi Ymarfer Corff ar yr iard i ddisgyblion y flwyddyn gyntaf.

Ond, diolch byth, yr oedd eithriadau. Byddai Walter Hughes, yr athro Cemeg, yn troi i'r Gymraeg ar ganol brawddeg, a John Pierce yntau, os nad yr athro Cymraeg gorau fu erioed, yn magu cariad at iaith a diwylliant, a chawsom weld ei nofel, *Blacmêl,* yn tyfu'n gyffrous o flaen ein llygaid yn yr ystafell ddosbarth. Fy hoff athro i oedd Cyffin Morris, gŵr llariaidd, caredig a diymhongar – er mai fo oedd y dyn mwyaf galluog yn yr ysgol. Ac mi ddysgodd y gŵr rhyfeddol hwnnw, F. G. Fisher, Gymraeg, a chynhyrchu dramâu yn yr ysgol yn ogystal â chwarae rhan amlwg yn sefydliad Theatr Fach Llangefni. Ac mi fûm i'n dipyn o ffefryn gan G.I. Jones, yr athro Cerddoriaeth, nes i fy llais i dorri.

Roedden ni'n cael ein rhannu'n ddwy ffrwd ar ddiwedd y flwyddyn gyntaf, ar ôl blwyddyn o ddysgu gallu cymysg.

Roedd y pymtheg cyntaf ym mhob ffrwd yn cael mynd i ffrwd A yn yr ail flwyddyn. Pedwerydd ar ddeg oeddwn i a thrwy groen fy nannedd y cyrhaeddais i 2A. Rhaid bod y cyfrwng Saesneg dieithr a'r rhychwant newydd o bynciau'n ormod i mi. Mi wellodd pethau ryw gymaint wrth i mi ddringo'r ysgol.

Arwynebol iawn oedd Seisnigrwydd Ysgol Sir Llangefni. Cymry gwerinol cefn gwlad Môn oedd ei disgyblion a Chymraeg oedd iaith y buarth a'r coridorau ar wahân i ambell ebychiad Saesneg gan Mr Young a'i debyg yn ein hannog i gerdded yn ddisgybledig. A'r hogia Cymraeg gwerinol hynny oedd yn gwneud eu marc mewn colegau a phrifysgolion.

Mae plant dosbarthiadau isaf ysgolion yn tueddu i edrych i fyny at y disgyblion hynaf a chreu arwyr o'u plith, a doeddwn i ddim gwahanol. Bechgyn talentog fel J. O. Roberts a Gwilym Owen (oedd yn actio mewn dramâu fel *Amlyn ac Amig* gan Saunders Lewis), neu Bedwyr Lewis Jones a Harri Pritchard Jones oedd fy arwyr innau. Ac roeddwn i'n edmygydd mawr o Alffi, sef Alfan Williams, Coed Anna, oedd yn gawr ar y cae pêl-droed ac yn her i ddisgyblaeth athrawon. Mae'n wir i Hywel Gwynfryn ymuno â'r ysgol yn ystod fy nghyfnod i, ond does 'na ddim lle i arwyr sy'n dod o ddosbarthiadau is yn oriel bechgyn ysgol!

Cymysg yw fy atgofion am Ysgol Llangefni. Mi gymerodd hi amser maith cyn imi setlo yno, ac roedd yn gas gen i'r daith droellog ar y bỳs bob dydd. Mae arogl diesel yn codi cyfog arna hyd heddiw, a dydw i ddim yn rhy hoff o hyd o deithio mewn bỳs. Ond yn sicr mae gen i ddyled fawr i lu o athrawon am ymestyn fy ngorwelion, ac edmygedd o genedlaethau o ddisgyblion a wrthododd blygu i gyfundrefn addysg estron.

## Atseiniau Rhyfel

Mae'n rhaid fy mod wedi gwisgo lledr gwadnau mwy nag un pâr o sgidiau ar fy hynt yn ôl ac ymlaen o'r Erw Ddu i'n tŷ ni. Tyddyn bychan un fuwch a hanner dwsin o ieir oedd Erw Ddu, heb fod yn ddigon o faint i roi bywoliaeth i ŵr y tŷ ond bod llefrith, menyn cartref a wyau yn gaffaeliad mawr adeg rhyfel. Roedd Idris yr Erw a minnau'n ffrindiau pennaf, ac anaml y gwelid un ohonom heb y llall y tu allan i oriau ysgol. Er bod Idris dros ddwy flynedd yn hŷn na mi, doedd y gwahaniaeth oed ddim yn llyffethair o gwbl a byddwn wrth fy modd yn rhannu dyletswyddau'r tyddyn fel hel cerrig, corddi a llosgi eithin, yn ogystal â gorchestion mabolgampaidd fel nofio, neidio a rhedeg ar Draeth Dinas.

Erys ambell ddiwrnod ym mywydau pawb ohonom yn un darn yn y cof tra bod wythnosau a misoedd cyfan weithiau'n mynd i lwyr ddifancoll, ac mae un diwrnod o blith yr ugeiniau a dreuliais yng nghwmni Idris yn sicr yn syrthio i'r categori dethol hwnnw. Roedd y ddau ohonom wedi bod wrthi'n brysur drwy'r pnawn yn lladd Jyrmans ac wedi hen alaru ar y gelyn dychmygol. Doedd yr un ohonom yn fodlon cogio bod yn 'jeri', felly roedd hi'n amhosib gallu cael ymladd go iawn, a bu'n rhaid bodloni ar saethu at dwmpathau eithin a lluchio bomiau tywyrch at foncyffion a llwyni drain.

'Be gawn ni 'i neud rŵan?'

'Gad i ni fynd i lawr at yr afon.'

Ac i lawr at yr afon â ni. Yno yr aem bob amser pan fyddai pob chwarae wedi colli ei flas. Nid afon oedd hi mewn gwirionedd ond nant fechan. Ond ar yr un egwyddor ag y gelwir Parys, Llwydiarth a Bodafon yn fynyddoedd ym Môn, yr oeddem ni'n galw hon yn afon. Fe elwid y darn arbennig yma'n Afon Ty'n Llan. Amrywiai ei henw o fferm i fferm gan nad oedd hi'n ddigon pwysig, hyd y gwn i, i gael un enw o'i tharddiad i'r môr.

Roedd ffordd y Tabernacl yn igam-ogamu heibio i'n tŷ ni, Siop y Tabernacl, Tan y Bryn, Tyddyn Sarjiant, Bryn Erw ac Erw Ddu – cartref Idris – hyd at Dy'n Llan, yna'n fforchio'n ddwy ar ôl croesi'r afon, y naill gangen yn mynd heibio i Eglwys Llanfair Mathafarn (cyn dirywio fwy neu lai'n llwybr trol) a'r llall yn nadreddu nes cyrraedd y ffordd fawr rhwng Bryn-teg a Marian-glas.

Fe redai'r afon ar hyd ffin terfyn un o gaeau Ty'n Llan a mynd dan y bont a oedd rhwng Ty'n Llan a'r eglwys. Fel arfer enwau digon cyffredin a roddid ar gaeau – Cae Dros Ffordd, Cae Pella, Cae Boncan, ond roedd enw digon barddonol i gae afon Ty'n Llan, sef y Dalar Arian. Rhaid bod rhyw fardd o amaethwr wedi gweld adlewyrchiad y lloer yn rhimyn arian ar ymyl y cae wrth gerdded ei gariad!

Dyma gyrraedd pont Afon Ty'n Llan. Doedd fawr o ddŵr yn yr afon – yn wir, prin ei bod hi'n rhedeg o gwbl. Ar ochr dde'r bont yn wynebu'r eglwys yr oedd cafn wedi ei gloddio yng ngwely'r afon gan Richard Williams, tenant Ty'n Llan, gyda grisiau cerrig yn arwain o'r ffordd gyda bôn y clawdd ato. Mi fyddai dŵr yr afon yn crynhoi ac yn gogr-droi yma, cyn disgyn yn bistyll bach i'r cae islaw. O'r fan yma y byddai Richard Williams yn codi dŵr i'r gwartheg.

Eisteddem ein dau ar wal y bont yn syllu ar y dŵr yn gweu ei ffordd drwy'r brigau a'r cerrig ar wely'r afon.

'Mi fydd Nhad yn dŵad adra ar *leave* ymhen y mis.'

'Fydd o?'

'Pryd mae dy dad di am gael dŵad adra?'

'Wn i ddim. Roedd Mam yn deud y medrith o ddŵad unrhyw adag.'

Doeddwn i ddim yn hoffi siarad am fy nhad efo fo. Nid fod gen i gywilydd ohono fo, ond roedd tad Idris yn sowldiwr go iawn yn cario gwn ac yn gwisgo iwnifform ac yn cwffio mewn gwlad bell, tra oedd Nhad yn gweithio yn Lloegr yn adeiladu dociau i ddiogelu porthladdoedd rhag sybmarîns y Jyrmans. Nid ei fai o oedd hynny – mi driodd ei orau, ond doedd ei iechyd o ddim digon cryf i fod yn sowldiwr felly fe fu'n rhaid iddo fo wneud defnydd o'i brofiad fel saer coed ac adeiladydd i gefnogi'r ymdrech ryfel.

Tynnodd Idris gyllell o boced ei drowsus a dechrau naddu darn o bren yn bwrpasol.

'Be 'ti'n neud?'

'Llong. *Battleship.*'

'Be ti'n mynd i neud efo hi?'

''I gollwng hi i'r afon i edrach ddoith hi drwodd dan y bont i'r ochor arall.'

'Gad i mi fenthyg dy gyllall di? Mi gawn ni ras wedyn.'

Ac wedi dethol darn arall o frigyn a naddu tipyn fe lwyddwyd i lunio dwy long. Dyma sefyll ein dau uwch ben yr afon ac anelu'n ofalus am y ffrwd.

'Os daw fy llong i drwodd,' medda Idris, 'mi ddaw fy nhad adra'n saff o Jyrmani cyn diwedd y mis.'

'Olreit 'ta, ac mi ddaw 'nhad inna adra'n iach hefyd.'

'Tafla di gynta.'

'Na, tafla di. Dy syniad di oedd o.'

'O, olreit 'ta.'

Taflodd ei long yn syth i'r dŵr. Trodd ataf yn fuddugoliaethus.

'Dy dwrn di rŵan.'

Anelais a thaflu.

'Hei, mae dy long di wedi disgyn ar garrag!'

'Damia! Dydi hynny ddim yn deg. Mae'n iawn i'r ddwy gael cychwyn.'

'Olreit 'ta, rho hwyth fach iddi hi efo'r ffon 'ma. Mi rydw i am fynd i aros am fy un i yr ochor arall.'

Rhoddais swadan go egar i'm llong nes ei bod yn diflannu o dan y bont a rhedeg i'r ochr arall at Idris. Buom yno am sbel hir yn syllu i'r düwch o dan waelod y ffordd ond nid oedd arlliw o'r ddwy long.

'Wyt ti'm meddwl y daw hi?'

'Mae'n rhaid bod y ddwy wedi bachu yn rhywbeth.'

'Wyt ti'n meddwl y byddan ni'n twyllo 'tasan ni'n taflu carrag fawr i'r dŵr yn y pen arall er mwyn creu ton go fawr?'

'Na fyddan siŵr. Dim ond helpu dipyn bach arnyn nhw fyddan ni. Aros di, mi ollynga i garrag o ben y wal.'

Ar ôl bustachu tipyn mi lwyddais i ryddhau carreg go fawr o ben y wal a'i gollwng hi'n syth i'r dŵr, nes bod hwnnw'n tasgu.

'Weli di rwbath?'

'Na, dim byd.'

'Weli di rwbath rŵan 'ta?'

'Na... Gwela! Mae 'na rwbath yn dŵad – fy llong i ydi hi. Diolch byth – fydd fy nhad yn saff rŵan.'

'Weli di f'un i?'

'Ddim eto, ond ma' hi'n siŵr o ddŵad.'

'Mae hi'n gythgam o hir.'

'Gad i ni gael trei efo carrag ne' ddwy eto.'

'Olreit 'ta.'

'Wyt ti'n barod?'

A dyma ryddhau carreg fwy fyth.

'Rargian, os symudith rhywbeth hi, mi neith hon.'

A dyma hyrddio'r garreg at y dŵr islaw.

'Weli di rywbeth?'

'Na dim byd. Tria un arall…'

'Y tacla bach drwg i chi. Be 'dach chi'n drio'i neud? Malu cloddia felna. Rhoswch i mi'ch dal chi, mi…'

Ond wnaethon ni ddim aros, dim ond rhedeg am ein bywyd. A rhedeg y buon ni nes i bigyn gwynt ein harafu ni bron i hanner milltir o Dy'n Llan. Doedd Richard Williams, er ei fod o'r dyn clenia'n fyw dan amodau arferol, ddim yn ddyn i'w groesi.

Y noson honno wrth gario'r gannwyll ar hyd y lobi hir i'm gwely, roedd cysgodion yn troi pethau cyfarwydd yn fwganod yn fflam anwadal y gannwyll. Ond er cymaint y brawiau a godai gorfod cysgu am y wal â'r fynwent, nid ofn oedd yn cael y lle blaenaf yn fy meddwl. Yr oeddwn i'n dal i weld y llong bren yn stond ar wely oer yr afon a chofio'r llw ffôl a wnes wrth ei lluchio hi i'r dŵr. Dadwisgais, ar ôl tynnu'r llenni'n ofalus, gwthio rhwng y cynfasau, cau fy llygaid a dweud fy mhader. Fyddai'r paderau ffyrbwt arferol ddim yn gwneud y tro heno. Codais drachefn a phenlinio wrth erchwyn y gwely a gweddïo o'r frest, fel y byddai blaenoriaid yn arfer gwneud, am i Dduw warchod fy nhad rhag derbyn unrhyw niwed. Ar ôl dechrau cloff, fe ddechreuodd y geiriau lifo.

Wedi i mi fynd yn ôl i 'ngwely, fedrwn i yn fy myw gysgu. Gorweddais ar wastad fy nghefn yn syllu i'r tywyllwch yn dychmygu pob mathau o ddamweiniau erchyll – bomiau'n disgyn gan chwalu'r dociau, awyrennau'n poeri tân, pob math o olygfeydd erchyll... Cyn hir daeth fy mam a'm chwaer i'w gwelyau yn y llofft gyferbyn. Clywais hwy'n symud yn araf dros lawr y llofft gan sibrwd siarad rhag ofn fy neffro i. Yna, ymhen y rhawg, syrthiodd tawelwch y nos.

Fu hi ddim yn hir na chlywais sŵn cyfarwydd awyren yn y pellter. Daeth yn nes ac yn nes a sŵn ei pheiriant fel cacynen fygythiol yn entrych yr awyr. Jyrman oedd hi tybed? Craffais ar ei sŵn nes fy argyhoeddi fy hun mai awyren o'r Almaen ydoedd. Roedd grŵn y peiriant yn fy argyhoeddi fwyfwy mai bomar o'r Almaen oedd hi, ac y byddai'n gollwng ei llwyth marwol ar ein pennau a'n chwythu ni i gyd i ebargofiant. Ond mynd heibio wnaeth hi. Rhaid ei bod hi ar ei ffordd yn ôl o Lerpwl neu Firmingham ac wedi bwrw ei llwyth yno. Efallai bod fy nhad yn gorwedd yn gelain yn y ddinas fawr honno, neu lle bynnag oedd o, o dan domen o rwbel, ac arna i y byddai'r bai am hynny...

Wn i ddim a gysgais i ai peidio, ond mae'n rhaid fy mod i wedi hepian. Rywdro rhwng nos a bore torrodd sŵn newydd ar fy nghlyw – rhyw 'phwt-phwt-phwt' rheolaidd oedd hwn. Yr oedd yn sŵn cyfarwydd rywsut ond fedrwn i yn fy myw â'i leoli. Ai'n gryfach ac yn gryfach, ac fel y trodd y gornel wrth groesffordd y Tabernacl gyferbyn â'r tŷ mi wyddwn i'n union beth oedd o. Rhuodd i fyny'r ffordd ac aros gyda sglefriad o flaen y tŷ.

Neidiais o'm gwely â dagrau o lawenydd yn powlio o'm llygaid. Curais ar ddrws llofft Mam a gweiddi:

'Mam, Marian, deffrwch! Mae Dad wedi dŵad adra. Deffrwch, mae o newydd gyrraedd ar 'i foto-beic.'

Ac mi gerddodd Nhad drwy'r drws yn 'i ddillad moto-beic a'i gogls. Rhedais ato, a chododd yntau fi'n un darn at y nenfwd.

'Mi rwyt ti'n mynd yn fwy o ddyn bob dydd,' meddai'n floesg, a wnaeth o mo 'ngollwg i o'i afael am hir.

Daeth Mam a Marian i mewn ar hynny ac fe fu hen gofleidio a dagrau.

Mae'n debyg i Nhad fod ar y ffordd am oriau ac iddo adael Birmingham ymhell cyn iddi nosi.

'Fûm i rioed mor falch o weld Pont y Borth,' medda fo, 'ac roedd yr hen feic yn cyflymu wrth i mi gyrraedd "bryniau a phantiau Pentraeth" ac agosáu at adra.'

Er cymaint ei ludded, chafodd o ddim mynd i'w wely am hydoedd – fy chwaer a minnau am y gorau'n holi cwestiynau, 'Fydd rhaid i chi fynd yn ôl? Am faint gewch chi aros?', a Mam yn gofyn, 'Oes 'na ryw arwydd bod yr hen ryfal ma'n dŵad i ben?'

Doedd dim cartra hapusach yn y byd na'n tŷ ni y noson honno.

Ac mi ddaeth Pyrs Owen, Erw Ddu, adra yn 'i ddillad sowldiwr gan roi gwên ar wyneb teulu arall, ac aeth y llongau rhyfel yn Afon Ty'n Llan yn angof llwyr am hanner can mlynedd a mwy.

## Gorchwylion Tenantiaid

Roedd dydd Sul yn ddiwrnod prysur i bob aelod o'r teulu. Mi fyddai Nhad yn codi'n blygeiniol bron i gynnau tân glo yn y festri a'r parlwr, a Mam hithau cyn y gwasanaeth deg o'r gloch yn paratoi cinio o gig, llysiau tatws berw a thatws rhost a phwdin reis ar gyfer rhyw weinidog neu'i gilydd, a Marian a minnau'n helpu fel y medrem ni. Yn y gaeaf, pan fyddai'r gwasanaethau yn y capel, roedd angen cynnau'r chwe stôf baraffin i dwymo'r adeilad a mynd i'w golwg nhw bob hyn a hyn rhag ofn eu bod nhw'n mygu. Byddai Nhad wedi eu llenwi â pharaffin y noson cynt. Roedd hi'n dipyn haws pan ddechreuwyd ar yr arferiad o gynnal y gwasanaethau yn yr ysgoldy dros y gaeaf. Ein gwaith ni fel plant oedd twtio a gwneud yn siŵr nad oedd dim byd amheus neu anweddus ar gyfer y Sabath yng ngŵydd y cyhoedd. Mi wellodd pethau pan ddaeth trydan i oleuo a thwymo adeiladau'r capel tua diwedd y pedwardegau.

Fel y soniais eisoes, dulliau digon llafurus oedd yna i wresogi'r tŷ a'r capel cyn i drydan gyrraedd ein rhan arbennig ni o'r ardal. Ond roedd dull goleuo'r capel a'r ysgoldy yn ei ddydd yn fentrus ac arloesol. Roedd nwy carbaid wedi ei bibellu drwy'r adeilad. Calon y gweithgarwch cynhyrchu nwy oedd 'y cwt gias'. Ynddo yr oedd fersiwn bychan o'r tanciau nwy anferth y mae modd eu gweld heddiw ar gyrion trefi mawrion. Mewn gwirionedd, yr oedd dau danc – un ar i fyny a'r llall ben ucha'n isaf drosto, gyda'r tanc uchaf yn rhedeg ar fath o bwli. Y tanciau yma oedd yn dal y nwy. Fe gynhyrchid nwy carbaid o ganlyniad i effaith dŵr ar y darnau cerrig carbaid. Ar ddwy ochr y tanciau roedd math o diwb neu beipen gyda diamedr o tua naw modfedd. Ynddynt fe roddid cewyll o wifren ddur yn llawn o'r cerrig carbaid, gwthio pob cawell i ben draw'r tiwb, yna selio'r cyfan efo caead a oedd yn cael ei dynhau efo nyten. Wedi llenwi'r ddwy ochr, gollyngid dŵr ar y carbaid a chreu nwy a fyddai'n ymgasglu yn y tanc, gan godi'r tanc uchaf ar bwli fel yr oedd yn llenwi. Yna fe roddid pwysau ar ben y tanc nes gwthio'r nwy ar hyd y pibellau i'r capel, y festri a'r ysgoldy – ond nid i'r tŷ.

Er nad oedd fflam ddisglair yn y lampau nwy, yr oedd ar y cyfan yn fwy diogel ac yn llai trafferthus na'r lampau paraffîn oedd yn y capeli eraill. Fel yr oeddwn yn tyfu'n hŷn, fy nhasg i fyddai llenwi a gwagio'r cewyll. Gwaith digon drewllyd a budr oedd o ac roedd effaith y dŵr ar y cerrig carbaid yn creu hylif gwyn yr oedd yn rhaid ei grafu o du mewn y ddau diwb a'i gario i'r domen y tu allan.

Roedd rhai manteision mewn bod yn gyfrifol am 'y cwt gias'. Fe gyrhaeddai'r carbaid mewn drymiau dur, pob un o'r drymiau efo caead tyn rhag ofn i leithder fynd at y carbaid. Er nad oeddwn i'n gallu rhoi fy nwylo ar gerrig carbaid di-ben-draw, fe allwn gael gafael ar ambell lond llaw heb i neb sylweddoli hynny. Roedd yn ddeunydd bargeinio da efo plant eraill, gan y gellid rhoi carbaid a dŵr mewn potel, gosod corcyn arni, ac yna byddai pwysau'r nwy yn chwythu'r corcyn allan fel ergyd o wn. Defnydd arall (ychydig yn fwy peryglus!) oedd rhoi darn o garbaid mewn tun triog gwag, ychwanegu ychydig bach o ddŵr, cau'r caead yn dynn, a gwneud twll o faint pìn yn ochr y tun. Yna dal matsen wrth y twll – ac achosi ffrwydrad!

Digwyddiadau anaml oedd mentrau masnachol o'r fath. Roedd dylanwad y Beibl fel cas lledr yn cau yn dynn o amgylch bywyd hogyn tŷ capel. Oedd, roedd gan grefydd bresenoldeb a oedd yn treiddio i bob agwedd a thwll a chornel o fywyd beunyddiol.

Roedd 'iaith capel' yn unigryw. Nid yn unig roedd iaith yr emynau a'r darlleniadau o'r Beibl yn goeth a chyhyrog, ond yr oedd iaith mynegiant y gweinidogion a'r blaenoriaid – yr iaith dydd Sul – yn enghreifftiau o'r iaith lafar ar ei gorau, hyd yn oed os oedd hi ychydig yn hen ffasiwn a braidd yn ystrydebol yng nghyhoeddiadau ambell un o'r blaenoriaid.

I mi, roedd geiriau fel 'gras', 'tangnefedd' a 'thragwyddoldeb' yn eiriau cyffredin. O ran amlder eu defnydd roeddynt yn eiriau cyfarwydd, hyd yn oed os oedd eu hystyron yn niwlog. I 'hogyn tair-gwaith-y-Sul', roedd cysyniadau fel 'Cyfiawnhad trwy Ffydd' a'r 'Iawn' yn athrawiaethau a oedd yn hofran ar ymylon dealltwriaeth. Ac os oedd 'tân uffern' wedi troi'n lludw llwyd, roedd 'pechod' yn wirionedd a 'chabledd' yn dal i fod yn achos dychryn ac ofn. Roedd y Deg Gorchymyn negyddol gyda'i 'na wna hyn' a 'na wna'r llall' yn llinyn mesur moesoldeb cymdeithas gapelyddol, ac i rai roedd y 'llo aur' yntau yn dal i fod yn fygythiad – yn enwedig i'r ifanc.

Fel plant, mae'n sicr bod y rhan fwyaf ohonom yn gwybod llawer iawn mwy am hanes gwlad Canaan nag am hanes Cymru. Roedd gorchestion a chwedloniaeth brenhinoedd fel Dafydd a Solomon yn llawer mwy cyfarwydd na Hywel Dda neu Lewelyn ein Llyw Olaf, Goliath yn fwy o gawr nag Ysbaddaden Bencawr, y tri llanc yn y ffwrn dân yn fwy o ryfeddod na Bendigeidfran yn cerdded dros y môr i Iwerddon ac yn llunio pont â'i gorff, Jiwdas Iscariot yn fwy o ddrwgweithredwr nag Efnisien, a Dafydd efo'i ffon dafl yn fwy dethe ei law na Lleu Llaw Gyffes. Y gwir plaen oedd na wyddem ni fel plant fawr ddim am Owain Glyndŵr a'i wrthryfel nac am chwedlau'r Mabinogi, oherwydd ein bod ni wedi etifeddu hanes a diwylliant estron yn gyfan gwbl bron ac am fod dysgeidiaeth yr Ysgol Sul a dylanwad y capel yn drech na chwricwlwm ysgol ddyddiol.

Ac roedd yr un peth yn wir am ein gwybodaeth ddaearyddol. Prin oedd ein gwybodaeth am leoedd y tu hwnt i Bont y Borth. Roedd lleoliad Jeriwsalem a Jerico, Capernaum a Bethesda yn wybyddus i ni ar fap o Wlad Canaan yn yr Ysgol Sul, tra bod Caerdydd, Abertawe a hyd yn oed Wrecsam a'r Wyddgrug yn fannau dieithr pellennig. Yr oedd y Rhyl, fodd bynnag, yn hynod o gyfarwydd, gan mai yma'n ddieithriad bron y byddai bysys Niwbwrch yn mynd â ni ar dripiau Ysgol Sul. Un peth a achosai benbleth i mi'n blentyn oedd bod pentrefi o'r enw Bethesda, Carmel a Cesarea i'w canfod yng Nghymru; sylweddoli wedyn, wrth gwrs, mai pentrefi wedi eu henwi ar ôl capeli oedden nhw.

Peth arall pwysig yr oedd hogyn Tŷ Capel yn ei etifeddu bron yn ddi-feth oedd cydwybod! Pa un a oedd o'n dda neu ddrwg wrth reddf neu wrth natur, yr oedd byw yng ngwynt crefydd yn rhoi iddo'r adnoddau angenrheidiol i wybod y gwahaniaeth rhwng da a drwg ac, yn dilyn hynny, i gael brath go egr ym mhlygion ei gydwybod os digwyddai dramgwyddo trwy dorri rhai o'r rheolau mwyaf sylfaenol.

Lawer gwaith mi fûm i'n edrych ar fy nhad a'm mam yn paratoi'r llestri a'r bara a'r gwin ar gyfer gwasanaeth y Cymun. Mi fyddai Nhad yn prynu gwin Cymun arbennig mewn siop yn Llangefni, gwin di-alcohol fel y deuthum i wybod yn ddiweddarach. Fe gedwid llestri arian y Cymun mewn cwpwrdd gwydr derw yn festri'r capel. Byddai Mam yn eu glanhau – y platiau bara, y daliwr gwydrau a'r tebot arian oedd yn dal y gwin – nes eu bod yn sgleinio fel swllt newydd, a byddai'n llathru'r gwydrau bychain nes eu bod fel grisial. Yna byddai'n torri tafellau gweddol denau o fara, torri'r crystyn ymaith, ac yna sgorio'r tafellau bara'n sgwariau bychain efo cyllell fel bod y gweinidog yn gallu 'torri'r bara' yn gymen yn y gwasanaeth. Fy nhad fyddai'n tywallt y gwin i'r llestr arian ac yn llenwi rhai o'r gwydrau bychain cyn y gwasanaeth. Gosodid y cyfan yn ddefodol wedyn ar liain bwrdd claerwyn ar fwrdd mewn man canolog yn y Sêt Fawr.

Ar bob sedd yn y capel roedd dolenni dur crwn gyferbyn â phob eisteddle, lle y gellid gadael y gwydrau a'r platiau bychain otanynt ar ôl y gwasanaeth. Fy ngwaith i a Marian fyddai casglu'r rhain wedi i'r gynulleidfa fynd adref. Yn ddieithriad, byddai pob gwydr gwin yn wag!

Mi fûm i'n dyheu sawl tro am gael blasu gwin cymun ond doedd dim yn tycio. Roedd y Cymun yn ddefod gysegredig ac fe fyddai'n rhaid i mi gael fy nerbyn 'yn gyflawn aelod' cyn cael profi'r gwin. Un diwrnod, a minnau yn y tŷ ar fy mhen fy hun, mi ddigwyddais sylwi ar botel win dri chwarter llawn yn y cwpwrdd gwydr yn y festri. Dyma agor y cwpwrdd, tynnu'r corcyn, ogleuo'r gwin ac yna cymryd joch sydyn. Siomedig iawn oedd y blas. Rhoddais y corcyn yn ei ôl yn ofalus a gosod y botel yn ei hôl yn yr union fan, ac aros. Ddigwyddodd dim. Yna fe ddechreuodd brath cydwybod gnoi ac achosi ofn y byddai Duw'n dial arnaf am gyflawni'r fath weithred. Am ddyddiau bwygilydd mi fûm i'n disgwyl dyrnod o'r entrychion, disgwyl am farn anochel Duw am fy nghamweddau cableddus. Ychydig cyn hynny yr oeddem ni wedi cael pregeth ar y proffwyd Amos ac fel yr oedd Duw yn dial am gamweddau pobl Israel os oeddynt yn gwyro yn eu hymddygiad. Disgwyl yn ofer y bûm i am i Dduw Amos, Duw cyfiawn yr Hen Destament, fy nghosbi – diolch am hynny.

Fel y crybwyllais eisoes, roedd mynd i'r capel dair gwaith y Sul ac i'r Seiat a'r Cyfarfod Gweddi yn ystod yr wythnos yn rheidrwydd, yn orfodaeth nad oedd modd ei hosgoi ond ar adegau o afiechyd difrifol fel y frech goch neu glwy'r pennau. Ers yr adeg y cawsom ni drydan i'r adeiladau (a hyd yn oed cyn hynny, os cofia i'n iawn), roedd hi'n arferiad gennym ni yn y Tabernacl aeafu yn llofft y capel – neu'r 'ysgoldy' fel y byddai rhai o'r blaenoriaid yn ei galw. Roedd amryw o resymau dros hyn. Y rheswm pennaf oedd un economaidd gan fod llofft y capel yn haws ac yn rhatach i'w thwymo. Ar ben hyn, mewn cyfnod o leihad mewn presenoldeb, fe edrychai cynulleidfa'n fwy yno gyda phawb yn nes at ei gilydd, yn hytrach na bod ar wasgar fesul un a dau yn eu seddi eu hunain yn adeilad mwy y capel. Ac roedd llai o flas 'Methodistiaid, pobol fawr' yn llofft y capel gan nad oedd neb yn berchen sêt, ac er bod pulpud yno doedd dim Sêt Fawr fel y cyfryw, dim ond tair mainc ar letraws lle'r eisteddai'r blaenoriaid. Meinciau cyffredin oedd y rheiny, yn union fel gweddill y meinciau. Mae'n wir bod y pulpud ychydig yn uwch na'r meinciau a bod clustog go grand ar sedd yr organyddes ond does yr un gymdeithas yn berffaith! Ar y cyfan, yr oeddem ni'n eithaf democrataidd. Gwneid un cyfaddawd go bwysig – câi clustogau seddi'r capel eu cario i'r ysgoldy, ond mater o hap a damwain oedd hi pwy oedd yn digwydd eistedd ar y glustog fwyaf cyfforddus.

Ys gwn i a fyddai, ac a fydd, meddyliau blaenoriaid a gweinidogion yn crwydro wrth wrando ar bregethau a gweddïau'r naill a'r llall? Rhaid i mi gyfaddef mai rhwng pedair wal capel y byddai fy meddwl i'n crwydro wylltaf a'm dychymyg yn aml iawn ar ei fwyaf toreithiog. Mae'n debyg bod hyn oll â'i wreiddiau yn y cyfnod gorfodol, y cyfnod pan oedd yn rhaid eistedd yn ddiddig drwy darlleniadau, gweddïau a phregethau a oedd ymhell y tu hwnt i'm hamgyffred. Mae'n debyg i'r meddwl, bryd hynny, ddyfeisio dulliau diddorol ac anghrefyddol o dreulio, a hyd yn oed o ladd, amser.

Un dull oedd gwneud pob math o symiau yn y pen ar sail rhifau'r emynau a'r tonau a fyddai'n cael eu dangos ar y bwrdd pren ar bwys y pulpud. Pa rif fyddai'n ymddangos amlaf, p'run oedd yr ail – 'ac ymlaen', fel y byddai ledwyr yr emynau hynny'n arfer ei ddweud! Yna fe ellid gwneud pob math o symiau lluosi, tynnu a rhannu nes y byddai'r meddwl yn chwil ac amser yn carlamu. Wedi dihysbyddu'r bwrdd emynau, fe ellid cyfrif faint o gwareli gwydr oedd ym mhob ffenestr a lluosi'r rhain er mwyn cael cyfanswm ar gyfer y capel cyfan. Ac, wrth gwrs, fe fyddid yn cyfrif sawl aelod oedd yn bresennol yn Sabothol ym mhob gwasanaeth. Digwyddai'r ymarferion cyfrif hyn gan mwyaf yn y capel mawr, ac mae'n syndod i mi na fyddwn wedi datblygu'n well mathemategydd.

Yn llofft y capel, roedd pob dim gymaint yn llai, o ran amlder a maint. Roedd llai o ffenestri a dim ond pedair cwarel fawr oedd ym mhob ffenest, ac roedd llai o seddau neu o feinciau. Hefyd, wrth gwrs, un llawr oedd i'r adeilad, ac mewn awyrgylch mor glòs roedd hi'n anodd troi eich pen i gyfrif pobol. A doedd dim bwrdd cyhoeddi rhifau emynau a thonau yno chwaith. O ganlyniad, roedd yn rhaid i'r dychymyg fod yn llawer mwy dyfeisgar yn yr ysgoldy.

Un fantais i lofft y capel, yn wahanol i'r capel mawr, oedd bod modd gweld y byd y tu allan drwy'r ffenestri. Drwyddynt roedd byd natur yn wrthrych haws ei werthfawrogi gan fod amser wrth gefn i sylwi ar newidiadau mewn lliwiau a thyfiant ac anwadalwch y gorwel. Ar ddiwrnod clir fe ellid gweld aruthredd mynyddoedd Eryri yn codi'n haen ar ben haen yn y pellter. Dro arall prin y gellid gweld y tu hwnt i Quarry Bank dri lled cae i ffwrdd. Fe fyddai detholiad da o adar yn mynd a dod ar eu rhawd: brân neu ddwy, gwylanod y Benllech a Moelfre ar dywydd drycin, drudwy yn gymylau duon yn eu tymor, ambell robin goch yn hawlio ei gynefin ac, yn llai aml, cudyll coch yn hofran cyn disgyn ar ei ysglyfaeth – a hynny ar ddydd Sul!

Prin oedd y ceir a fyddai'n mynd heibio. Er bod modd gweld darn o'r brif ffordd rhwng Llangefni a'r Benllech, fe allech fynd am dri chwarter pregeth heb weld yr un car. Ond yr oeddynt yn werth aros amdanynt. Roedd nam yng ngwydr un ffenest – ploryn o chwydd yn y gwydr – ac os digwyddech ddilyn car ar hyd y ffordd, fe fyddai'n rhoi sbonc sydyn wrth gyrraedd y llecyn hwnnw cyn parhau'n wastad lyfn am weddill ei daith. Digwyddiad cyffrous ac arbennig oedd gweld 'car sbonc'.

Dro arall fe fyddai fy nychymyg yn cael penrhyddid llwyr. Yn amlach na pheidio y symbyliad cyntaf fyddai gair neu enw yng nghorff y bregeth, a gallai hwnnw arwain i unrhyw le ac i bobman. Fe allai'r gair 'torf', er enghraifft, esgor ar gêm bêl-droed a minnau'n arwr torf anferth ar gae Bangor yn ergydio'r bêl i gefn y rhwyd. Gallai 'pysgotwyr dynion' droi'n ôl yn bysgotwyr pysgod, a minnau'n tynnu lein a 'sbinnar'o gefn cwch injan a phentwr o fecryll yn gwingo wrth fy nhraed. A byddai'r gair 'tystiolaeth' yn mynd â fi i fyd ditectifs fel John Aubrey a oedd yn datrys lladradau a llofruddiaethau. Bryd hynny, ni fyddai llais y gweinidog yn ddim namyn grŵn pell yn y cefndir...

## Pregethwrs a Blaenoriaid

Fynnwn i ddim am y byd greu'r argraff bod pob Sul yn ddiflas, pob pregethwr a gweinidog yn syrffedus hirwyntog, a phob blaenor y tu hwnt i amgyffred a dirnadaeth plentyn. Dim o gwbl. Mae'n wir bod 'na rai gweinidogion hirwyntog diflas oedd yn gallu gwneud i amser rygnu neu hyd yn oed aros yn ei unfan ond, ar yr un pryd, roedd 'na gyfarwyddiaid o weinidogion oedd yn gallu creu darluniau byw, disglair a chofiadwy efo geiriau. Roedd 'hogyn tair-gwaith-y-Sul' yn gallu dweud y gwahaniaeth rhwng y rhain yn bur dda, ac fe ddysgodd profiad sut i adnabod y rhai hirfaith a diflas o'r foment y byddent yn ymddangos yn y pulpud am y tro cyntaf. Roedd rhywbeth dadlennol mewn osgo corff, yn nhôn llais ac ym mhryd a gwedd y gwrthrych a fyddai'n datgan bron yn ddi-feth pa fath o bregethwr fyddai o.

Fe fyddai'r pregethwyr *gwaethaf* yn dechrau'r gwasanaeth i'r eiliad ar ben yr awr. Byddai ei ddarlleniad, gan amlaf, bum munud neu ddeg yn feithach na'r arfer. Ni fyddai'n darllen yr emynau'n llawn, dim ond darllen llinell neu ddwy a dweud 'ac ymlaen', neu 'mi ganwn ni'r emyn drwyddi'. Byddai'r weddi'n para am gryn ugain munud ac yn llawn dyfyniadau digon digyswllt o adnodau ac emynau, nes gwneud dilyn trywydd meddyliau'r gweddïwr yn anodd. Tua phum munud ar hugain i'r awr fe gychwynnid

61

ar y bregeth ei hun. Yn bur aml fe fyddai pedwar pen yn hytrach na thri, ac fe fyddai'r rhain yn cael eu hailadrodd fel tiwn gron. Ni fyddai unrhyw arwydd am orffen ar yr awr na hyd yn oed bum neu ddeng munud wedi'r awr. Tua 'chwartar wedi', byddai synau cau pen y mwdwl yn dechrau dod i'n clyw – rhyw newid yn y llais, ymgais at grynhoi ac ailadrodd amlach. Ond bob tro y teimlech ei fod am ddiweddu, mi fyddai fel rhedwr marathon yn cael ail wynt ac yn ailgychwyn. Rhwng ugain munud a phum munud ar hugain wedi'r awr fe ddeuai diwedd sydyn – annisgwyl braidd – ond mi fyddai hi'n rhyddhad mawr cael 'mynd ymlaen' i ganu'r emyn olaf, hyd yn oed os oeddem ni'n 'canu'r emyn drwyddi'.

Ond nid dyna'r cyfan! Yn amlach na pheidio fe fyddai pregethwr tila yn berchen ar lais amhersain ac undonog, oedd yn mynnu dilyn rhyw diwn ddi-diwn ddiflas fyddai'n llesteirio gwrando ac yn cymylu deall. Prin bod ganddo na theimlad at iaith nac at rin geiriau, ac roedd rhythmau naturiol mynegiant llafar yn beth cwbl ddieithr iddo.

Mor wahanol, yn ôl y brith gof sydd gennyf, oedd pregeth gan Tom Nefyn mewn cyfarfod pregethu yn y capel mawr. Roedd y capel yn orlawn, a minnau – yn groes i bob arfer – wedi cael mynd i eistedd i'r galeri. O'r cychwyn cyntaf, roedd y Tom Nefyn 'ma'n siarad efo ni, yn cyfathrebu efo ni yn blant ac oedolion ar draws pob rhychwant gallu. Chofia i mo'i bregeth o – doeddwn i fawr o beth ar y pryd – ond mi gofia i iddo gyfarch cymeriadau o'r Beibl yn y capel. Rhywbeth fel:

'Helô, Pedr! *Ti* sydd yna…?'

Fe daerech fod Pedr yn eistedd ar ganllaw'r pulpud! Ac

fe ddaeth disgyblion eraill a Phawl ei hun i'r galeri o fewn deg llath i mi. Anghofia i byth ddrama'r amgylchiad.

Un arall a allai wefreiddio efo geiriau oedd Idwal Jones, Llanrwst – awdur *SOS Galw Gari Tryfan*. Roedd yntau heb ei ail am ddweud stori, am wneud y cymhleth yn syml a'r dyrys yn ddiddorol. Roedd ganddo fo a Thom Nefyn leisiau swynol a pharch at rythmau naturiol iaith a chariad at eiriau. Eithriadau, yn anffodus, oedd y math yma o bregethwr.

Pobl gyffredin oedd y blaenoriaid i gyd, dynion bob un. Seiri coed oedd tri ohonynt – H. R. Rowlands, Awelon; Owen Llewelyn Williams, Bryn Neuadd (tad Gwyn Llewelyn, y darlledwr), a Nhad. Yna tri ffermwr – Owen Williams, Tyn-y-gongl Ffarm; John Williams, Ty'n Tro, a Robert Roberts, Brynhyrddin. Y ddau arall oedd W. D. Williams, Hafod Wyn, siopwr wedi ymddeol, a T. H. Hughes, a oedd yn ysgolfeistr ar ysgol Llaneugrad. Ar wahân i Owen Llewelyn Williams a T. H. Hughes, nid oedd gan yr un ohonynt ddawn gyhoeddus arbennig ond gwnaent y gorau o'r doniau a gawsant; ble collent mewn graen gyhoeddus 'broffesiynol', enillent mewn naturioldeb a diffuantrwydd.

Does gen i ddim cof o gwbl i mi glywed Mr Rowlands, Awelon na W. D Williams, Hafod Wyn, yn cymryd rhan yn gyhoeddus. Fel 'Wil Dan' y byddid yn cyfeirio at yr olaf y tu ôl i'w gefn, ac mi fyddai rhai yn ychwanegu sillaf arall go aflednais ar ôl y Dan. Roedd WD wedi ymddeol ac yn byw ar ei arian pan oeddwn i'n ei gofio fo. Roedd o'n un o'r ychydig oedd yn berchen car, Awstin 12 du. Roedd o'n gefnogwr pêl-droed brwd ac ar adegau mi fyddai Nhad a minnau'n cael mynd efo fo ar ddydd Sadwrn i weld Dinas

Bangor yn chwarae. Tâl fyddai hyn fel arfer am gymwynas a wnaed gan fy nhad fel saer coed.

Gŵr gweddw oedd John Williams, Ty'n Tro, ac roedd ganddo un ferch mewn oed, Serah Ann, a oedd ychydig bach yn syml. Byddai Serah Ann yn arfer galw ambell waith cyn yr oedfa ar nos Sul, ac yn ddieithriad ar ôl yr oedfa i aros i'w thad orffen trafodaethau a smôc y blaenoriaid yn y festri. Roedd John Williams yn weddïwr huawdl a gwreiddiol, ac ambell waith fe glywid y pethau rhyfeddaf ganddo pan fyddai'n bwrw ei lid ar bechaduriaid yr oes.

Gan fod y Benllech yn bentref glan môr poblogaidd, roedd Saeson ar wyliau haf wedi bod yn torri'r Saboth yn deilchion ers tro byd, gan ymdrochi a thorheulo a dangos rhannau helaeth o'u cyrff ar y Sul. Yn fwy diweddar, roedd pobl frodorol y sir wedi dechrau eu hefelychu a chyrchu i'r traeth ar y Sul, a byddai byseidiau ohonynt yn cyrraedd bob prynhawn Sul heulog o haf. Fyddai wiw i ni blant y capel fynd yn agos i'r un traeth ar y Sul, er bod rhai cyplau caru yn mynd am dro i gyfeiriad y môr ambell nos Sul ar ôl yr oedfa. Rhaid bod hyn yn achosi cryn boen meddwl i John Williams. Meddai yn ystod ei weddi mewn cyfarfod gweddi un nos Sul: 'Gwarchod ni, O! Dduw Dad, rhag cabledd yr oes sydd ohoni. Pobol Niwbwrch yn heigio i ddraethau'r Benllech yn eu bysys, a'r diafol wrth y llyw.'

Yn ei henaint fe aeth yr hen John Williams yn ddigon rhyfedd. Bob nos Sul, fe gâi Mam a fy chwaer a minnau saga'r garreg fedd gan Serah Ann.

'Wyddoch chi be, Mrs Owen bach, mae Tada wedi dewis darn o lechan fel carrag fedd iddo fo'i hun, ac mae o wrthi bob cyfla geith o yn siapio ac yn llyfnu'r garrag. Does dim modd dal pen rheswm efo fo.'

Ymhen peth amser fe ailgydiai yn ei stori:

'Wyddoch chi be mae o'n 'i wneud rŵan?'

Distawrwydd dramatig.

'Mae o wedi dechra torri ei enw yn y llechan: "John Williams, Tyddyn Tro".'

Beth amser yn ddiweddarach: 'Mae o wedi gorffan ei enw'n ddigon destlus. Mae o wrthi rŵan yn torri adnod o'r Beibl.'

Ac yna, ymhen rhai wythnosau: 'Mae o wedi gorffen sgwennu ar y garreg ei enw, enw'r tŷ a'r adnod – ond dydi o ddim wedi rhoi'r dyddiad eto'!

Does dim byd gwaeth ac anos i'w reoli na chwerthin mewn lle o addoliad. Yn amlach na pheidio fe all y rheswm dros y chwerthin fod yn un digon tila, ond bod parchusrwydd a'r ymdeimlad o barchedig ofn sydd yn rhan o'r amgylchedd, a'r orfodaeth – yn wir, y rheidrwydd – i ymatal rhag chwerthin yn gwneud y sefyllfa'n ganmil gwaeth. Cymaint yw'r awydd i ffrwyno'r chwerthin nes y bydd yn siŵr o orffen mewn ffrwydrad swnllyd maes o law.

Mi gefais i ffit o chwerthin fwy nag unwaith yn y capel mawr, ond roedd ffit o'r fath yn ystod gwasanaeth yn *llofft* y capel yn waeth o lawer, gan fod pawb yn gymaint nes at ei gilydd a dim modd cuddio na mygu'r chwerthin na'i droi yn ffit o besychu.

Cyfarfod gweddi fore Sul oedd hi, a mwy nag un o'r blaenoriaid wedi cymryd rhan. Yna fe gododd Owen Williams, Tyn-y-gongl Ffarm, i ledio emyn. Gwyddwn cyn iddo fo agor ei geg beth fyddai ei ddewis emyn a doedd hi fawr o gamp fy mod i wedi canfod yr union dudalen cyn iddo fo gyhoeddi rhif yr emyn fel 'saith gant pewar deg ag un'. Yr un emyn fyddai ganddo bob amser, a rhaid ei fod o'n ei gwybod hi ar dafod leferydd.

Tan y bore arbennig hwnnw nid oeddwn wedi sylwi ar eironi'r geiriau pan oedd o yn eu traddodi. Fel y llafarganai'r cwpled:

> 'Mor hawdd yw rhifo'r tywod,
> Neu'r gwallt sydd ar fy mhen...'

fe ddaeth pwl afreolus o chwerthin drosof. Doedd gan Owen Williams brin flewyn ar ei ben; roedd o mor foel a llyfn â phen-ôl babi. Mewn sefyllfa normal mi fyddai sylweddoliad o'r fath yn haeddu gwên fechan, dim mwy. Fe ddechreuodd y chwerthin rywle tua gwaelodion fy 'sennau. Gwesgais gefn y fainc o'm blaen nes oedd fy migyrnau'n wyn a brathais fy ngwefus hyd at waed i geisio atal yr hwrdd anochel o chwerthin, ond i ddim pwrpas. Mi ffrwydrodd 'na bwff swnllyd nes bod pennau'n troi a llygaid yn ceryddu. Drwy drugaredd fe ddechreuodd yr organ ganu'r arweiniad i'r emyn, a chyn pen dim ymunodd y lleisiau â hi nes boddi fy synau i. Drwy'r weddi a oedd yn dilyn, gyda chymorth cadach poced yn fy ngheg, fe aeth y plyciau chwerthin yn llai ac yn llai nes marw mewn sobrwydd llwyr.

Llithrais allan rhag wynebu fy nhad ond fe ddilynodd fi i'r gegin a mynnu cael eglurhad am fy ymddygiad. Pan ddywedais wrtho'r rheswm dros fy chwerthin, chwerthin wnaeth yntau, nes bod Mam a Marian, fy chwaer yn sbïo'n wirion ar y ddau ohonom.

# Yr Ysgoldy

Ond nid defnydd caeth grefyddol oedd i lofft y capel yn ddieithriad. Yr oedd ar adegau yn ganolfan ac yn fan cyfarfod cymdeithasol i'r ardal ehangach, ac yn wir yn ganolfan dra eciwmenaidd gan ei bod yn denu Annibynwyr, Bedyddwyr ac Eglwyswyr.

Yno, cyn eisteddfodau, y byddai Côr Bro Goronwy yn ymarfer – côr cymysg bryd hynny o dan arweiniad J. C. Parry. Byddai'r cantorion yn cyrraedd fesul un a dau o gwmpas wyth o'r gloch fin nos. Cerddent i mewn drwy'n drws ffrynt ni ac yna dringo'r grisiau coed i'r ysgoldy.

Fûm i erioed yn llygad dyst i ymarfer côr ond fe glywais ugeiniau ohonynt gan fod sain y gerddoriaeth yn treiddio i lawr drwy'r nenfwd i'r gegin a thrwy'r parwydydd i'm llofft. Byddai JC yn rhoi'r sopranos, yr altos, y tenoriaid a'r baswyr drwy eu pethau yn eu tro. Weithiau fe fyddid yn rhygnu ar yr un cymal dro ar ôl tro nes ei berffeithio. Bryd hynny, byddai llais JC yn llwyddo i'w amlygu ei hun er gwaethaf y llu o leisiau oedd yn bresennol.

Pan fyddai cystadleuaeth eisteddfod yn agosáu byddai'r ymarferiadau'n amlach ac yn llawer meithach. Mae'n debyg i mi syrthio i gysgu yn sŵn 'Teyrnasoedd y Ddaear' fwy nag unwaith.

Gweithgarwch cymdeithasol arall, er ei fod yn perthyn i'r capel, oedd y Sosial. Wn i ddim pam y glynwyd at yr enw Saesneg arno gan fod yr achlysur ei hun yn un cwbl Gymraeg – noson gymdeithasol o fwyta ac adloniant cartref.

Cyn gynted ag y byddai Nhad adref o'i waith fe fyddem yn mynd ati i baratoi'r ysgoldy ar gyfer yr achlysur. Roedd angen troi'r meinciau yn barau i wynebu ei gilydd a gosod y byrddau tresel rhyngddynt. Yna byddai Mam a Marian yn gosod llieiniau ar y byrddau pren a thynnu llestri'r capel allan o'r fasged wellt – llestri efo 'Capel y Tabernacl M.C.' wedi eu stampio arnynt. Yna byddid yn cynnau tân yn y grât ac yn llenwi'r wrn haearn efo dŵr, a'i gosod ar y tân i ferwi mewn da bryd. Rywbryd yn ystod y bore byddai cyflenwad o fara tun gwyn a bara brith wedi cyrraedd o fecws Marian-glas.

Yn gynnar gyda'r nos byddai merched y Capel yn cyrraedd â'u basgedi'n llwythog o gacennau, past cig, wyau wedi'u berwi'n galed, llefrith, siwgr a menyn. Yn eu plith roedd Mrs Rowlands, Awelon; Mrs Roberts, Quarry Bank; Mrs Owen, Olgra Fawr; Bet Thomas, Penmeysydd (oedd hefyd yn gyfeilyddes ac yn dwyn yr enw barddol 'Eryl y Môr' yng Ngorsedd Môn); Mrs Parry, Bodlondeb, a Mrs Owen, North – byddin o ferched fyddai'n mynd ati i baratoi bwyd ar gyfer porthi'r lluoedd.

Byddai'r rhain yn torri'r bara'n dafellau cymen, yn taenu'r menyn, yn eu llenwi â chaws a wyau a phast cig, ac yn eu pentyrru ar blatiau. Hwy fyddai'n gosod y byrddau, a phan gyrhaeddai'r gynulleidfa, hwy fyddai'n gweini'r danteithion gan dywallt cwpaneidiau o de berwedig o debotiau metel o faint tegell, ac yn cymell pawb i 'estyn am y bwyd'.

Fe fyddid yn gwledda am awr a mwy nes bod boliau

pawb yn grwn. Yna fe fyddid yn clirio'r byrddau, yn rhoi'r byrddau tresel o'r neilltu ac yn troi'r meinciau i wynebu'r pulpud, a oedd i wasanaethu fel llwyfan ar gyfer y cyngerdd.

Cymysgfa ddiddorol fyddai hwnnw fel arfer. Rhai o'r plant yn canu ac yn adrodd – cynnyrch y Gylchwyl neu ambell ymgais aflwyddiannus o Eisteddfod Marian-glas, a minnau yn eu mysg. Yna fe geid cystadleuaeth darllen darn heb ei atalnodi a oedd yn creu doniolwch wrth i frawddegau redeg i'w gilydd a chreu penbleth i'r darllenwyr. Fel arfer, byddai Marian a Mam yn adrodd. Byddai ambell un yn dweud stori ddoniol, llawer ohonynt yn rhai cyfarwydd, neu adrodd stori celwydd golau. Ymysg y goreuon roedd Ned, Tan y Bryn, oedd hefyd yn faswr o fri, ac fe fyddai ei dad, Richard Jones, yn chwarae alawon ar yr organ geg. Unwaith fe ddaeth rhyw ddyn diarth yno a oedd yn canu alawon ar li drwy dynnu bwa ffidil dros ei meingefn a phlygu'r lli ar ei lin i greu'r nodau. Un o uchafbwyntiau'r noson oedd pan godai John Ty'n Lôn i ganu 'Cloch y Llan' yn ei denor soniarus, efo un llygad ar gau ac yntau wedi ymgolli'n llwyr yn nheimladrwydd y gân.

Uchafbwynt pendant arall oedd pan godai Richard Davies i adrodd. Deryn brith oedd Richard Davies a dreuliodd ran o'i fywyd fel crwydryn. Cafodd ei gyflogi fel gwas yn Tudor Villa, ac yn ystod y cyfnod yma fe gafodd dröedigaeth grefyddol. Daeth yn aelod gyda'r Bedyddwyr yn Seion, ac roedd yn weddïwr gwlithog a gwreiddiol. Un adroddiad oedd ganddo, sef 'Mae Popeth Wedi Codi', ond roedd o'n adroddiad newydd bob tro gan fod Richard Davies yn ychwanegu ato'n fyrfyfyr wrth fynd ymlaen gan restru nwyddau fel bisgedi, sigaréts a baco, sgidiau ac yn y blaen at y pethau oedd wedi codi yn eu pris, heb drafferthu i barchu na mydr nac odl. Dyn diniwed oedd o ond dyn diffuant, ac roedd y gynulleidfa'n chwerthin efo fo yn hytrach nag am ei ben.

Mawredd y nosweithiau hynny oedd bod y gymdeithas yn dod at ei gilydd i weld a chlywed pobl leol yn perfformio – 'sosial' yng ngwir ystyr y gair!

# Y Fynwent

Roedd y fynwent yn ymestyn o ddrws cefn Tŷ Capel yn rhimyn gweddol gul ar hyd cefn y capel ei hun, gan ymledu gyda'r talcen pellaf ac ymestyn hyd at led cae o'r lôn fawr rhwng y Benllech a Bryn-teg. Roedd y darn wrth y drws cefn yn hen ac yn cynnwys beddi cist gan mwyaf, gyda charreg lwyd weddol drwchus yn llunio copa ac ochrau'r cistiau. Erbyn fy nghyfnod i roedd y gwynt a'r glaw a'r rhew wedi erydu'r ysgrifen oddi ar y beddi hynaf neu roedd cen wedi tyfu ar wyneb y garreg, fel ei bod yn anodd os nad yn amhosibl darllen y cofiant i'r meirw. Yma ac acw roedd ambell fedd llai uchelgeisiol gyda charreg grom isel weddol syml, a fawr ddim i ddangos ffiniau'r bedd.

Yn y llecyn hwn yr oedd un bedd digon mawreddog o farmor cochddu ar ffurf colofn, gydag ysgrifen ar bedair ochr y golofn a chadwyn haearn a phileri carreg yn cylchu ffiniau bedd a oedd yn fwy na dwbl maint bedd arferol – bedd teulu cyfan go gefnog. Fel y dynesid at dalcen y capel, roedd y beddi cist – er yn dal yn boblogaidd – yn tueddu i fod o lechfaen glas, a'r ysgrifen arnynt yn fwy darllenadwy. Cofiaf fod ochr un o'r beddi cist wedi syrthio'n agored gan amlygu pridd coch y fynwent, a chywiro'r gred oedd gennyf bod yr arch yn y gist. Cymraeg gan mwyaf oedd yr ysgrifen ar y beddi cynnar.

Wrth droi cornel talcen y capel roedd y beddi'n dod yn fwy confensiynol – carreg gefn o farmor neu lechfaen ac yna ymylon o'r un garreg yn dangos ffiniau'r bedd. Yn amlach na pheidio roedd yno ffiol ar gyfer dal blodau, ond dim ond ar y beddi diweddar y gwelid olion blodau. Ar y beddi hyn byddai llythrennau o aur, a chofiaf wylio crefftwr fwy nag unwaith yn torri enw newydd ac yn euro'r llythrennau.

Roedd torri bedd yn y fynwent yn waith trwm llafurus gan mai clai oedd y pridd dan yr wyneb. Gan amlaf John Jones, Bryn Awel, fyddai'n gyfrifol am y gwaith caled hwn. Byddai'n cyrraedd yn fore gyda'i gaib a'i raw, yn marcio'r bedd, ac yn dechrau cloddio. Roedd John Jones y math o weithiwr a allai ddal ati drwy'r dydd gan weithio'n ddyfal wrth ei bwysau. Fy nhasg i fyddai mynd â phaned ddeg iddo fo. Byddai wedi gadael ei biser efo Mam, gyda the a siwgr yn barod yn ei waelod. Byddwn innau, wedi i Mam dywallt dŵr berwedig arno, yn cario'r trwyth berwedig i'r fynwent, ac yntau yn ychwanegu llefrith o botel fechan yn ei fag bwyd ac yn yfed y te o gaead y piser.

Erbyn hynny byddai John Jones at ei benliniau yn y bedd newydd, a'r clai coch a melyn yn tyfu'n domen ar yr ymyl pellaf.

'Sut mae pethau'n mynd, John Jones?'

'Ara deg ar y naw, John bach – clai a cherrig ym mhob man.'

'Mi rydw i wedi dŵad â'r piser i chi gael paned, ac mae Mam yn rhoi dwy dafell o fara brith ichi.'

'Chwarae teg i'w chalon hi. Un dda ydi dy fam am gacen. Paid a dŵad yn *rhy* agos, mae'r clai 'ma'n llithrig.

Wneith hi mo'r tro i ti syrthio i mewn i'r bedd fel y gwnest ti'r tro dwytha!'

Chawn i byth anghofio'r tro anffodus pan syrthiais i i mewn i waelod bedd go ddwfn a gorfod cael fy nghodi allan yn glai i gyd.

'Dim ffiars o beryg, mi gadwa i'n ddigon pell.'

Gwaith blinedig oedd cloddio yn y clai. Bob yn hyn a hyn mi fyddwn i'n galw heibio efo llond piser newydd o de. Erbyn diwedd y prynhawn byddai John Jones o'r golwg yn y bedd, a blaen ei raw yn ymddangos bob hyn a hyn.

'Bron â gorffen, John Jones?'

'Bron iawn. Dydi o ddim *cweit* ddigon tyfn. Pasia'r ysgol 'na i mi, 'ngwas i, i mi gael dringo i dir y byw.'

Erbyn i mi alw cyn noswyl, byddai John Jones wedi gorffen cloddio ac wedi gosod tua chwe rhes o frics ar waelod y bedd, yr un siâp a maint â'r arch, ac wedi gosod dwy styllen tua throedfedd o led ar hyd ymylon y bedd.

Achlysuron traddodiadol eu naws yn llawn defod oedd angladdau pan oeddwn i'n blentyn. Roedd y pwyslais yn ddieithriad ar ddilyn confensiwn a dangos parch yn hytrach na dathlu bywydau unigolion. Roedd amrywiadau yn y patrwm, wrth gwrs: angladdau mawr a fyddai'n agored i'r cyhoedd yn ddiwahân, angladdau i ddynion yn unig (er nad oedd y rhain yn gyffredin iawn yn Sir Fôn), ac angladdau preifat a oedd yn gyfyngedig i'r teulu a chyfeillion agos.

Tua awr cyn angladd – neu 'gynhebrwng' fel y byddem ni'n ei ddweud yn lleol – byddai Mam yn cau llenni'r gegin, y llofftydd a'r parlwr fel arwydd o barch. Byddai'r tai cyfagos i gyd yn gwneud yr un peth. Byddai'r hers yn cael ei gyrru i mewn i gowt y capel ac ymlaen at giât ddwbl y fynwent. Pan ddefnyddid y capel i gynnal gwasanaeth angladdol fe fyddid yn cludo'r arch ar elor i flaen y capel, a hyd at y Sêt Fawr. Fel arall, eid yn syth i'r fynwent a glan y bedd. Fel arfer, byddai o leiaf un cynrychiolydd o bob teulu yn y gymdogaeth leol yn bresennol.

Byddai pawb yn gwisgo du neu ddillad tywyll, a gweddwon yn gwisgo dillad parch am gyfnod go faith ar ôl yr angladd. Anaml y gwelid plant mewn angladd yn y cyfnod hwnnw os nad oeddynt yn berthnasau agos, a hyd yn oed wedyn y duedd oedd cadw plant gartref. Er i mi fyw rhan gyntaf fy oes mewn tŷ capel, yn ystod fy nghyfnod i yno fûm i erioed mewn gwasanaeth angladd, dim ond gweld y gorymdeithiau'n mynd heibio trwy fwlch yn llenni'r gegin. Roedd allanolion confensiwn galar yn bwysig, a gwae neb a fyddai'n meiddio torri ar yr arferion cydnabyddedig.

Er bod y gymdeithas yn un Gristionogol ei naws, yr oedd llawer iawn o ofergoeliaeth yn parhau ynglŷn â marwolaeth a mynwentydd. Fe ddywedid y byddai cyn-berchennog y Tŷ Capel yn clywed sŵn carnau ceffylau ac olwynion hers cyn pob angladd, ac fe honnai fy nhad iddo glywed sŵn crafu ar do'r tŷ pan fyddai rhywun wedi marw. Roedd straeon am 'dderyn corff' ac ysbrydion yn gyffredin, ac fe honnai ficer lleol iddo weld cylchoedd tân yn dilyn marwolaeth ei frawd.

Byddai llawer o'r plant lleol yn ofnus wrth fynd heibio'r fynwent liw nos. Ond, i mi, wnaeth agosrwydd y fynwent erioed godi ofn arna i – roedd hi'n bresennol barhaus, ac wedi tyfu'n rhan o'r tirlun a'r amgylchfyd. Ond cofiwch, doeddwn i ddim yn *rhy* hyderus wrth fynd i'r tŷ bach a oedd wrth y drws cefn, ac ar bwys y fynwent, yn y tywyllwch.

## Mam a Nhad

Dynes fain eiddil oedd Mam, gwraig a oedd yn byw ar ei nerfau. Bu'n wael am ran helaeth o'i hoes – nid o waeledd difrifol, ond o fân afiechydon a gwendid. Roedd hi'n un o naw o blant. Er bod y teulu'n hanu o Garmel yn ymyl Llannerch-y-medd, fe gafodd fy mam ei magu gyda'i thaid a'i nain yn Llanfechell, ac roedd dylanwad uniaith Gymraeg ei thaid a'i nain yn drwm ar ei hiaith a'i hymadroddion hithau. Roedd ei hiaith yn frith o eiriau tafodieithol y sir, fel 'pipidown' am dop, 'llyffanta' am godi o'ch gwely ac oeri ar lawr y llofft, 'hen sinach' am ddyn go aflednais, a 'dreigia' am fellt oedd yn fflachio o gwmwl i gwmwl.

Fe wyddai ar dafod leferydd eiriau nifer helaeth o ganeuon gwerin, caneuon fel 'Titrwm Tatrwm' a 'Mae 'Nghariad i'n Fenws', ac roedd ganddi hi amrywiad na chlywais i mohono gan neb arall yn ail gwpled y pennill:

> 'Mae 'nghariad i'n Fenws,
> Mae 'nghariad i'n lân,
> A'i dannedd cyn wynned
> *Â phric dafad gwlân.'*

Roedd Mam yn arfer cystadlu ar adrodd yn eithaf llwyddiannus mewn eisteddfodau ac roedd ganddi gof eithriadol am rigymau a barddoniaeth. Ganddi hi y clywais i 'englynion' a chwpledi'r Bardd Cocos gyntaf. Rhaid bod campweithiau'r hen fardd wedi treiddio'n helaeth i iaith lafar Môn. Ei sylw'n ddiwahân pan fyddai'n tywallt y glaw fyddai:

> Roedd hi'n bwrw fel o grwc,
> Ond roedd Noah yn yr arch, wrth lwc.

Un o fy hoff weithiau i o blith cerddi'r Bardd Cocos oedd yr 'englyn' beddargraff yma i'w dad. Mi fyddai'n gwneud englynion pum llinell fel arfer, ond mae hwn yn hir a thoddaid o englyn! Dyma fo, fel y clywais i o gan Mam:

> Hen ŵr oedd fy nhad yn byw yn y Borth
> Yn gyrru cwch i'r dŵr, i mi a Mam gael torth.
> Ond heno mae o'n huno'n hynod
> Gyda'r graean a'r cacynod.
> Afiechyd oedd ei waeledd
> A marw wnaeth o'r diwedd:
> Pridd ar ei draws a phridd ar ei hyd,
> A dyna lle bydd o tan ddiwedd y byd.

A phrin bod cwpled yn yr iaith Gymraeg yn fwy cynhwysfawr na:

> Fydd yr awen ddim yn fflash
> Heb fwstash.

Mi fyddai Mam yn feunyddiol bron yn adrodd hen benillion fel:

> Llannerch-y-medd y bondo
> Lle claddwyd Brenin Pabo,
> A'r frenhines deg ei gwedd
> Yn Llannerch-y-medd mae honno.

– pennill hen dros ben, yn ôl Bedwyr Lewis Jones, pennill sydd â'i wreiddiau'n ddwfn yn hanes Môn.

Ffefryn arall ganddi hi oedd y rhigwm athronyddol praff, 'Had Maip Môn':

> Had maip Môn,
> Heuwch nhw'n gynnar, mi ddôn;
> Ac os y dôn nhw, ddôn nhw ddim,
> Ac os na ddôn nhw, mi ddôn.

Cyfeirio at fynd a dŵad brain y mae'r 'nhw' yn y pennill, yn ôl yr arbenigwyr. Efallai mai gwir hynny, ond i mi mae 'na ryw oddefgarwch heintus hirymarhous yn neges y rhigwm, rhyw agwedd ffwrdd-â-hi at ddigwyddiadau bywyd – adlais o'r agwedd *mañana* tuag at fyw sydd i'w ganfod mewn gwledydd fel Sbaen a Groeg.

Nid yn unig fe fyddai hi'n llafarganu rhigymau cyfrif – rhigymau diddanu babis a phlant bach – fel 'Modryb y Fawd, Bys yr Uwd' a 'Si Hei Lwli', ond mi fyddai ganddi hefyd rigymau mwys fyddai'n dod â gwên i wyneb rhywun, fel:

> *Doh ray me, ray soh fah,*
> Cei dithau res o bys!

Roedd ganddi hi gyfoeth o rigymau, adroddiadau, emynau a geiriau alawon gwerin ar ei chof, a dawn arbennig i'w hadrodd. Byddai doniau adrodd Mam yn dod i'r amlwg yn 'sosials' y capel. Mi fedrwn i eistedd yn ddigon bodlon a gwrando ar Marian yn adrodd, ac ni fyddai canu alaw werin neu ddwy fy hun yn poeni fawr ddim arna i, ond roedd gwrando ar Mam yn adrodd yn gyrru iasau i lawr fy nghefn i ac yn gwneud i mi deimlo'n annifyr. Wn i ddim pam. Efallai mai am fod personoliaeth

Mam yn newid yn gyfan gwbl pan fyddai hi'n adrodd. Mi fyddai hi'n sefyll yno fel adroddwraig go iawn, ei dwy law yn cydio yn ei gilydd a'i llygaid yn syllu'n syth o'i blaen. Ac mi fyddai tôn ei llais hi'n troi'n hyderus ac yn ddieithr.

Fel arfer, mi fyddai hi'n adrodd darnau ysgafn troad y ganrif am 'Pat yn Mynd i Lundain', neu ddarnau dramatig am y 'Royal Charter' a oedd yn ddigon i gynhyrfu'r gwan. Dim ond un darn wnes i ei hoffi erioed ganddi hi a hwnnw oedd 'Cymru' Gwenallt, er y byddai llinellau fel:

> A bu'r Ysbryd Glân yn nythu
> Fel colomen yn dy goed

ychydig bach yn felodramatig ganddi. Ond roedd grym y geiriau a'r briodas rhwng ystyr a theimlad yn argyhoeddi. Mae'n debyg i Llew Llwydiarth (Derwydd Gweinyddol Gorsedd Môn, a arferai ei dysgu i adrodd cyn eisteddfodau o bwys) gael dylanwad go drwm arni hi.

Os oedd fy mam yn gallu blodeuo'n gyhoeddus, nid felly fy nhad. Er iddo gael ei godi'n flaenor (ar ôl cryn berswâd), prin oedd ei ddoniau cyhoeddus. Dyn ymarferol di-flewyn-ar-dafod oedd Nhad, un gwyllt fel matsen yn ôl rhai o'i gyd-weithwyr, ond dyn meddal teimladwy a llawn hiwmor yn y bôn.

Wrth ei alwedigaeth fel saer coed, bu'n gweithio am ran helaethaf ei oes i William Henry Parry, Bryn Mair. Byddai'n treulio ei amser rhwng gwaith adeiladu a chyfnodau yn y gweithdy ym Mryn Mair, ble byddai – ymysg pethau eraill – yn gwneud eirch.

Doedd o ddim yn hoff iawn o'r gwaith eirch ac fe wrthodai'n lân â mynd i fesur cyrff marw i'w cartrefi. Mae'n debyg bod hynny'n mynd yn ôl i'r profiad a gafodd o fel prentis. Pan fu farw un o drigolion yr ardal aeth

William Henry Parry â Nhad gydag o i dŷ'r ymadawedig i fesur y corff. Roedd y gŵr marw i fyny grisiau cul mewn llofft dywyll. Yn anffodus, roedd y truan wedi marw yn ei gwrcwd ac ar ei ochr, fel nad oedd modd mesur ei hyd yn gywir.

'Tro fo ar ei gefn, 'ngwas i,' meddai William Henry.

'Pwy, fi?' oedd ateb pryderus Nhad.

'Wela i neb arall yma,' oedd yr ateb, 'a digon o waith y bydd o'n fodlon troi ohono'i hun.'

Gafaelodd Nhad yn betrus yn ei ddau ben-lin a'i ddroi o ar wastad ei gefn.

'Da ti, 'rhen hogyn. Rŵan, gwthia ar i lawr ar ei ddau ben-lin o i'w sythu fo.'

Gwthiodd Nhad yn ufudd, ond yn lle sythu fe gododd wyneb y corff at ei wyneb yntau. Rhoddodd un sgrech a'i heglu hi oddi yno am ei fywyd. Byth ers hynny, doedd dim modd ei gael i fesur cyrff, na'u gosod yn eu heirch, dim ond gwneud y gwaith coed angenrheidiol yn y gweithdy.

Roedd ganddo stori am ddyn go gynnil yn dod i'r gweithdy at William Henry Parry i geisio taro bargen am arch iddo fo'i hun. Dechreuodd y dyn ddadlau ynglŷn â phrisiau eirch, a'r saer yn ei ateb:

'Dim ond y coed gorau fyddwn ni'n eu defnyddio, a dau bris sydd gennym ni – mae'r eirch derw, yn naturiol, ychydig bach yn ddrytach.'

'Ond William bach, mae 'na ddyn ym Mangor yn cynnig eirch am chwarter y pris. Pam mae dy brisiau di mor ddrud?'

'Fel y deudais i, mi rydan ni'n defnyddio'r coed gora. Os nad wyt ti'n fodlon, pryna arch gan y dyn yna o Fangor. Mi fydd dy din di drwyddi hi cyn pen tri mis.'

Roedd Nhad yn ei elfen yn adeiladu tai ac roedd ganddo'r ddawn i lunio ac i ddarllen cynlluniau. Pan oedd o'n hogyn ysgol mi lwyddodd i basio'r 'sgolarship' ond doedd gan ei deulu, ac yntau'n un o bump o blant, mo'r modd i'w anfon o i ysgol ramadeg.

Fe ddechreuodd drwy weithio ar y tir yn ardal Rhosgoch cyn penderfynu bod yn brentis saer coed. Bu cyfnod cynnar ei fywyd yn eithaf tlodaidd, a doedd pethau fawr gwell yn y tridegau pan oedd gwaith adeiladu'n brin ac yntau'n ddi-waith am gyfnodau. Er na ddywedwyd hynny wrthyf erioed, mi gredaf mai mater o angen yn hytrach na dewis oedd symud i fyw fel gofalwyr Tŷ Capel y Tabernacl ddiwedd y tridegau. Er gwaethaf ei ddiffyg addysg, roedd Nhad yn ddyn deallus a chanddo afael dda ar bynciau'r dydd. Roedd o'n gefnogwr brwd i'r Blaid Lafur ac rwy'n ei gofio'n canfasio dros Cledwyn Hughes pan gipiodd Cledwyn etholaeth Môn oddi ar Megan Lloyd George, a'i orfoledd mawr oherwydd y fuddugoliaeth bryd hynny. Roedd ei feic adeg y canfasio'n rhubanau coch i gyd.

Roedd o'n ddyn cryf, cryf o gorff ac o ran personoliaeth, ac fe safai ar egwyddor waeth beth fyddai'r gost bersonol iddo fo. Anaml y byddai'n dangos ei deimladau; fe lwyddai'n ddieithriad bron i guddio'i ddyheadau a'i siomedigaethau fel ei gilydd. Yn y cyfnod pan oeddwn i'n sefyll arholiadau Safon O, y drefn oedd cyhoeddi'r canlyniadau yn y *Daily Post* yn hytrach na chyflwyno'r wybodaeth yn yr ysgolion. Cofiaf i mi godi'n gynnar y bore hwnnw a gwibio ar fy meic i'r Benllech i brynu papur. Rhyddhad oedd 'mod i wedi gwneud yn well na'r disgwyl. Cyrraedd adref a dweud y newydd wrth Mam, a hithau wrth ei bodd.

'Well i ti fynd i ddeud wrth dy dad,' meddai hi toc. 'Mi fydd o siŵr o fod ar binna fel finna.'

Bryd hynny, roedd Nhad yn gweithio ar res o dai cyngor newydd ym Mryn-teg a dyma neidio ar fy meic a theithio'r tri chwarter milltir fwy neu lai at safle'r tai newydd. Fe ddeuai sŵn morthwylio prysur o un o'r tai a thybiais yn gywir mai yno'r oedd fy nhad. Dyna lle'r oedd o ar ei liniau yn gosod 'styllod ar lawr cegin.

'Nhad!'

Peidiodd y morthwylio.

'O, ti sy 'na. Be 'ti'n dda yma'r adag yma o'r bora?'

'Wedi dŵad â chanlyniadau'r Lefel O i chi eu gweld.'

'Felly! Gad i mi weld, 'ta.' Cydiodd yn y papur a darllen yn hamddenol. 'Diawch, *wyth* pwnc – mi wnest ti'n rhagorol.'

'Mam yn meddwl y basach chi'n hoffi cael gwbod.'

'Wyddost ti be? Roedd dy fam yn llygad 'i lle…'

Daeth llais arall o'r tu cefn i mi.

'Paid â gwrando arno fo, John bach, mae o'n gwbod ers cyn saith. Y peth cynta wnaeth o bora 'ma oedd mynd ar 'i feic i'r Benllach i brynu papur. Mae o wedi bod fel ci efo dwy gynffon ers hynny. Da iawn ti'r hogyn. Hwda, dyma i ti rywbeth bach iti ddathlu.'

Un o'i gyd-weithwyr o oedd yno. Roedd ei eiriau mor agos at y gwir nes i Nhad brysuro i droi'r stori; un fel yna oedd o.

## Olgra Fawr

Mae'n od fel yr ydym ni'n tueddu i dderbyn enwau lleoedd, tai a ffermydd yn ddi-gwestiwn – derbyn heb holi pam a sut y daeth enw i fod, hyd yn oed os yw amser wedi llygru'r enw, neu gamynganu dros genedlaethau wedi dieithrio'r gwreiddiol. Yn aml iawn, nid yw'r boblogaeth leol yn gallu cynnig ystyr i enw lle, ac os ydynt, mae mwy o ddychymyg nag o ffaith yn yr ystyron a gynigir. Yn gyffredinol yng nghefn gwlad, enwau ydi enwau, a'u prif swyddogaeth yw bod yn label cywir ar fan arbennig – 'ydynt yr hyn ydynt'.

Does gen i fawr o gof imi holi erioed beth oedd union ystyr Plas Sglatar, Tyddyn Tlodion neu Bant y Saer, na chysidro pam y galwyd dwy fferm gyfagos yn Tudor Villa a Quarry Bank mewn ardal mor Gymreig. Dim ond derbyn mai fel yna yr oedd pethau. Ond, yn ddiweddar, mi dyfodd rhyw chwilfrydedd ynof ynglŷn ag ystyr y gair Olgra, yn gymaint felly nes i mi, trwy gyfrwng ffrind, geisio barn yr Athro Hywel Wyn Owen yn Adran Ymchwil Enwau Lleoedd, Coleg Prifysgol Cymru, Bangor. Mae'n werth dyfynnu yn ei grynswth esboniad difyr a manwl yr Athro:

> Enwau dwy fferm ym mhlwyf Llanddyfnan, Llanfair Mathafarn Eithaf, Môn, yw Olgra Fawr ac Olgra Fach. Fe wn i hefyd am Olgra Terrace yn Llanberis.
>
> Yr elfen gyntaf yw 'ôl', yn yr ystyr llwybr. Ond beth am

yr ail elfen? Mae'r Olgra yn Llanddyfnan i'w weld yn 1520 fel Olgre. Ai cryf neu gre' – llwybr cadarn solet? Rhywbeth tebyg i sarn, efallai? Mae hynny'n gweddu i ffermydd Olgra Fawr a Fach gan bod rhaid croesi Afon Marchogion i fynd o'r naill i'r llall. Enw arall ar Olgra Fach yw Olgra Gerrig, sy'n cryfhau'r ddamcaniaeth mai sarn neu lwybr o gerrig yw ystyr Olgra.

Ond mae gair arall yn gweddu'n well fyth, sef y gair 'gre' – gyrr o feirch neu o wartheg. 'Ôl-gre' felly fyddai llwybr ceffylau neu wartheg. A yw hyn yn rhoi arwyddocâd i Afon Marchogion rhwng Olgra Fawr ac Olgra Fach (neu Olgra Gerrig)? Mae rhywun yn meddwl am Ôl-march ger Tregaron ac am yr 'eb-hynt' – llwybr yr eb(olion) – a roddodd i ni Epynt.

Felly llwybr ceffylau, mae'n debyg, yw Olgra.

Alla i ond rhyfeddu at gwmpas gwybodaeth Hywel Wyn Owen a 'niffyg gwybodaeth i fy hun am fan mor gyfarwydd. Mae ei eglurhad yn argyhoeddi'n llwyr er nad oes gen i gof am neb yn galw Olgra Fach ar y fferm – Olgra Gerrig oedd hi i ni. A wyddwn i ddim mai Afon Marchogion oedd enw'r afonig rhwng y ddwy ffarm – Afon Bwlch oedd enw'r darn oedd gyferbyn â'n tŷ ni. Dydi'r traddodiad llafar ddim yn hirhoedlog bob amser!

Roedd yr Olgra Fawr led ffordd a lled cae o'r Tŷ Capel. Seth a Polly Owen oedd yn ffermio'r Olgra Fawr pan oeddwn i'n blentyn – mae'n amheus gen i a wyddent hwythau ystyr enw'r fferm. Roedd y ffermdy ei hun yn ymddangos yn hen iawn. Ar un talcen (y talcen agosaf at y Tŷ Capel) roedd stabl, cartref y ddwy gaseg wedd. Yna fe redai'r tŷ ei hun gyda'r parlwr a'r ystafell fwyta y naill ochr i ddrws y ffrynt, ac yna'r beudy – y cyfan dan yr unto. Ni chofiaf i mi erioed weld neb yn defnyddio drws y ffrynt.

Roedd ffrynt y ffarm yn wynebu'r brif ffordd o Fryn-teg i'r Benllech. Ar bwys wal y ffordd, yn ymestyn o'r giât at goeden anferth ar y dde, roedd pwll hwyaid crwn, fwy neu lai. Roedd y dŵr ynddo yn ddu ac yn drwchus fel triog, a pha ryfedd gan fod y biswail o'r beudy a'r stabl wedi rhedeg iddo ers blynyddoedd. Yn y cefn yr oedd y llofft granar, y sgubor a'r drws cefn a oedd yn arwain heibio i'r tŷ llaeth i'r gegin. Y drefn oedd rhoi cnoc ar y drws, gweiddi 'Oes 'ma bobol?' a cherdded i mewn. Yn y cefn, hefyd, roedd buarth arall lle byddai'r ieir yn crafu ac yn clwcian, a'r ardd ŷd. Llecyn yn cynnwys tas ŷd, tas wellt a thŷ gwair, gyda wal garreg yn amgylchynu'r cyfan, oedd yr ardd ŷd – y rhan honno o'r fferm a elwir mewn ardaloedd eraill yn 'gadlas' neu 'ydlan'.

Rhaid fy mod i wedi croesi'r cae i'r Olgra Fawr filoedd o weithiau ar ryw neges neu'i gilydd – nôl menyn cartref, wyau, ambell lond piser o laeth enwyn. Dim ond yn dilyn tywydd gwlyb, pan fyddai wyneb y cae yn fwd i gyd, y byddwn i'n cerdded ar hyd y ffordd. Roedd y ddau deulu'n fwy na chymdogion – roedden ni'n gyfeillion agos.

Yn fuan wedi i'r rhyfel dorri fe dderbyniodd Seth a Polly Owen ddwy faciwî o Lerpwl – Margaret a Dorothy Jackson – i'w haelwyd, a rhoi cartref gwerth chweil i'r ddwy. Fe ddychwelodd Margaret, yr hynaf o'r ddwy, i Lerpwl ar ôl y rhyfel, ond fe arhosodd Dorothy yn yr Olgra nes iddi gyrraedd ei harddegau. Erbyn hynny roedd hi'n rhugl ei Chymraeg.

Pan fyddai'r tywydd yn wael mi fyddai Mam, Marian a minnau, a Polly Owen, Margaret a Dorothy wrthi fel lladd nadredd yn helpu Seth Owen i drin y gwair. Gwaith araf oedd chwilio'r rhenciau am gudynnau gwlyb o wair, eu hysgwyd a'u chwalu efo picwarch a'u gosod i sychu yn llygad yr haul. Unwaith y byddai'r gwair yn dderbyniol sych, byddai Seth Owen yn cribinio'r gwair yn rhenciau efo'r gribyn fawr a oedd yn cael ei llusgo gan Seren y gaseg. Ein gwaith ni wedyn fyddai gwneud cocynnau o'r rhenciau yn barod ar gyfer y cario. Ganol y pnawn mi fyddai Polly Owen yn diflannu am gryn hanner awr cyn dychwelyd gyda basgedaid o frechdanau a chacennau a llond piser o de melys chwilboeth. Dyna lle byddem ni i gyd yn eistedd yn lluddedig ym môn y clawdd yng nghysgod y gwrych i fwyta. Mae gwell blas ar fwyd yn yr awyr agored, ac er y byddai swigod ar fy mysedd ar ôl trin y bicwarch a phigau ysgall yn fy nghnawd, fel diwrnodau dedwydd y mae'r cyfnod wedi aros yn y cof.

Fel arfer, ar ôl i Nhad ddod adref o'i waith y byddai'r cario'n dechrau. Weithiau dim ond y ddau – Nhad a Seth Owen – fyddai wrthi'n cario; dro arall mi fyddai un neu ddau o gymdogion yn rhoi help llaw. Mi fyddai Seth Owen wedi paratoi'r drol ymlaen llaw drwy osod y garfan arni er mwyn iddi ddal mwy o lwyth. Fy nhad fyddai'n llwytho a Seth Owen yn derbyn ac yn adeiladu'r llwyth ar ben y drol. Mi fyddwn i'n cael y fraint o dywys Seren, a oedd yn gaseg hynod o ddof, o gocyn i gocyn. Roedd fy nhad yn ddyn nerthol ac fe allai godi cocyn cyfan i ben y llwyth yn ddiymdrech. Pan fyddai'r drol yn llawn, mi fyddwn i'n cael fy nghodi i ben y llwyth i fwynhau'r daith esmwyth yn ôl i'r Olgra Fawr.

Wedi i ni gyrraedd yr Olgra, Nhad fyddai'n dadlwytho o ben y drol a Seth Owen yn derbyn ac yn gwasgar y gwair yn gyson a threfnus yn y tŷ gwair. Mi gawn innau neidio ar y gwair i'w gywasgu.

Ni fyddai arian byth yn cyfnewid dwylo yn dâl am unrhyw waith y byddai Nhad yn ei wneud. Roedd cael arian sychion o groen ffarmwr fel tynnu gwaed allan o garreg! Talu mewn tatws a wyau ac ambell ffowlyn oedd y drefn, neu câi Nhad hanner rhes o datws. Yn hyn o beth roedd Seth Owen yn hael, ac mae'n eithaf tebyg y byddai'r hyn a dderbyniem yn werth mwy nag arian sychion. P'un bynnag, doedd neb yn cyfrif. Fel yna roedd pethau rhwng cymdogion.

Ond diwrnod mawr y flwyddyn amaethyddol oedd diwrnod dyrnu. Byddai nifer o ffermwyr lleol, cymdogion o fewn cylch o bron i filltir, ynghyd ag ambell lafurwr oedd angen diwrnod o waith ac yn canlyn y dyrnwr o fferm i fferm, yn cynnig eu llafur gan gadw at hen hen batrwm yn y gymdogaeth. I'r Olgra Fawr fe ddeuai Rolant Jones, Ysgubor Fadog; Huw Owen, Tyddyn Sarjant; Capten Roberts, Quarry Bank; a Twm, Ty'n Felin, ymysg eraill. Perchennog y dyrnwr oedd William Roberts, Betws, a fo ynghyd â Wil ei fab fyddai'n trefnu'r diwrnod.

Byddai Polly Owen (fel y gwnâi Mam adeg Sasiwn yn y capel) yn gofalu paratoi ymhell ymlaen llaw. Roedd angen bwydo'r holl ddynion – pryd poeth o datws a chig a phwdin ganol dydd, a the mawr o frechdanau a chacennau a bara brith at ddiwedd y prynhawn. Roedd hi'n dipyn o gystadleuaeth ymhlith gwragedd y ffermydd i weld pwy fyddai'n darparu'r arlwy gorau, a sarhad oedd cael enw drwg am fwyd sâl neu arlwy crintachlyd.

Mi fyddai'r dyrnwr mawr yn cyrraedd yn hwyr y noson cynt. Gellid clywed sŵn y tracsion yn dod o bell, gan fod ei olwynion haearn yn crinshian tarmacadam y ffordd a gadael patrwm yr olwynion arni am hydoedd. Ac roedd chwisl stêm ar yr injan oedd â'i gwich i'w chlywed o bellteroedd. Byddai hyn yn ddigon i ddenu amryw o blant bychain a rhai hŷn at giât yr Olgra i hebrwng y dyrnwr i'r ardd ŷd. Yna gosodid y dyrnwr, ar ôl cryn symud yn ôl a blaen, mor agos a phosib at y das. Golygfa frawychus braidd oedd gweld y ddau anghenfil fel dau ddeinosor yn llechu yn llwyd-olau'r ardd ŷd.

Fore trannoeth, cyn i mi godi, mi fyddai William Roberts, Betws, wedi cynnau tân o dan fwyleri'r injan stêm a'i fab wrthi'n tynnu'r nithlan orchudd a tho brwyn y das ŷd yn barod ar gyfer y fyddin o weithwyr. Mi fyddid yn gosod nithlan o dan fol y dyrnwr i ddal y peiswyn, bachu'r sachau yn y pinnau ar gefn y dyrnwr i dderbyn y grawn (byddai lle i bedwar sach), a gosod y strap lledr ar ffurf ffigwr wyth rhwng olwyn yrru'r tracsion ac olwyn dderbyn y dyrnwr. Fel y byddai'r gwlith yn codi, mi fyddai'r ffermwyr lleol a'r 'helpwrs' yn cyrraedd ar droed, fesul un a dau.

William Roberts y mab fyddai'n trefnu'r gweithwyr, tra byddai William Roberts y tad yn piltran efo'r injan stêm ac yn cadw llygad barcud ar wahanol elfennau'r dyrnwr ei hun. Y mab fyddai ar ben y dyrnwr yn bwydo'r ŷd i'r hopran fawr, tra byddai un arall yno gydag ef yn torri'r llinyn beindar ar bob ysgub cyn eu trosglwyddo iddo fo. Byddai dau arall ar ben y das yn taflu'r sgubau i ben y dyrnwr, a dau arall wedyn yn cadw llygad ar y grawn yn llifo i'r sachau ac yn gosod sach newydd pan fyddai'r sachau'n rhwydd lawn, cyn eu cario i fyny'r grisiau cerrig i lofft y granar a'u tywallt ar y llawr coed yno. Mi fyddai 'na hefyd ddau yn cario'r gwellt o ben arall y dyrnwr ac yn dechrau adeiladu tas newydd, ac un ar ei rawd yn cario'r llond nithlan o beiswyn fyddai wedi casglu o dan fol y dyrnwr.

Ar un adeg, mi fyddid yn defnyddio'r peiswyn i lenwi clustogau a matresi gwely gwellt. Casglu peiswyn, yn ôl yr hanes, oedd gwaith y Bardd Cocos, yn ogystal â hel cocos ar Draeth Lafan – a barddoni!

Dynion gwydn, byr o gorff oedd y ffermwyr gan mwyaf (ar wahân i Capten Roberts, oedd yn ddyn go dal). Pob un ohonynt yn ei drowsus ribs brown tyn, a chrys gwlanen streipiog heb goler. Gwisgai ambell un sach rownd gwaelod ei drowsus wedi ei glymu efo llinyn beindar, a llinyn beindar hefyd fyddai'n dal trowsus ambell un rhag syrthio. Roedd llinyn beindar yn dra defnyddiol. Dros y crys fe fyddai gwasgod llewys byr. Gweithwyr hamddenol a diffwdan oeddynt, ar wahân i ambell ddiogyn fyddai'n osgoi gwaith; yr oeddynt yr un mor egnïol ar ddiwedd diwrnod gwaith ag yr oeddynt ar ei ddechrau. Roedd oes o lafurio wedi creu dygnwch mewn corff a meddwl.

Ar y cyrion yn mwynhau newydd-deb y gweithgarwch y byddai Frank Quarry Bank a minnau. Mab ieuengaf Capten Roberts oedd Frank, ac roedd tua'r un oed â mi. Mi fyddai 'na gryn dipyn o dynnu coes a herio ymysg y gweithwyr. Un cast oedd gosod carreg drom yn y sach ŷd heb i'r cariwr wybod. Tro Twm Ty'n Felin oedd hi i gael ei dwyllo. Roedd un o'r llafnau ifanc wedi gosod carreg go fawr yn y sach hanner llawn, ac wedi i lif y ceirch ei gorchuddio ac i'r sach rwydd lenwi, dyma droi at Twm.

' Twm! Dy dro di ydi hi – fi gariodd y sach dwytha.'

Roedd Twm yn ddyn cydnerth, os ychydig bach yn ddiniwed, a chydiodd yn y sach, ei osod ar ei gefn a cherdded yn dalog i fyny'r grisiau i lofft y granar. Ymhen rhai eiliadau fe glywyd y rhegfeydd mwyaf dychrynllyd o'r granar. Rhywbeth yn debyg i hyn:

'Y ffernols drwg i chi – mae'n ddigon i mi gario ceirch, heb orfod cario hanner yr ardd ŷd yn ogystal. Mi ddarn ladda i bwy bynnag wnaeth hyn.'

Ymddangosai Twm yn gynddeiriog ar ben grisiau'r llofft granar, ond pan sylweddolodd fod pawb yn chwerthin ac yn cael hwyl fawr mi ddechreuodd yntau chwerthin, a diflannodd ei gynddaredd yn o sydyn.

'Aros di, Quarry Bank, neu pwy bynnag wnaeth hyn. Mi ro i ti lawr hopran y dyrnwr ac mi fyddwn ni'n dy gario di adra mewn sacha.'

Roedd Twm, er ei fod ychydig yn syml ei feddwl, yn ffraeth ei dafod ac yn gryf ei araith.

Fel yr âi'r bore rhagddo, âi edrych ar ddynion yn gweithio yn llai deniadol, ac fe ddechreuai Frank a minnau greu ein hadloniant ein hunain. Hysian y cŵn ar ôl y llygod bach a oedd yn dechrau gadael diogelwch y das ŷd; creu ras redeg o amgylch y dyrnwr, y tracsion, y das a'r tŷ gwair – unrhyw beth, yn wir, oedd o fewn ffiniau'r ardd ŷd – ond heb ddilyn yr un llwybr fwy nag unwaith.

Roeddwn i'n rhedeg ar y blaen i Frank rhwng y dyrnwr a'r tracsion un tro pan gydiodd llaw giaidd yn fy ngwegil a'm codi'n un darn i'r awyr.

'Be haru ti'r twmffat gwirion? Paid ti *byth* â mynd yn agos at strap y dyrnwr.'

Twm Ty'n Felin oedd yno yn fy ysgwyd i fel taswn i'n ddol glwt.

'Wyddat ti ddim y galla'r strap 'na dorri dy ben di fatha llafn pladur, ne' dy sugno di i berfedd y dyrnwr nes y bydda dy gnawd di'n tywallt yn dameidia i mewn i'r sachau 'na?'

'Be sy'n bod, Twm?' holodd Seth Owen.

'Newydd achub bywyd yr hogyn gwirion yma ydw i, Seth. Mi fu ond y dim iddo gael hollti corn ei wddw.'

Doedd dim iws dadlau na fûm i ddim nes na dwy droedfedd at y tipyn strap, a 'mod i'n gwybod yn union be roeddwn i'n ei wneud. Siarsiodd Twm ni i gadw draw oddi wrth y dyrnwr ac fe awgrymodd Seth Owen, er mwyn cadw'r heddwch, ein bod ni'n chwarae rywle arall. Dwi'n cofio gobeithio y byddai rhywun arall yn rhoi carreg anferth yn sach Twm Ty'n Felin, ac y byddai yntau o ganlyniad yn disgyn wysg ei din o ben y grisiau cerrig. Y noson honno fe gornelodd o Nhad, ac fe fu'n edliw iddo sut y bu iddo achub bywyd ei fab anystyriol.

Cyn bod y cloc wedi troi hanner dydd daeth sŵn y gloch ginio, ac fel un gŵr rhoddodd y dynion y gorau i'w gorchwylion a throi i gyfeiriad y tŷ, gan adael i William Roberts ddiffodd yr olwyn oedd yn gyrru'r dyrnwr a rheoli'r stêm yn y bwyler. Arweiniwyd y dynion i'r ystafell ffrynt lle roedd Polly Owen, Mam, Margaret a Dorothy wedi hwylio'r bwrdd yn barod ac yn cymell y dynion i 'ymestyn at' y bwyd. Roedd gan Polly Owen enw da am fwyd, ac fe osodwyd plateidiau o gig eidion, moron, pys a thatws rhost gerbron y dynion – a phwdin reis a chacen afal i ddilyn. Oherwydd diffyg lle yn yr ystafell ffrynt – neu rhag ofn i'n clustiau diniwed gael eu halogi gan sgwrs y dynion – fe gafodd Frank a minnau, er mawr siom i ni, ein bwyd ar fwrdd y gegin.

Yr un prysurdeb oedd yno drwy'r pnawn. Fel yr âi'r das ŷd yn llai fe dyfai'r das wellt. Roedd yr ysgubau bellach hyd picwarch o ben y dyrnwr. Rhag croesi Twm Ty'n Felin, fe aeth Frank a minnau i edmygu'r injan stêm a chael gwers

gan William Roberts ar y ffordd orau i yrru'r anghenfil –
sut i droi i'r chwith neu i'r dde ag ati – ac egluro inni sut yr
oedd pwysau'r stêm o'r bwyler yn ddigon nerthol i yrru'r
peiriant. Diddordeb bywyd William Roberts a'i fab oedd
peiriannau stêm, ac edrychent ar eu holau gan ymlid pob
arlliw o rwd oddi arnynt a llathru'r pres nes ei fod fel
ceiniog newydd. Roedd ganddo fwy nag un peiriant adra
yn y Betws, medda fo, ac roedd croeso i ni alw heibio i'w
gweld.

Llusgo wnaeth y pnawn hwnnw gan fod gweithgarwch
y dynion braidd yn ailadroddus a diflas. Diwrnod gwaith,
os diwrnod anarferol, oedd diwrnod dyrnu iddynt hwy.
Aeth y das ŷd yn llai ac yn llai nes i eithin a rhedyn sylfaen
y das ddod i'r golwg ac i'r llygod bach ei gadael hi fel gadael
llong yn suddo. Fel roedd y dynion yn cymoni'r ardd ŷd fe
ddaeth galwad y gloch de, ac aeth y dynion am y tŷ unwaith
eto – y tro hwn i gladdu brechdanau cig a samwn tun,
cacennau, bara brith, ffrwythau tun a hufen. Ymhen hir a
hwyr, a llawer o roi'r byd yn ei le, cododd pawb oddi wrth
y bwrdd â'u boliau'n dynn dan y wasgod a'r llinyn beindar
wedi ei lacio fodfedd a mwy, a'i throi hi am adref ar gyfer
godro hwyr a phorthi.

Trist oedd gweld llusgo'r dyrnwr mawr o'r ardd ŷd
drwy'r buarth i'r ffordd fawr ar ei daith i'r ffarm nesaf, a
diwrnod arall o ddyrnu i rywun.

Pan ddaeth Nhad adref y peth cyntaf ofynnodd o i mi
oedd:

'Be wnest ti i gynddeiriogi Twm Ty'n Felin?'

'Dim o bwys. Dydi'r dyn ddim yn gall; mae hanner ei
farblis o ar goll.'

'Paid ti *byth* â siarad fel yna am neb. Ella bod Twm

ychydig yn ddiniwed ond dy les di oedd ganddo fo mewn golwg.'

'Doeddwn i ddim yn agos at y strap. Doedd dim angen iddo fo afael yn fy ngwegil i a bytheirio fel dyn gwyllt.'

'Un fel yna ydi Twm, un braidd yn fyrbwyll a diniwed, ond mae ganddo fo ddawn efo geiriau.'

'*Rhegi* ydach chi'n feddwl?'

'Na – er 'i fod o'n hoff o ambell i reg. Wyddost ti na fedar o ddim darllen na sgwennu? Ond mi all ddeud ei feddwl cystal â neb mewn iaith ddigon lliwgar. Mae 'na wreiddioldeb mawr yn yr hen Dwm.'

Roedd Twm wedi ei fagu efo'i fam weddw ar dyddyn a oedd prin yn ddigon mawr i roi bywoliaeth i'r ddau. Ei fam fyddai'n gwneud pob dim drostyn nhw, tra byddai Twm, a oedd yn llefnyn cryf, yn rhedeg y tyddyn ac yn chwilio am ddiwrnod neu ddau o waith ar ffermydd cyfagos. Pan fu farw'r hen wraig ei fam, yr oedd Twm ar goll yn lân gan na allai na golchi na smwddio, glanhau na choginio. Yn ffodus iddo fo, roedd o'n byw mewn cymdogaeth lawn gofal ac fe ofalai'r merched nad oedd Twm yn llwgu.

Un flwyddyn, a'r Nadolig yn agosáu, mi gafodd Twm bwdin Nadolig yn anrheg. Roedd y pwdin mewn powlen â chadach yn gaead arni, ac fe siarsiwyd Twm i ferwi'r pwdin am ddwy awr cyn meddwl am ei fwyta. Mi benderfynodd Twm wahodd ei gyfeillion agosaf i'w gartref i rannu'r pwdin – Ap Thelwal, y Parchedig David Poole a Nhad.

Roedd yn rhaid dilyn y cyfarwyddiadau i'r manylyn lleiaf. Gosododd Twm sosban â'i llond o ddŵr ar y tân i ferwi. Pan oedd yn fodlon bod y dŵr yn berwi go iawn, mi osododd y pwdin yn ei bowlen yn y sosban. Gwaith fy nhad, gan ei fod yn berchen wats, oedd sicrhau nad oedd y pwdin yn berwi am ddim mwy, na dim llai, na dwy awr.

Fe fu hi'n ddwy awr faith. Pawb yn gwrando ar y dŵr yn ffrwtian heb feiddio gadael i'r sgwrs grwydro'n rhy bell.

'Faint o ferwi mae o wedi gael rŵan, Bob?'

'Ugain munud, Twm.'

'Wyt ti'n siŵr?'

'Ydw, yn berffaith siŵr.'

'Diawch, mae o'n berwi'n ara deg.'

Mi fu'r pedwar yn mân siarad am ychydig nes i Twm ofyn:

'Faint rŵan, Bob?'

'Pum munud ar hugain, Twm.'

Felly y bu pethau, gyda Twm yn gwneud ei oraü glas i gyflymu treigl amser.

Toc dyma Ap Thelwal yn awgrymu:

'Well i ti roi chydig mwy o ddŵr yn y sosban?'

'I be ddiawl wnawn i beth felly?'

'Wel, rhag ofn iddi ferwi'n sych. Os na wnei di, mi fydd crac yn y bowlen a'r pwdin yn llosgi.'

'Wyt ti'n siŵr, Thelwal?'

Pan gytunodd y ddau arall, fe roddodd Twm hanner llond jwg o ddŵr oer yn y sosban.

Llusgodd y noson yn ei blaen gyda Twm yn ychwanegu dŵr pan oedd angen. Fel yr âi hanner awr yn awr, llwyddodd Twm i roi ffrwyn ar ddiffyg amynedd ac aeth y sgwrs yn fwy naturiol, a chyflymodd bysedd wats fy nhad nes iddo allu cyhoeddi yn y diwedd bod y pwdin yn barod.

Aeth Twm â'r pwdin i'r pantri a chyn hir fe glywyd rhegfeydd dychrynllyd.

'Be sy'n bod, Twm?' meddai Ap Thelwal.

'Mae'r diawl peth yn chwilboeth,' atebodd Twm. 'Well i ni aros am dipyn iddo fo gael oeri.'

Daeth yn ei ôl yn waglaw ac eistedd yn anniddig am ddeng munud a mwy er mwyn i'r pwdin oeri.

'Mi ddylsa fod yn iawn rŵan,' meddai, a dychwelyd i'r pantri. Daeth yn ei ôl efo'r pwdin ar blât a thwca yn ei law. Torrodd y pwdin yn bedwar efo'r twca a gafael â'i law fawr yn y chwarter cyntaf.

'Hwda, Poole,' meddai, '*ti* gynta gan mai ti ydi'r gweinidog.' Yna 'Hwda, Thelwal a hwda ditha, Bob', cyn cydio yn y darn olaf a'i stwffio i'w geg ei hun.

Oedd, roedd Twm yn perthyn i oes y tracsion a'r dyrnwr mawr pan oedd cymdeithas yn malio a gofal a chydweithredu yn hanfod bodolaeth, a phan oedd bod yn wahanol yn dderbyniol.

Syndod i'r ardal gyfan oedd clywed bod Twm yn mynd i briodi. Yn ôl y stori, roedd Twm wedi datgan fwy nag unwaith wrth Ap Thelwal ei fod yn unig a'i fod o angen rhywun i edrych ar ôl y tŷ. Methodd pob ymdrech i ddenu morwyn. Ap Thelwal a awgrymodd y dylai chwilio am wraig.

'Sut gythral y gwna i beth felly?' oedd ymateb Twm.

Awgrymodd Ap Thelwal ei fod yn gosod hysbyseb am wraig yn y wasg. Gan mai ei syniad o oedd o, fe gafodd Ap Thelwal y dasg o lunio'r hysbyseb Saesneg a'i hanfon at y papur newydd. Roedd ambell grechwen yn dilyn hyn, a neb yn credu y byddai Twm yn bachu gwraig. Ond fe ddaeth ateb o ardal Wrecsam – Cymraes o fath, er nad oedd Twm yn deall ei Chymraeg od hi. Ond er gwaetha'r diffyg cyfathrebu fe lwyddodd i'w chael yn wraig iddo ac fe briodwyd y ddau gan y Parchedig David Poole yng Nghapel y Tabernacl mewn priodas gofiadwy.

Does gen i ddim cof am weld cystal sbloet o flodau yn y capel erioed: roeddynt yn disgyn yn gawodydd lliwgar o'r galeri ac yn blethiadau cymen o amgylch colofnau, ac roedd y Sêt Fawr a'r pulpud yn perarogli ac yn wledd i'r llygad. Ar y dydd ei hun roedd llawr y capel yn llawn, rhai yn sicr yn boddhau eu hawydd i fusnesa a chrechwenu (sylw a glywais i fwy nag unwaith y diwrnod hwnnw oedd 'Mae 'na frân i bob brân...') – ond y mwyafrif o ddigon yno i ddymuno'n dda i'r pâr canol oed anarferol.

# 'Sioe Bach' y Benllech

Gwyliau Cristionogol a throad rhod y byd amaethyddol oedd yn gosod patrwm digwyddiadau ein bywydau, ac yr oedd i bob digwyddiad ac achlysur ei dymor yng nghalendr y capeli neu'r drefn flynyddol amaethyddol.

Ond nid felly roedd hi'n ddieithriad. Bob haf, yn ystod Gorffennaf ac Awst, fe ddeuai'r Sioe Bach (nid y Sioe *F*ach, sylwch!) i bwt o gae ar ochr y lôn rhwng Tyn-y-gongl a'r Benllech. Bob haf hefyd fe chwyddai poblogaeth y cylch oherwydd bod traethau'r Benllech, Traeth Coch, Lligwy, Moelfre a'r Traeth Bychan yn denu ymwelwyr wrth eu cannoedd. Nid oedd llawer o westai mawrion yn y cylch ac roedd hi'n arferiad gan y trigolion, yn dai annedd a ffermydd fel ei gilydd, i 'gadw fisitors' a gosod ystafelloedd eu cartrefi i ymwelwyr. Yn wir, yr oedd mwy nag un teulu yn byw mewn tai allan neu gytiau pren dros yr haf er mwyn manteisio ar y mewnlifiad drwy gadw ymwelwyr. Yr oedd un gŵr o'r enw Hewitt wedi ei gweld hi, gan iddo brynu aceri o dir creigiog di-werth ar fin y môr yn y Benllech – am bris rhesymol, yn ôl pob sôn – a gosod ugeiniau lawer o garafannau rhad arno. Rhaid bod poblogaeth yr ardal yn mwy na dyblu yn ystod yr haf.

Nid oedd dim byd crefyddol nac amaethyddol yn perthyn i'r Sioe Bach – i'r gwrthwyneb. Roedd peiriannau hapchwarae yn codi gwg capelwyr a'r ffair yn cael ei hystyried yn fwy o ffair wagedd nag o adloniant diniwed, ac roedd yn denu ceiniogau crintachlyd plant y ffermydd. Yn ddiamau, yr ymwelwyr oedd yn gyfrifol bod y Sioe yn gwneud ei thaith flynyddol o Gaergybi i gyrion y Benllech. Busnes teulu oedd o a byddai'r perchnogion yn byw fel sipsiwn mewn carafannau lliwgar oedd wedi eu gosod yn gylch, fel wagenni cowbois o amgylch gwersyll rhag ymosodiadau'r Indiaid Cochion. Johnny a Sam a'u gwragedd a'u plant a'u rhieni oedd yn gyfrifol am osod a rhedeg yr holl weithgareddau. Roedd peth o ddylanwad y sipsiwn i'w weld hefyd ar y lliwiau llachar – y coch, glas, gwyrdd a melyn oedd yn addurno'r stondinau a'r peiriannau adloniant.

Roedd swyn arbennig i mi yn y Sioe Bach. Cyhoeddid ei phresenoldeb drwy chwarae cerddoriaeth boblogaidd Saesneg yn fyddarol, rhywbeth oedd yn fwy effeithiol i ddenu cynulleidfa na'r un gloch eglwys. Roedd hi'n symbol o ryfyg a menter, o siawns a hapchwarae, o fesur dewrder, medr a nerth braich, ac yn herio culni traddodiadol y capeli. Roedd yno rywbeth at ddant pawb, heblaw'r piwritan mwyaf eithafol. Roedd dau chwrligwgan, neu feri-go-rownd – un efo teganau fel tractors a bysus a cheir rasio ar gyfer y plant bach (a honno'n troi yn hamddenol ar un lefel), a'r llall efo'r ceffylau bach traddodiadol yn mynd ar duth ac yn codi ac yn gostwng gan adael stumogau'r marchogion ar ôl. Yr un modd efo'r ddwy siglen – siglen sidêt i'r plant bach, a siglenni ar ffurf cychod (a gâi eu gyrru gan nerth braich trwy dynnu ar raff) ar gyfer plant hŷn ac oedolion. Fe fyddai'r hogia mawr yn gyrru'r siglen i'w heithaf nes bod y ffrâm bren yn crynu. Bryd hynny mi fyddai merch y sioe yn arafu ei hynt drwy godi llorp pren at waelod y cwch i'w arafu.

Y prif atyniad oedd y ceir bach – y 'dodgems' – y ceir trydan oedd yn gweu'n gynddeiriog drwy'i gilydd. Yn ôl y rheolau, osgoi oedd pwrpas y chwarae, ond taro, a tharo'n galed a rhyfelgar, oedd anian pob gyrrwr. Roedd dyn y sioe yn ffromi, ac yn wir yn gwahardd unrhyw ergydio bwriadol, ond prin bod neb yn cymryd sylw ohono. Roedd hi'n ormod o demtasiwn mynd yn benben i ganol tagfa a rhoi sgydfa go dda i ambell Sais ffroenuchel.

Ac yna mi roedd y gyfnewidfa arian a'r babell ddwyn ceiniogau. Yno roedd bwth lle y gellid newid papur chweugain, hanner coron neu bishyn swllt yn geiniogau – nid i arbed eu gwario, ond i oedi rhyw ychydig ar eu diflaniad. Roedd y babell yn llawn o beiriannau llyncu ceiniogau (peiriannau bagatel), ble byddai marblen ddur yn syrthio i'r cafn coch, cafn y colli'n ddieithriad, gan lwyddo'n rhyfeddol i osgoi'r cafnau gwyrddion. Ac roedd bwrdd yno'n llwythog o geiniogau'n driphlith draphlith tu ôl i len wydr, a hwnnw'n symud yn ôl ac ymlaen gan fygwth gyrru'r ceiniogau dros y dibyn ac i gafn yr enillwyr. Gallech daeru y byddai gollwng un geiniog yn ddigon i wthio pentwr o geiniogau i'r cyfeiriad iawn. Ond ar yn ôl y disgynnai pob ceiniog bron, i ddifancoll drwy hopran fawr i grombil y peiriant.

Ac yr oedd yno graen, craen cadarn yr olwg (eto mewn câs gwydr), y gallech am bishyn chwech ei gyfeirio at bob math o ddanteithion disglair, yn deganau ac yn siocledi. Rhoi'r chwech yn y bwlch a throi'r olwyn at gar bach coch nes bod bysedd y craen yn cau'n garuaidd amdano, ac yna'n ei godi'n araf at y twll crwn a'r byd mawr y tu allan.

Ond rywsut, ar ôl trin y craen mor fedrus byddai'r car coch, a phob gwrthrych arall o ran hynny, yn disgyn yn ddiniwed wrth ymylon y twll.

Roedd mwy na ffawd yn eich atal rhag ennill. Roedd y cnau coco wedi eu sodro'n sefydlog ar y pyst er gwaetha'r sioe o lwch lli oddi tanynt; prin bod lle i'r cylchoedd ddisgyn dros wddw gwrthrych i ennill gwobr hŵp-la, ac roedd hi'n dipyn o strach taflu pêl ping-pong i geg powlen wydr ac ennill pysgodyn aur.

Ond roedd 'na un stondin ble roedd modd i berson medrus ennill. A deud y gwir, *dwy* stondin ochr yn ochr â'i gilydd oedden nhw, yn cael eu gwarchod gan yr un wraig. Y dasg yn y naill oedd taflu dartiau ar gardiau chwarae wedi eu gludo ar wal gefn y stondin gyda hanner modfedd dda rhwng pob cerdyn. Pe llwyddid i daflu tri dart a tharo tri cherdyn, yna fe geid gwobr fechan, tegan neu ornament rhad. I'r dartwyr da, gellid derbyn cerdyn gwobr a chasglu'r cardiau dros gyfnod a derbyn gwobr fwy sylweddol ar y diwedd. Hawdd, meddech – ond tueddai'r trydydd dart i syrthio i'r bwlch rhwng y cardiau. Roedd pob camp yn y Sioe Bach yn ffafrio'r perchnogion. Gwelais ambell un oedd wedi hen arfer chwarae dartiau yn gadael y stondin honno'n llwythog ryfeddol, ond roedd mwy o lawer yn rhoi'r bai ar y dartiau.

Drws nesaf i'r dartiau roedd stondin y gynnau – gynnau oedd yn saethu dartiau bychain pigfain. Y gamp oedd sgorio 21 neu fwy drwy gael o leiaf dri dart yng nghylch mewnol y bwl a roddai sgôr o bump yr un, ac un yn y bwl ei hun i sgorio chwech. Hon oedd fy hoff stondin i, ac yn ystod yr haf mi fyddwn yn gwario ambell ddarn chwech gan gasglu cardiau er mwyn ennill set o lestri te i Mam. Mi fyddwn i'n defnyddio'r un gwn bob tro, ac ar ôl ychydig o ymarfer, anaml y byddwn i'n methu. Erbyn diwedd yr haf roedd y wraig yn fy adnabod wrth fy enw, ac os byddai dart ar ymyl eithaf y cylch, mi fyddwn i'n siŵr o gerdyn. Ar ddiwedd un haf, mi gadwodd set o'i llestri gorau i mi eu rhoi'n anrheg i Mam.

Roedd sŵn ac arogl arbennig i'r Sioe Bach – sŵn rhialtwch a cherddoriaeth fyddarol, ac arogl diesel, llwch lli tamp, candi fflos a nionod yr 'hot dogs'. Roedd yno her i foddio pob blys, cryfder bôn braich, medrusrwydd mewn anelu a saethu, a pheth wmbredd o ddiddanwch a chyfle i ddangos eich hun – am bris.

# Pytiau

Ymhlith y prif atgofion sydd gan bawb ohonom o ddyddiau'n plentyndod, daw hefyd rai pethau i'r cof nad ydyn nhw'n llawn haeddu cael eu galw'n atgofion. Rhyw bytiau byrion ydyn nhw sydd wedi goroesi'n dameidiog rywsut, gan fflachio fel dreigiau ar ffurfafen y cof. Er mor anghyflawn a thameidiog ydyn nhw, *maen* nhw'n bod, felly barnaf eu bod hwythau'n haeddu eu lle yma!

Mae gen i ryw frith gof o weld rhywbeth a ddaeth i'r wyneb ar dywod un ai Traeth Bychan neu Draeth Coch, a thwr o bobl wedi ymgasglu i edrych arno. Rai blynyddoedd yn ôl, mi soniodd ewythr i mi, f'ewyrth John o Bermo, iddo fynd â fi i weld llong danfor y *Theutus* a oedd wedi mynd i drafferthion ym Mae Lerpwl, ac a ddaeth i'r wyneb yn Sir Fôn. Ond doeddwn i fawr mwy na babi ar y pryd! Tybed...?

Mae gen i well cof am goelcerth ar Bonc Pant Bugail, coelcerth a daniwyd i ddathlu diwedd yr Ail Ryfel Byd. Roedd hi'n anferth o goelcerth efo delw o Hitler ar bolyn ar ei phen. Mi fu'n llosgi am rai dyddiau, ac ardal gyfan wedi casglu o gwmpas y goelcerth i ganu emynau a dathlu diwedd cyfnod du yn ein hanes.

Cofio hefyd bod mewn cwch modur efo Glyn Bay View yn llusgo 'spinner' ar lein y tu ôl i'r cwch a mynd i ganol haig o fecryll. Roedd y môr yn corddi efo nhw, wrth iddyn nhw geisio llarpio'r pysgod bychain gloyw oedd yn sleifio am eu bywyd ar hyd wyneb y dŵr. Cofio cael ffrae iawn am gyrraedd adref yn hwyr – a wnaeth hanner dwsin o fecryll ffres *ddim* i liniaru llid fy mam.

Cofio helpu i gorddi yn nhŷ llaeth Erw Ddu efo Idris. Troi a throi nes bod bôn braich yn brifo. Edrych drwy'r ffenast wydr ar y corddwr bob egwyl i weld a oedd y llefrith 'di suro wedi troi'n fenyn. Yr egwylion yn mynd yn hwy ac yn amlach, a'r newid llaw a newid troellwr y corddwr yn mynd yn amlach fyth. Yna rhyfeddod gweld lympiau bychain o fenyn fel aur ar wyneb y llaeth enwyn.

Un o'r golygfeydd fydd yn aros efo mi tra bydda i ydi gweld Seren, caseg Olgra Fawr, yn rhoi genedigaeth i ebol. Roedd gan Seth Owen, Olgra Fawr, ddau geffyl gwedd ond y ffefryn gan bawb oedd Seren, y gaseg wen. Mi oedd hi wedi ei rhoi i bori yn y cae-dros-lôn ers rhai wythnosau oherwydd ei bod hi'n feichiog. Un diwrnod, o flaen fy llygaid, fe roddodd enedigaeth i ebol bychan, a dyna lle bu hi'n llyfu ei hepil yn famaidd am hydoedd. Toc, cododd hwnnw'n betrus ar ei draed heglog a cherdded yn simsan ac yn goesau i gyd ar ôl ei fam.

Cofio eistedd ar bwt o graig yn y Wig ger traeth y Benllech ar ddiwrnod trymaidd o haf ym mis Awst. Doedd dim crych ar wyneb y môr llaethog ac roedd tawch ysgafn yn cyfyngu'r gorwel i fod ddim ond ychydig y tu hwnt i Drwyn Penmon. Synhwyro yn hytrach na gweld y llanw'n dod i mewn wnes i gan nad oedd ton i'w gweld yn unman, ac roedd yn rhaid craffu i glywed sŵn y dŵr yn llepian yn erbyn y graig a'r gro mân. Roedd fel petai'r tywod a'r gro yn sugno'r llanw i'w anterth. Welais i erioed fôr mor llonydd na gweld adlewyrchiad llun mor berffaith o greigiau'r Benllech yn y dŵr.

# Gadael

Pan oeddwn i'n bymtheg mlwydd oed, roedd fy nhad yn gweithio ar adeiladu tai cyngor newydd ym Mryn-teg. Daeth adref un diwrnod a dweud ei fod ag awydd gwneud cais am un o'r tai. Mi fu Mam ac yntau'n trafod yn faith. Roedd sgwrio lloriau'r capel a'r ysgoldy'n dechrau mynd yn drech na Mam, roedd fy chwaer wedi dechrau gyrfa fel nyrs yn Lerpwl, roedd y tŷ mawr yn damp (y talcen agosaf at y lôn yn gollwng fel gogor pan fyddai'r gwynt yn gyrru glaw ato), a'r ffaith ei fod gymaint ar wasgar yn ei wneud yn anodd i'w ddwymo ac yn faich i'w gadw'n lân. Byddai llawer o fanteision mewn symud.

Y diwedd fu i ni wneud cais a llwyddo i gael tŷ newydd sbon. Roeddwn i wrth fy modd. O'r diwedd fe fyddem ni â'n tŷ ein hunain – er ei fod yn dŷ rhent – tŷ cynnes, hawdd ei gadw'n lân, efo ystafell ymolchi go iawn. O'r diwedd hefyd fe fyddwn i'n gallu diosg cochl 'hogyn tŷ capel', a chael bod yn fi fy hun.

Fe ddaeth lorri William Henry Parry, Bryn Mair, i gario ein buddiannau bydol y tri chwarter milltir i Fryn-teg. Gollyngdod oedd cael sefyll ar gefn y lorri, yn gadarnhad ein bod fel teulu yn gadael Tŷ Capel y Tabernacl o'r diwedd. Nid yn unig yr oeddwn yn cefnu ar adeilad, ond roeddwn hefyd yn cefnu ar ffordd o fyw a oedd – yn fy marn i ar y pryd – yn gaethiwus braidd. Yn well na dim, byddai terfyn am byth ar fod yn wasaidd i aelodau a blaenoriaid.

Ond nid profiad syml, wrth gwrs, oedd gadael. Fuaswn i ddim am y byd yn dewis bod heb y llu profiadau cyfoethog a gefais i fel hogyn Tŷ Capel. Bu bod yn aelod ffyddlon o Ysgol Sul a holl wasanaethau'r capel yn addysg werthfawr a oedd yn ymestyn y tu hwnt i grefydd gonfensiynol i gwmpasu iaith a diwylliant ac adnabyddiaeth o bobl garedig a diddorol, er bod yn eu plith ambell ragrithiwr wyneb-galed. Mi gefais gyfle i gymryd rhan yn gyhoeddus a magu hyder o flaen cynulleidfa. Mi ddysgais adnodau o raid, a llu o emynau heb sylweddoli hynny, ac mae'r rhain yn dal i ganu yn fy mhen hanner canrif a mwy yn ddiweddarach. Ac ar y cyfan yr oeddem yn troi ymysg pobl garedig a chyfeillgar, pobl a oedd yn malio.

Cymerodd beth amser inni setlo yn Gwenallt, Bryn-teg. Wedi byw mewn tŷ helaeth llawn lobïau a grisiau a nenfydau uchel, ble byddai rhywun – yn gymydog neu aelod o'r capel – yn galw byth a hefyd, roedd tawelwch cyfyng y tŷ newydd yn brofiad dieithr. Ond roedd y newid mwyaf ar y Sul. Bellach doedd dim rhaid codi'n fore i gynnau tân yn y parlwr, y festri ac ysgoldy'r capel. Doedd dim *rhaid*, hyd yn oed, mynd i'r gwasanaeth ar gyfer deg. Ar ôl y mudo, mae'n debyg i mi wrthryfela yn erbyn amserlen oes a pheidio â mynd ar gyfyl y capel am wythnosau!

Os cymerodd hi rai wythnosau i mi ddygymod â 'nghartref newydd, cymerodd lawer iawn hirach i mi golli'r label 'John Tŷ Capel'. Mae'n debyg y bydd hwnnw efo mi weddill fy oes mewn rhai mannau. Wedi dyheu cymaint am gael gadael y Tŷ Capel, doedd y newid pan ddigwyddodd o ddim mor bell gyrhaeddgar, nac mor syfrdanol, â'r disgwyl.

## Diwedd Plentyndod

Ond mae 'na fath arall hefyd o atgof. Hwnnw ydi'r un sydd wedi ei serio am byth ar y cof, a phob eiliad boenus ohono wedi dal y pum synnwyr yn gwbl effro. Ni ellir fyth roi mynegiant uniongyrchol i'r math hwnnw o atgof, a hyd yn oed pe gellid, ni fyddid yn dymuno gwneud hynny.

Cerddais drwy'r drws cefn fel y gwneuthum ganwaith o'r blaen, ac i lawr heibio i Siop Bryn-teg a thua sgwâr y pentref. Drwy drugaredd doedd neb o gwmpas a sefais yn nrws tafarn y Califfornia i ddisgwyl am y bỳs. Doeddwn i ddim yn teimlo fel siarad â neb. Daeth y bỳs, fel arfer, bum munud yn hwyr. Yn rhyfedd iawn, roedd *popeth* fel arfer. Roedd y bỳs yn dri chwarter gwag a cherddais heb edrych ar neb ac eistedd yn y sedd flaen wag. Roeddwn yn ymwybodol iawn ohonof fy hun – fel pe bawn i'r tu allan, rywsut, yn gwylio pob un symudiad o'r eiddof. Eisteddais ar y chwith i gefn y gyrrwr a theimlo ar unwaith bod o leiaf un pâr o lygaid wedi eu hoelio ar fy ngwegil i.

Cychwynnodd y bỳs a cheisiais innau anwybyddu'r llygaid drwy ganolbwyntio ar y ffordd o'm blaen. Roedd Capel Soar yn dal ar y chwith a'r Werydd o hyd ar y dde. Ond er pob ymdrech fedrwn i yn fy myw anwybyddu lleisiau'r ddwy wraig oedd yn fy nhrin yn huawdl ryw dair sedd y tu ôl i mi.

'Naddo, chlywais i ddim.'

' 'I dad o wedi marw neithiwr.'

'Tewch! Be oedd matar?'

'Ciansar ar y lyngs, glywais i.'

'Tewch da chi! Hogyn pwy ydi o, deudwch?'

'Hogyn Bob Saer. 'Doeddan nhw'n arfar byw yn Nhŷ Capel y Tabernacl.'

'Nid y fo ydi'r hogyn bach oedd yn arfer canu?'

'Ia, dyna chi. Roedd o'n arfer bod yn yr un fform â Huw ni yn y Cownti Sgŵl.'

'O! Lle mae o'n gweithio felly?'

'Gweithio! Weithiodd o rioed yn 'i fywyd. Dal yn 'rysgol tua Llangefni 'na mae o. A Huw bach yn ennill cyflog del ers bron i flwyddyn.'

'Wn i ddim be sy *haru* rhai rhieni, na wn i wir. Yn cadw'u plant yn yr ysgol nes 'u bod nhw'n llarpia mawr diog.'

'Mi fydd hi'n newid byd arno fo rŵan. Yn ôl be glywis i mi fydd hi'n o fain arnyn nhw, a nhwtha newydd symud i Dŷ Cownsil newydd ym Mryn-teg.'

Aeth y lleisiau croch ymlaen yn fydol ddoeth i drafod swm a sylwedd ein meddiannau daearol ni, a gwiriondeb fy rhieni'n fy nghadw i ymlaen yn yr ysgol. Er nad oeddynt yn gywir yr oedd eu geiriau'n fy mrifo i'r byw. Fy nhad oedd yn gyfrifol am imi aros yn yr ysgol, ac er i mi wrthryfela, gwyddwn yn y bôn mai fo oedd yn iawn. Pe bawn i'n gorfod nodi'r amser y peidiais i â bod yn blentyn, credaf y byddai rywbryd yn ystod y daith honno ar y bỳs i Langefni.

Erstalwm oedd hynny – yr erstalwm hwnnw pan oedd y Beibl yn wir bob gair a Mam yn hollwybodol, haul yn tywynnu trwy bob haf ac afalau yn y berllan, a thonnau diog yn llyfu aur Traeth Llugwy.

Bellach, mae 'na ysgolheigion Beiblaidd sy'n amau

dilysrwydd geiriau'r Beibl, a doedd hollwybodolrwydd Mam ddim yn ddi-ben-draw chwaith. Ers dyddiau fy mhlentyndod i, cawsom sawl haf gwlyb ac oer yn ogystal ag ambell un tanbaid, a chawn bellach ein bygwth gan dwymo byd-eang a nwyon tŷ gwydr. Ac er bod tonnau'n dal i lyfu Traeth Llugwy, aeth y traeth yn fwy o gyrchfan ymwelwyr, yn fwy o fenter fasnachol ble y codir tâl am barcio ceir ac amlder cyrff estron yn pylu peth ar wawr yr aur. A rywsut, fe grebachodd y byd mawr crwn nes bod ei derfynau mwyaf diarffordd o fewn taith awyren.

Ond o fewn diddosrwydd fy meddwl i, mae'r darn tir rhwng Llanbedr-goch a Marian-glas, y Califfornia a'r môr yn dal i fod yn dalp mawr o'm hetifeddiaeth, ac yn 'llond y nefoedd, llond y byd' pan mae'r dychymyg ar waith. Mae'n debyg na wna i byth eto adnabod ardal mor drylwyr ag yr adnabûm i filltir sgwâr fy mhlentyndod. Er i mi fyw yn hapus ddigon am dros ddeugain mlynedd yng nghyffiniau Dinbych, dydw i ddim yn gwybod nac yn cofio enw pob tŷ yn y rhan o'r dref y trigaf ynddi, nac yn adnabod caeau cyfagos wrth eu henwau. Dydw i ddim chwaith yn gallu camu i mewn i fwy nag un neu ddau o dai drwy agor y drws a gweiddi 'Oes 'ma bobol?' Pa un bynnag, mae larymau a goleuadau diogelwch ac arwyddion gwarchod cymdogaeth wedi rhoi terfyn digon swta ar yr hen arferiad cymdogol hwnnw.

Efallai, wir, fy mod i'n rhamantu dros rychwant amser, ac yn delfrydu cyfnod nad oedd na gwell na gwaeth nag unrhyw gyfnod arall, dim ond ei fod yn wahanol. Ond un peth a wn i'n sicr: i blentyn, roedd o'n gyfnod pan oedd y pum synnwyr yn effro a'r dychymyg yn fyw, a phan oedd hygoeledd a diniweidrwydd yn ddiderfyn.